"So you were just bluffing.

He looked at her. "Do you know how incredibly dangerous that is? How foolish, to threaten an unknown intruder the way you did me with a weapon when you're not even certain of its status?"

Irritated, she blasted back, "There's no need to lose your mind about it. I only had the gun as a deterrent. I was never going to hurt anyone."

He shook his head. "But what if it hadn't been me, Giselle? Because if Markus had seen the useless thing and perceived you as a threat, he would've shot you down without a moment's hesitation."

Feeling her face heat, she said, "You know, I've done just fine on my own for almost three years without you mansplaining my survival for me."

"If you can't see the difference between mansplaining and discussing reasonable precautions when we're on our way to confront a serial killer, you ought to be *really* grateful I'm here to point out the difference."

As the rain intensified, her grip on the wheel tightened. "When this is over, I hope you'll remind me to throw you and your ego a parade."

Dear Reader,

When a person is grieving the death of a loved one, as rancher Malcolm Colton has spent the past three and a half years doing, it is only natural to instinctively avoid reminders of both the traumatic event and the person whose loss has caused him so much pain. This has been exactly how Malcolm has coped, throwing himself not only into his family's ranching operation but also into volunteer work with his trailing rescue K-9, Pacer, whose companionship has provided a welcome distraction from memories of the boat accident that cost his fiancée's life—and Malcolm's own failure to save her.

But when his hunt for a murderous fugitive brings him face-to-face with the only other survivor of the tragedy, his fiancée's beautiful younger sister, Giselle Dowling, Malcolm must protect the celebrity ghostwriter from the very real danger now on the loose.

In the end, they must ask themselves the question that each of us does when weighing our deepest wounds against the very human need to cling to the hope for better.

Do we allow the memory of past pain to imprison us within the boundaries of a diminished present, or do we choose to face whatever the future has to offer, accepting the gifts and sorrows of each day as they come?

I'm ending this message with the hope that those of you reading will navigate future chapters of your own lives with courage—and many a good book at your side.

Colleen Thompson

COLTON'S K-9 RESCUE

COLLEEN THOMPSON

Harlequin

ROMANTIC SUSPENSE

Special thanks and acknowledgment are given to
Colleen Thompson for her contribution to
The Coltons of Owl Creek miniseries.

Harlequin®
ROMANTIC
SUSPENSE™

Recycling programs
for this product may
not exist in your area.

ISBN-13: 978-1-335-50261-2

Colton's K-9 Rescue

Harlequin Enterprises ULC
22 Adelaide St. West, 41st Floor
Toronto, Ontario M5H 4E3, Canada
www.Harlequin.com

Printed in Lithuania

MIX
Paper | Supporting
responsible forestry
FSC® C021394

The Texas-based author of more than thirty novels and novellas, **Colleen Thompson** is a former teacher with a passion for reading, hiking, kayaking and the last-chance rescue dogs she and her husband have welcomed into their home. With a National Readers' Choice Award and multiple nominations for the RITA® Award, she has also appeared on the Amazon, BookScan and Barnes & Noble bestseller lists. Visit her online at www.colleen-thompson.com.

Books by Colleen Thompson

Harlequin Romantic Suspense

The Coltons of Owl Creek

Colton's K-9 Rescue

Lost Legacy

Danger at Clearwater Crossing
Ambush at Heartbreak Ridge
Secrets of Lost Hope Canyon

Colton 911: Chicago

Colton 911: Hidden Target

Passion to Protect
Lone Star Redemption
Lone Star Survivor
Deadly Texas Summer
First Responders on Deadly Ground

Visit the Author Profile page
at Harlequin.com for more titles.

To all the dogs who fill our lives with love, warmth and loyalty...but especially to those occasional rapscallions who arrive on the scene to keep us on our toes and season our days with a ration of laughter.

Chapter 1

Breeze ruffling his shaggy, dark-brown hair, Malcolm Colton adjusted his cap and zipped the collar of his tactical all-weather jacket higher as the wind shifted and the fine mist turned to drizzle. If Pacer, his K-9 search-and-rescue partner—and often, his only reason for getting out of bed these past three years—felt the deepening chill through his thick coat and working vest, he gave no indication. The red-and-black German shepherd mix, whose DNA contained just enough hound to make his ears floppy and his nose exquisite, was far too intent on dragging Malcolm to follow the scent trail he'd picked up, several miles from the area where the task force had previously chased.

This unsanctioned mission had come courtesy of a new tip from a citizen. It was a tip that Malcolm had risked everything—including his future volunteering with Owl Creek, Idaho Search and Rescue—to pursue on his own after shutting off his phone and disabling his GPS tracker so no one would have any way to find him. He felt even worse about lying to his family, telling his dad over their morning coffee that he was making the two-hour drive to Boise to meet up with a friend for the weekend. "If you can spare me on the ranch for a couple days, that is," he'd added, as if his father hadn't been practically begging him to take time for a getaway since the tragic drowning of Malcolm's fiancée three years earlier.

Beaming over the rim of his mug, Buck Colton had nodded his approval and reached over to scrub Pacer's thick ruff affectionately with his free hand. "Don't you worry, son. The ranch can spare you for a few days, especially with Greg and Wade both here to help me. And you know I'll have fun spoiling your buddy while you're gone—if he's not too busy playing with Betty Jane to give me the time of day." He chuckled warmly at the reference to the way his cousin Wade's dog and Pacer would wrestle when both K-9s were off duty.

"Oh, I'm taking Pacer with me," Malcolm had told him, racking his brain to come up with a reason that would throw off any suspicion about the dangerous idea that had taken root in his mind. "This friend of mine is quite the fan of animals, and to be honest, she's asked specifically if she could meet him."

Laughing, his dad—who was currently head-over-heels in love and convinced that everyone else should be—set down his mug and clapped Malcolm on the shoulder. "You sly dog, you! So, who's the lucky woman? And how long have you been hiding this big news from me?"

"This is exactly the reason I didn't tell you, Dad. It's still early days and very casual, so I don't need you making a huge deal of this. Or telling anyone else in the family before I'm ready. Got it?"

His father mimed locking his mouth and tossing away the key, a gesture so totally unlike him that Malcolm chuckled and shook his head remembering it now. Still, he felt another surge of guilt for getting the man's hopes up, because every time Malcolm so much as thought of putting himself out there in the dating world again, he broke out in a cold sweat, remembering the moment he'd finally caught the eye of one of the EMTs who'd been working frantically to revive Kate beside Blackbird Lake that horrendous August day. Remembering the bitter truth he'd seen there as he'd listened to the other Dowling sister screaming.

He still heard those heartrending screams in his nightmares. Screams forever etched into his memory.

Malcolm staggered to a stop as Pacer abruptly pulled up short, raising his head and sniffing the breeze deeply. A trailing rather than a tracking dog, he didn't follow the footprints of the criminal who was their quarry—which was a damned good thing since Malcolm hadn't spotted any in the hard-packed, rocky ground at this elevation. Instead, the well-trained K-9 sought out the scent cones that floated in the air or attached to items their quarry brushed against, such as vegetation or rocky outcrops.

Jerking his head sharply to the right, Pacer barked and lunged again, indicating that he'd caught another strong whiff of the scent matching that of the old T-shirt belonging to the subject. Thinking of where the item had been collected and the damage the man had done to Malcolm's family had him telling himself that *nobody* got to cause his loved ones so much pain and then use the cover of some freak storm to disappear forever. Because at this point, Malcolm cared far less about his own personal safety—this storm and Markus Acker's track record of putting Coltons in the ground be damned—than he did about ending the nightmare that had held his family in its grip for far too long now.

As Pacer led the way, Malcolm kept his bearings using various trails they crossed in the normally popular recreational area. They crested a hill, and the sight of a familiar ridgeline had him catching his breath, though it hurt like hell to remember those vibrant, sky-blue days when he and Kate had hiked out from her family's ski cabin, one of the many in the area, to enjoy the scenery. With the cold rain pattering down around him, he could almost hear the echo of lost laughter among the rocks and trees. Could almost see the tears gleaming in Kate's beautiful gray eyes as she had clapped her hands together, saying, "Of course I'll marry you! Even if you hadn't adopted the most adorable puppy in all Idaho, can't you see I'm absolutely crazy about you, Malcolm? And you know how much I love your family."

Shoving aside the painful memory, Malcolm reached up to switch on his headlamp against an afternoon that had grown as dark as that day had been brilliant. Driven by a bitter wind, the rain blew straight into his face. Half blinded by the worsening conditions—the very reason that Ajay Wright, the officer in charge of the SAR operation, had ordered the team to hold off instead of heading out here—Malcolm missed seeing a hole underfoot and yelped as he found himself unexpectedly hurtling forward.

Throwing out his hands to save his face, he heard the crack before he felt it when the two outermost fingers of his left hand caught a small rock and snapped back sharply.

"It's okay, boy," he told Pacer, who had circled back and shoved his face directly into Malcolm's, his deep brown eyes worried. "I'll be fine."

Apparently not buying it, Pacer whined and snuffled and licked at Malcolm's face, warm breath pluming in the chilly air around them.

"I'd be a lot more flattered by your concern," said Malcolm, "if I didn't know you're just eager to go find yourself a bad man."

Pacer barked loudly, bouncing on his front paws, reminding Malcolm never to use the word *find* unless he was well and truly ready to get moving.

"Sorry, boy. Give me a minute. Settle," Malcolm said, before testing his injury by carefully flexing the hand—which turned out to be an even worse idea. Once he'd finished seeing stars at the agony arcing across his knuckles and letting fly with a curse, he slipped off his backpack and fished out the first aid kit he had brought along.

With the rain growing even colder by the minute, he quickly abandoned thoughts of attempting to immobilize the hand, figuring he'd only make a mess of the bandage trying to wrap it under these conditions. Instead, he swallowed a couple of ibuprofen with some water, hoping the pills would at least delay the pain and swelling—because there was no way in the world he was turning on his phone to beg for help after disobeying orders.

Not as long as his dog, his legs, and his right hand were all working—and he had the pistol he'd brought along in case he unexpectedly found himself face-to-face with Acker.

Soon, he and Pacer were on their way again, Malcolm's effort to tune out the ache in his hand aided by his need to concentrate on where he put his feet next on the steep uphill incline. But between the heavy run-off and the encroaching darkness, he was quickly forced to rely on Pacer's superior senses to guide them safely through the intensifying storm.

Just as he was beginning to worry this had all been a fool's errand, they emerged near a gravel road, where Pacer wagged excitedly as he sniffed a clump of weeds.

He looked up at Malcolm, his brown eyes smiling before he gave a hound-like howl of pure joy. His entire body vibrating with anticipation, he charged off barking, head held low.

"That's a boy. I'm coming," Malcolm said, practically tripping over his own feet in his effort to respond to the pulling. But as they began passing ski cabins, many already closed up with the recent spring thaw, he began to wonder if it was possible that his dog was following not his nose, but a memory from when he was last here as a tiny pup.

Surely, he can't recall that far back. He has to be on Acker's scent. Look at him.

But as Pacer unerringly continued heading in an undeniably familiar direction, he asked himself if it was possible that, of all the places Markus could have decided to hole up to ride out this weather, he could have really chosen, by pure coincidence, the one spot that Pacer had visited before.

"Ridiculous," Malcolm muttered as they turned up the long, tree-lined driveway.

Though he saw no sign of a vehicle, he knew one could be parked either behind the cabin or inside the small, detached garage. As he and Pacer started up the evergreen-studded slope, he soon made out the warm yellow glow of the lights in the single-story log dwelling's windows. With the wind making the steady rain feel even colder, that familiar light carried him back in time, promising comfort and welcome. He pictured Kate, her beautiful face illuminated by her phone as she checked her schedule at the clinic or shot a quick text to her writer sister down in Palm Springs. Or maybe Kate was curled up in her favorite overstuffed chair by the living room picture window, watching the rain fall over the valley. The same valley where, on a clear day, one could plainly see the shimmering sapphire eye of the same lake destined to take her life in one cruel blink.

Jolted back to reality, Malcolm cursed his foolishness. Painful as it was, she was three-and-a-half years gone now, and if he didn't want to join her before his time had come, he had damned well better pay attention. Because between his dog's behavior, the lights, and what he'd almost swear was the scent of something warm and fragrant cooking, he was 100 percent certain that there was someone in this house now.

And that someone might very well be Markus Acker, who, already alerted by Pacer's ruckus and his own headlamp, might be taking aim from some unseen position. Or were they still too distant?

Eager to improve their odds, Malcolm switched off his light and gave the command, "Hush," before shortening Pacer's lead to allow for better control.

His K-9 whined in protest, the hound in him wanting his say about the importance of his mission, but with a few freeze-dried chicken treats Malcolm had brought along as bribes, he was able to convince his partner to keep his peace.

With only the steady patter of cold rain for company, they continued toward a back patio dimly illuminated by rectangles of soft interior light spilling out from the panes of the rear door's windows. The real question was, had Markus's path led him up those porch steps, where he'd forced entry through that same door? Or had he bypassed the cabin, perhaps to hide out as close as the garage downslope to the rear?

Crouching low, Malcolm pressed forward, his heart

pounding as he strained to hear another door or window opening. As they reached the bottom of the three porch steps, a loud crack—what he took for gunfire—had him shouting in alarm, nearly jumping out of his skin.

He felt like a damned fool when a bright flash lit the sky at the same moment before thunder pealed again.

Legs shaking like a newborn foal's, he grabbed the handrail and let out a curse before quietly reassuring Pacer—who seemed uncharacteristically jittery as well. "It's only a lightning strike, boy. We're going to be all right."

"You're right about the lightning," said a female voice, positioned just behind him. A voice with a volume and a confidence that carried over the fury of the storm. "But as for the question of whether you're *really* all right, that very much depends on whether you make any sudden moves. And on whether you keep a firm grip on your animal as well."

"Owl Creek Search and Rescue," Malcolm identified himself and Pacer, his heart pounding at the clear warning in her words. "And I swear to you, we're here looking for a wanted criminal who may be in the area and not to do you any har—"

"Malcolm?"

The astonishment ripping through that single word stripped away the threatening tone, allowing him to hear something impossibly familiar. Something he'd thought lost forever, causing him to spin around to face the woman who was already lowering the handgun she'd been aiming at him...

The same woman whose limp body he himself had pulled too late from the lake more than three years before. He saw that his fiancée's once chin-length blond hair now nearly reached the shoulders of the old, green fatigue sweater she wore with a pair of jeans that molded to her slim form. She seemed oddly tall as well, but maybe that was because his perspective was off, shifting as he back-pedaled to avoid the gun, the raw shame, and this impossible hallucination.

His feet tangled with the dog's lead, drawing a pained yelp as he stepped on Pacer's paw. Instinctively reacting but already off-balance, Malcolm ended up sprawling on his back.

In the next bright flash that followed, he found himself staring up not at a ghost, as his shell-shocked mind first thought, but what he'd belatedly realized was a damned *ghostwriter* instead.

Chapter 2

It struck Giselle Dowling like a body blow, having the man who had played a starring role in so many of her nightmares invade her sanctuary.

Yet in that split-second of strobe-lit illumination, she saw the emotions parade across her sister's fiancé's face: the pain and confusion quickly giving way to horror and revulsion.

So it's the same for him, she barely had time to think before more thunder rumbled, so close and so deafening she felt its vibration in her sternum. Or maybe that was only the pounding of her heart.

Whichever it might be, she was darn well freezing out here, and quickly getting soaked since she'd grabbed her grandfather's old revolver and run outside without a jacket when her cell phone pinged an alert activated by one of the outdoor security cameras. She'd initially assumed it was a bear making a nuisance of itself, since the animals occasionally came looking for an easy snack this time of year after emerging from hibernation. Normally, she would have simply grabbed the air horn she kept to run off the hairy intruders. But one glance at the man-and-dog-shaped silhouettes on her screen had had her running for the gun.

Surely, what he'd said couldn't be right, could it?

"You're tracking a wanted criminal?" Shaking her head, she tried—and failed—to make sense of what he'd told her. "You're definitely the first trespasser my security cameras have picked up on. Maybe you're a little lost? Or was the temptation to check out the old place while you were in the neighborhood simply too much for you?"

"You can't honestly think I'd willingly get within ten miles of this place if I had any choice in the matter," he fired back, looking and sounding outraged by her suggestion. "Anyway, why aren't you back hobnobbing with your rich celebrity clients and those air-kissing suck-ups you hang out with back in Palm Springs? I heard you sold this place three years ago. Couldn't wait to put the bad memories as far behind you as possible."

Using the gun, she gestured shakily toward the house. "If we have to t-talk about this, can't we d-do it inside?" she began, her teeth chattering. "I can't imagine your team wouldn't want you seeking shelter, at least until this lightning passes anyway, right?"

He hesitated before gesturing toward her gun. "I'll make you a deal. I'll come in if you quit waving that thing around like some maniac. And then maybe we can check that camera footage? You have a way to do that, don't you?"

Lowering her weapon, she nodded. "Sure—and there's no need to be so dramatic. I wasn't even pointing at you that time."

But when she reached down to grasp his hand, he jerked it back with a pained grunt.

"You're injured?" she asked, alarmed as his dog sprang between them, hackles rising, as it eyed her with obvious suspicion.

Wincing in answer, he told his dog, "Settle down, boy. It's okay."

"Sorry if I hurt you." As she wiped the cold rain from her face, she realized that she meant it. Though his presence was an almost unbearable reminder of the most traumatic moments of her life, seeing him in pain only turned up the volume on her own discomfort.

Help him, Zella, her sister insisted. Giselle felt lightheaded for a moment, her eyes stinging because it had been so long since she'd even thought about the childhood nickname, much less heard Kate's voice, so clearly that she might have been standing right beside her.

Using his apparently uninjured right hand, Malcolm awkwardly pushed himself to his feet, his expression unsettled as his gaze swept over Giselle's hair, her eyes, her clothing. As if he were cataloging the differences between her and the woman she had once been—the one who'd put a premium on things like manicures, makeup and fashion. "Believe me, an aching hand's the least of my worries at the moment."

Shaking off her dizziness, Giselle motioned for him to follow her, taking him around to the side door that led to a combination mudroom/laundry area with the same golden-brown split log interior walls as the remainder of the cabin. Once inside, she laid the pistol on top of the dryer before opening a dark-green cabinet to grab a stack of folded towels.

"Here you go, for yourself and your hairy friend there," she said, passing him a few.

When the top towel tumbled to the floor, she said, "Let me help you with that."

"I can manage," he said, a bit brusquely. "You're dripping wet yourself, and I can see you shivering. Whoa there, buddy."

"Ugh!" She turned away, raising an arm uselessly as the big shepherd shook himself, showering her—and most of the room—with mud and cold droplets.

"Sorry," Malcolm struggled to cover the animal, who ducked the end of the towel before snatching it in his teeth and giving it a playful shake. "Pacer, knock it off."

"Wait a minute." As the dog relinquished his prize, she dried her face. "*Pacer?* You aren't telling me this is really the same sweet pup from back when—when I came out to visit Kate after you had just adopted..." The rest caught in her throat as she recalled the sounds of her big sister's laughter and the happy puppy yips of a rousing game of keep-away.

Malcolm's green eyes warmed, some of the tension easing in a face she had to acknowledge was still as handsome as ever in his mid-thirties, despite the addition of what looked like a few days' worth of dark stubble and the lines of tension etched across his forehead. "It's him, all right. Pacer in the flesh."

Giselle wrapped herself in the thick blue towel she'd been using and kicked off sodden sneakers to slip her cold feet into a pair of dry, lined moccasins she kept stashed beneath a bench. "He was mostly all floppy ears and fluff back then. But now, just look at him." She gestured toward the logo on Pacer's vest. "An actual search and rescue dog."

"A trailing dog, specifically—and a damned fine one." She heard the pride in Malcolm's voice as he squatted to dry his K-9 partner. "But you haven't told me how—and *why*—you're here and not back in the desert dressed to the nines and lunching with your social-climbing friends."

She scowled but stopped short of defending her Palm Springs crowd, since none of them had checked in on her in ages—or even returned her last few texts since word had gotten out about the implosion of her professional reputation. Banishing the traitors from her mind, she sighed. "After the—after the services"— she still couldn't say the word *funeral* in reference to her sister without her throat closing up—"I packed up a few things and went back to work."

"I know you had that major deadline coming." The window behind him flashing bright with lightning, Malcolm shook his head, his tone hinting that he still disapproved of how quickly she had fled her hometown.

Recalling how alien it had felt to her, with every last member of her family gone, she swallowed past a painful lump in her throat. "After losing both my sister and my boyfriend—"

"I'd argue that the latter was no great loss," he said angrily. "If it weren't for that irresponsible son of a bitch..."

Her cheeks burned. "Did you know that Kyle *died* last year? I heard he was killed in an auto-pedestrian accident. Hit after stumbling drunk into the street following an evening of heavy partying in Vegas."

"So your old boyfriend never *did* learn to watch for traffic," Malcolm said, his judgment as harsh as his anger was enduring. "Or when it was important to stay sober."

"Doesn't sound that way," she murmured, too ashamed of having been involved with such a person, however briefly—and of having been so utterly oblivious as to the potential consequences of the always charming, witty, and well-dressed Kyle's chronic lack of accountability— and tolerance for boredom—to do anything but quickly change the subject. "As I was saying, after everything that happened, I figured I'd be better off throwing myself back into my work—and there was a lot riding on that project for the other parties involved as well."

"So in other words, you were under pressure to fulfill your obligations," he guessed.

"That was certainly part of it," she admitted. "But then the buyer's financing on this place fell through at the eleventh hour."

"So what did you do then?"

She shrugged. "Asked my real estate agent to put the cabin back on the market so I'd never have to face those memories again." *And my guilt*, she wanted to add but didn't, unable to imagine ever again drawing a breath free of its crushing weight.

"That's understandable," he said, coming to his feet, "and I want you to know how damned sorry I am…"

As caught up as she was in her explanation, his words barely registered. "But the problems just kept coming," she continued. "Issues with the foundation and then the cabin's plumbing, which shorted out the old electrical wiring as well. By the time it was all fixed, interest rates had skyrocketed."

Malcolm blotted his face with another towel. "So you couldn't sell the place?"

She threw her hands up before admitting, "I'm sure I eventually could have, but the bigger problem was I couldn't sell *myself* any longer on glamorizing the escapades of some rich, entitled musical 'genius' even more famous for his appalling treatment of everyone around him—especially the women—than what some consider talent."

"Wait a minute," he said. "Don't tell me your big ghost-writing job involved that singularly named guy with all the lawsuits people can't seem to stop talking about? As if I could care less about his latest awards-show meltdown or which famous friend's wife he's sleeping with this week."

"The very one, I'm afraid." The one good thing about being blackballed from New York to Hollywood was that confidentiality agreements no longer really applied. "Or at least it was before I walked out on him—because every second I spent catering to Nico's ridiculous whims or dodging his tantrums, every hour I wasted trying to humanize that absolute *polyp* on the colon of humanity, the more upset I became that someone as kind and sweet as Kate could be gone while someone so horrible keeps right on hurting people."

"You're absolutely right. It *isn't* fair she's gone," Malcolm agreed, his face stretching into a pained-looking grimace. Then one side of his mouth twitched, amusement sparking in his green eyes. "But did I just hear you call Nico a *polyp* on the colon of humanity?"

"You'd have been treated to a lot worse, I'm afraid, if you'd been around before I ran out on him." Her stomach tightened as she recalled the incident that resulted in the destruction of a reputation that had made her one of the most sought-after younger ghostwriters in the country.

"Surely, it was provoked," Malcolm said.

She waved it off. "What *he* did isn't the point. What matters is that after I went nuclear the way I did—I couldn't get work ghosting for a D-list cartoon spokes-animal, let alone a celebrity of the caliber I'd spent years working with before this happened. And I needed a place to lie low and lick my wounds—to write about the only person whose life story I still care enough about to put to paper."

"You mean you've been writing about *Kate*?"

"Trying to," she admitted, knowing it wasn't talking

about Kate's *life* but her death instead that was the problem. Or the enormity of Giselle's own role in it.

"But how can you bear being here alone, with all these memories of your family? That has to be so—"

Glimpsing the concern in his face, she turned away as images tumbled through her memory. *A flash of sunlight off a steel blade, a coil of long, blond hair wrapped like a tentacle around a towrope in the water. The hair she'd once taken so much pride in, dragging her into the blue depths...*

She felt her shoulders stiffen, along with her resolve. "Maybe at some point." She was barely conscious of reaching behind herself to touch the tip of a finger across the faint, horizontal scar on her lower neck, one barely hidden by her hair. "I realized it was no more than I had coming. Now let's get you out of that wet hat and coat so I can take a look at your hand."

Shaking his head, he said, "Hold on a minute. *What* did you say? Why on earth would you imagine *you* deserved to suffer?"

"Didn't you want to check that camera footage?" Giselle rushed to say, hating the rising note of panic she heard in her own voice. "Make sure that criminal you've been tracking isn't right here after all?"

"Of course I do, but—"

"I'll pull up the cameras' live feed on my computer in the second bedroom—I've shoved a little worktable into one corner for a makeshift office. If you need any help figuring it out, I'll be in the kitchen."

She then turned and fled the room—leaving the question he had asked her still hanging in the air.

Chapter 3

Malcolm stared after Giselle's retreating form, a hollow opening in the pit of his stomach as he realized that Kate's death had impacted far more than her ability to work. He tried telling himself that his responsibility to her ended with the need to warn her about the dangerous fugitive on the loose in these mountains, but seeing the contrast between her current misery and the confidence and spirit she'd once embodied hit him far harder than he would have imagined. He told himself he only cared for Kate's sake, knowing how painful she would have found seeing her beloved younger sister struggling instead of moving forward with her life.

Reminded of his own inadequacies in that department, he removed his hat and jacket, along with Pacer's vest, before drying himself and his dog as best he could, a slow and clumsy process with his throbbing hand.

After finishing, he hurried down the hallway in his socked feet, Pacer close behind him. Anxious as he was to check Giselle's computer for any evidence that Markus had set foot on the property, Malcolm hesitated outside the bedroom doorway, steeling himself before stepping into the space that Giselle and Kate had shared as children. Though the bunkbeds they had slept in had long since been replaced with a desk and pullout sofa, the room still felt haunted by the distant past, its walls adorned with framed photos of the two blond sisters growing up. Other pictures featured the grandparents who had raised them, and still others, the young parents who'd fallen victim to an avalanche while skiing in these mountains when Giselle was still an infant and Kate was attending pre-school.

Wondering how Giselle could even think of writing among so many ghosts, he averted his eyes before seating himself at her computer. When he touched the mouse, a split-screen popped up on the monitor, showing a live feed featuring three views and one blanked-out spot in the lower right-hand corner.

As the rain outside beat against the windows, he spent the next twenty minutes playing with the settings and clicking through recorded footage until Giselle tapped at the doorframe and stepped into the room. To his profound relief, he saw that she'd changed out of the cozy, forest green sweatshirt he'd immediately recognized as one of Kate's old cabin favorites and into a dry, navy sweater she'd paired with a pair of dark-gray joggers.

"So how're things going? Did you spot anybody out there?" she asked.

As she reached to pet Pacer, who had gotten up to greet her, the angle of her shoulder—or perhaps it was the way her wheat-colored hair swung forward—had his brain's warning lights all flashing. Internal sirens blared out the name of the woman he should be married to, perhaps even starting a family with, by this time. Yet when Giselle glanced up at him a moment later, she shifted back into herself again, leaving him scrambling to push back grief's shadow, to anchor himself to the present.

"No," he said, raising his voice to speak over the rumbling of thunder. "I haven't seen any sign of an intruder. But did you know you have a camera out?"

"Let me guess." She padded over to the desk. "The garage again, right?"

Pointing out the screen's blank quadrant, he concentrated on keeping both his voice and his hand from shaking. "So you've been having trouble with it lately?"

"Something's chewed through the wiring out there a couple of times, beginning last summer. I tell myself it's squirrels or chipmunks. But my neighbor's been suggesting I might want to adopt a mouser from the shelter—or invest in traps and peanut butter." She made a face, nose crinkling in distaste at the thought.

"I'll want to go check things out just to be sure," he said. "It should be easy enough to tell the difference between a gnawed wire and a cut one, if that's what we're dealing with."

"Knock yourself out. I'm pretty sure those rodents don't have scissors, though."

"I'd love for you to be right," he said, turning in his seat to look up at her, "but we can't discount that scent trail Pacer and I tracked up here. Makes me wonder if your vehicle's still really in your garage."

"Oh, I'm sure it's still there," Giselle said. "I have one of those antitheft apps hooked up to my car alarm. My cell phone would be wailing if someone tampered with it."

"You use a car alarm way up here?" he asked, somehow surprised, since people tended to be casual about such things in this lightly populated vacation area.

She shrugged. "I had a car stolen once, back when I lived in California."

"I'd forgotten that little red convertible you used to drive."

She grimaced. "Well, I definitely haven't, so I take reasonable precautions, the same way as I lock my doors and use security cameras to help keep an eye out on the property."

"Makes perfect sense," he said, "especially since you're so far from anyone you can call for help way up here."

"I take care of myself these days," she said, a bitter edge to her voice, "so, please, don't ever feel obligated to come running to my rescue. Not again…"

"Is that what you believe you are to me," he asked, hurt by the stinging tone of her rejection, "just some kind of…*obligation*?"

"What else am I supposed to think, when you came out of your way to head over here to warn me about some supposed danger?"

"Like I said before, it *wasn't* out of my way. Pacer led me here, on the scent, and I figured it would be a new homeowner." Pushing back from the desk, he stood to face her. "Someone *grateful* to be warned that a desperate fugitive might be on the property."

"I *do* appreciate the warning. Please don't get me wrong. It's just that—" Her shoulders drooped. "It's just that seeing you again here, I'm afraid it's…it's…more root canal than roller coaster."

He frowned. "Root canal, huh?"

"Don't take it personally," she said, a plea in her blue eyes.

"Only if you won't when I tell you it's the same for me," he admitted.

"That's definitely understandable," she conceded. "But

this criminal you and your dog were following, he's definitely not here."

"Not that we can see now, maybe, but I'll still need to check your garage to be certain."

"Can't that at least wait until this weather's passed? This storm sounds like it's getting worse." She looked toward the window, where lightning flickered, and an intensifying rain pummeled the glass.

"I'm not trying to frighten you unnecessarily, but this fugitive I'm tracking's no garden-variety criminal. Markus Acker's smart enough to elude authorities and smooth enough to con followers into willingly signing over all their assets. But when push comes to shove, he'll take out anybody who gets in his way."

"So he's killed before, you're saying?"

Malcolm felt a coldness unfurl deep within his chest. "He was behind my uncle Robert's death last June."

"I'm *so* sorry," she said, her beautiful eyes brimming with compassion.

"And only two weeks ago, he shot my mother dead as well."

"You—your *mother*?" She reached out, her hand skimming the surface of his upper arm before pulling away as if she'd accidentally touched hot metal.

He shook his head, "We'd been estranged for decades."

"Kate mentioned that she left your father and you and your siblings a long time ago and that during most of your childhood, there was no contact. That must have been so difficult."

"My mother wasn't exactly a blameless victim of Acker's, either," Malcolm said grimly. "She'd gotten herself caught up in his cult, to the point where she was possibly tied up in what happened to my uncle Robert and some scheme to get my family's money."

"In some ways, I imagine that's even worse," Giselle said, sounding sympathetic, "grieving someone when your relationship's been so…complicated."

"I couldn't even really call it a relationship. But that still doesn't mean I'm about to let Acker get away with the hell he's put my family through this past year. Or use the cover of this storm to disappear. It's why I couldn't sit around and wait out this weather so the rest of the team could join me before I—"

"Wait a minute," Giselle said. "You mean to tell me you came up here all *alone*, without permission?"

"I had to. Don't you see? I couldn't allow him the chance to go on as if my family's suffering meant nothing and start up his same scam elsewhere, the way he has before. If that happens, before you know it, he'll be brainwashing and fleecing other people—until he's backed into another corner and starts killing once again."

"And you really think this man could be hiding in my garage?" she asked, a look of horror coming over her as if the personal threat had for the first time become real to her.

He considered for a moment before answering, "To be honest, I'd be surprised at this point. Pacer here can't help barking when he's on a scent trail, and I'm sure Acker would be listening for dogs."

"I imagine he might've heard us talking outside, too," she said.

Malcolm nodded. "Unless I miss my guess, he'll be trying to put as much distance as he can between us in the hopes that this storm will give him the cover he needs to shake off his pursuit. Only I can't let that happen, so

I'll need to get going while you pack your things to head down—"

"Pack up to head down where?" she asked, sounding bewildered.

"You can't possibly stay here on your own now. Not with a desperate murderer on the loose."

"Are you serious?" She shook her head. "I'm not leaving my home, especially not in this awful weather. I'll just keep my doors locked and my gun handy."

"No, please," he said, sensing that despite her talk of taking care of herself, she would be no match for a remorseless and experienced killer like Acker. "Just drive slowly and carefully and head down to the ranch. We have plenty of room there, and we'd be glad to have you as our guest until Markus is—"

"Didn't you hear me? I said I'll be fine right here. Just check my garage to make sure he's off my property and I'll stay—"

"You can't."

"Stop it right now, Malcolm," she said sharply.

"Stop what?"

"Acting as if Kate left you in charge of my life somehow."

"I'm not trying to be in charge of you, I swear it," he said. "But I can't help remembering how much you meant to her. I'm absolutely certain she'd never want you to be here alone under these circumstances."

"You—you *really* want me to be okay, Malcolm?" As a fresh tear trailed down her cheek, Giselle ran a hand beneath the fringe of blond hair near her lower nape, not far from the spot where he'd once sawed through her tangled locks to save her life. "Then the minute that it's safe to, you can go back to your manhunt. Go back to your life and leave me here to mine, *please*. Because I never asked to see you. Never asked to and hope to heaven that I never will again."

As Giselle started to walk out of the room, a blinding flash lit up the window, followed by a booming thunderclap that had her jumping in response. The computer chirped in protest, and she turned back in time to see its screen go blank as the lights died.

The house's interior went deathly quiet, the storm outside sounding even fiercer against the sudden hush.

"I suppose I should've seen that coming," she said, hugging herself and rubbing at the rising gooseflesh on her arms. "At least I have surge protectors to keep my electronics from getting fried."

"Do you have a good flashlight?" Malcolm asked.

"In the kitchen, with my lanterns."

As she headed in that direction, his footsteps came immediately behind her. Despite the fact that only moments before, she'd wanted nothing more than to see the back of him forever, she felt a certain comfort in his presence now, with the fiercest storm she'd heard in years lashing the cabin's exterior.

"Oof, watch yourself there, Pacer," Malcolm said, stepping around his dog.

"Is he afraid of storms?" Giselle asked.

"Pacer would scent-trail through a hurricane. He's probably just anxious to get back out there and back to work."

"You can't be thinking of going back out in that now, though, are you?" she asked, feeling anxious at the thought. "As bad as it sounds, you could be electrocuted."

Malcolm frowned. "You're probably right. We'd be

better off waiting out the worst of the storm here—that is, if we wouldn't be too much in your way."

Guilt twisted inside her as she grabbed a flashlight from the drawer and passed it to him. "Listen, what I said before—I'm sorry for the way it came out. It's just that—"

He waved off the apology. "Don't worry about it. I can't imagine I would've taken it any better if some walking root canal had turned up on my doorstep, either."

The laughter that bubbled up—a little rusty from disuse—surprised her. Still, she kept her focus on the match she'd just pulled out and struck.

After using it to light a lantern from a shelf lined with glass jars filled with canned fruits and vegetables, she said, "Please, stay until it's safe again. I'll even feed you. There's plenty here." She gestured toward the soup and the loaf of bread she'd pulled from the oven just prior to his arrival. "If Pacer can have a little sourdough and soup, I'll fix him up a bowl, too."

"He'll be better off sticking with the food I brought along for him, but I'd definitely love to have some. Thanks," Malcolm said. "I'd better go wash up first, though, and maybe try to wrap this hand of mine before it swells any worse."

"Why didn't you say something sooner?" she asked. "Let me help you with that before we eat."

"You don't have to—"

"Please," she said. "Allow me the illusion of feeling like living up here like a hermit hasn't turned me into a completely awful person."

"You're not an awful person," he protested.

She snorted. "High praise indeed, for someone who could barely tolerate me even when I *did* have social graces."

"Barely tolerate you? What in the world ever gave you that idea?"

"Oh, come on," she said. "You might've loved my sister too much not to rub it in her face, but you clearly were less than thrilled whenever I came to stay for the weekend."

"If I ever for a second made you feel anything less than welcome around Kate and me, I apologize," he said, though the flickering light from the lantern made it hard to read his expression.

"It wasn't that you were ever rude. I mean, you always went through all the motions," she assured him. "It's just a vibe that I got, when Kate and I—"

"—Stayed up all night chattering about the old days or any celebrity gossip she could squeeze out of you so she could share it with her work friends?"

"I imagine we both got carried away and left you out of our conversations sometimes," Giselle said, thinking back on it and frowning. "And I know I liked to tease you sometimes. Maybe a little too mercilessly, on occasion, about your moo-cow wrangling?"

"Ranching," he corrected before shaking his head. "And seriously, after growing up surrounded by three take-no-prisoners siblings and a bunch of cousins, did you really expect me to be impressed with that kind of weak sauce razzing, Miss Green Cuisine?"

"Oh, wait a minute," she said. "We're getting warmer now, aren't we? Back in those days, when I was still so new to it, I expended a lot of energy trying to convince people to come over to the veggie side with me. If I was ever obnoxious about your carnivorous ways, I *sincerely* apologize."

"I honestly don't remember you ever being *that* bad."

"High praise indeed," she joked. "But I know I kind of could be. I'm embarrassed now even thinking back on it."

"We all have our regrets. And mine's getting a little jealous of how much attention my fiancée gave her little sister every time the three of us all got together, when all I wanted was to enjoy some time alone with her. Just thinking back on *that* now makes me feel a little childish."

She shook her head. "I'll admit that I sometimes felt the same way, when she'd go on about how incredible it was, what the two of you had together, and how excited she was to spend the rest of her life with you. I used to worry she'd forget all about me, especially once the two of you got busy raising your own…"

Seeing grief twist his expression, she used the distraction of another growl of thunder as an excuse to change the subject. "Come on. Let's head to the bathroom and look for those first aid supplies to take care of your hand."

"Sure thing. You lie down and stay here, Pacer," Malcolm said.

Lifting the lantern carefully, Giselle led Malcolm down the hall and entered the room ahead of him. Once she'd taken an elastic bandage, antibiotic ointment, and fresh towels out of the closet and set the lantern in front of the mirror, she grew uncomfortably aware of how tight the space was with the two of them both standing in it.

But considering how long she'd been living alone, she reminded herself that being squeezed into such a tight space with anyone was bound to feel claustrophobic to her.

"May I take a look?" she asked him.

Grimacing, he laid down the lit flashlight before hesitantly extending his left hand. "Careful—it's the knuckles where the pain's worst."

"From the looks of this, I'm not surprised." She grimaced in sympathy at the deepening browns and purples of fresh bruising. "Can you turn it over—this way?" Touching him gingerly, she caught his sharp intake of breath as he moved his swollen hand.

"When I fell, I caught a rock and bent those last two fingers halfway back to my wrist."

"That looks super-painful," she said.

"Is that your professional opinion?"

"As an unemployed ghostwriter? Sure, for whatever *that's* worth. But if I were you, I'd get to a real expert with it as soon as you're able because it sure looks like you could have some kind of fracture or dislocation."

"I've seen enough of those kinds of injuries on the ranch that I wouldn't bet against it."

"Okay, then," she said. "If I'm remembering from way back in my first aid classes in school, we'll want to wrap it in a compression bandage and maybe elevate it with some ice to help reduce the swelling. And I have some over-the-counter pain tablets you can take, too."

"Thanks, but the bandage will do for now," he said, pushing up his sleeve. "I've already taken a couple ibuprofen out on the trail. And I'll want to try washing some of this mud off before we wrap it."

Once he'd cleaned up, she helped him gently blot the injured arm dry and wind the bandage around his hand and forearm to immobilize it. With the sounds of the raging storm outside, she felt as if they'd been dropped into the distant past and imagined that as soon as she finished helping him, they'd go out and find Kate in the kitchen, putting the finishing touches on a dinner the three of them would share.

But the sadness in his green eyes, when she caught

him looking at her for just a moment in the mirror, re-minded her those days were as irretrievable as her own dreams of happiness.

"That isn't too tight, is it?" she asked as she finished with the bandage.

"Actually, you're pretty good at this," he said.

She dredged up a half smile. "Kate used to insist on practicing on me when she was still in nursing school, so I couldn't help picking up a few things."

He nodded. "Well, I really appreciate the TLC. And the offer of dinner, too."

"You do realize I may have given up the lectures, but I still don't eat—"

"—Anything that had a mother. How could I forget?" He flashed a grin. "But meatless or not, whatever you've been cooking smells amazing. And besides, I'm almost hungry enough to choke down…a tofu smoothie." He made a face.

"As entertaining as it might be to make you put your money where your mouth is, that's not on tonight's menu. But let's go check out what is."

Some time later, as Malcolm used the heel of the sour-dough to sop up the last of the vegetable stew from the bowl, she raised her voice to be heard above the storm to ask, "Another helping?"

He shook his head. "Thanks, but I really should've stopped already. Would have, except I can't say when I've enjoyed a meal so much. Meatless or not."

"All that trekking through the mountains probably worked up quite an appetite," she said, waving off the praise.

"Pacer and I both burned off some serious calories out there." He glanced toward his dog, who was picking distractedly at a bowl of the food Malcolm had put down for him. "But don't sell your cooking short. Or your company."

She laughed, "My company? You're full of something other than the stew. We've hardly managed two words since we sat down together."

"It's been a little noisy for much conversation," he said. "But I really need to talk to you. Seriously, Giselle, about evacuation. With the power out, especially, it doesn't feel safe leaving you way out here on your own."

She shook her head. "I have a portable generator. I'll go get it out of the garage as soon as the storm dies down and you've checked for boogeymen. We have outages up here all the time. It's made me very self-reliant."

"Enough to handle Markus Acker if he comes back this way?"

She shrugged. "I guess I'll find out, if the situation arises."

Malcolm stared at her as if she'd lost her mind, causing her to add, "Don't look at me like that. You already said he's most likely moved on."

"Are you really willing to gamble with your life that I'm right?"

"It's *my* life," she reminded him.

"So why do I care more than you do about what happens to it?" he demanded, leaving her too stunned to answer. When she left the statement unchallenged, he pressed harder, saying, "That's it, isn't it? You've lost your sister and you've lost your way, so now you're not sure it's worth the bother of fighting for the life Kate would've given anything to still have."

"Stop it, Malcolm—just *stop*," she said sharply, her eyes gleaming. "If you'd really wanted Kate, you should've let go the moment you realized it was me instead of her you grabbed when my hand managed to break the water's surface. You should've left me there and gone and found her. Because I've wished every single day since then that you had."

Chapter 4

Malcolm's stomach pitched, his mind reeling with the horrifying realization that Giselle *knew*. She understood that despite the fact that once he had shouted back over his shoulder for Kyle—that useless piece of garbage—to dial 9-1-1 and get in the damned water with a life ring to help him, that there had been a moment after he'd spotted her that he'd been certain it *was* Kate he'd caught hold of, recognizing the deep purple of her bikini as she'd struggled beneath the surface.

An instant later, the horror of the tangled hair—far too much of it hopelessly trapping her head beneath the surface—had reminded him how Giselle had borrowed her sister's swimsuit after forgetting to pack her own for this trip.... And in that single, shocking instant, to his utter shame, he'd been tempted to let go of Kate's annoying younger sibling and swim on, to pretend he'd never made the contact, or even seen her struggling.

Still, it haunted him, the knowledge that if he had done so, no one would have ever been the wiser and Kate would likely be alive. But when he'd looked down through a foot of water to see the primal terror in Giselle's face, he'd only tightened his grip on her instead. And ducked his head beneath the water to share with her the breath from his own lungs…

"There's fault enough to go around in what happened that day, but as far as I can figure, none of it was yours," Malcolm told her. "I wasn't lying back then when I told the sheriff's investigators, when I told *you*, I caught a glimpse of Kate floating in her life vest as I was struggling to help you." He would never forget his last sidelong look at the woman he'd loved with all his heart, not as long as he lived. Nor would he forgive himself for not making damned well certain that Kyle had been coherent enough to act on his shouted order to go see to her safety. "But she was slumped like she was dazed or something. Still, she seemed safe enough for the moment that I thought there was time to save you—or that help would come to—"

He remembered looking back at that same spot on the water, as he had finally lifted Giselle, who was choking and gagging—and bleeding from the back of her neck, where he'd nicked her with his knife while sawing away her hair—to the surface. Remembered his heart's deep dive when he had spotted his fiancée's life vest floating on its own.

"It was *never* your fault," Giselle insisted, tears now streaming down her face. "*I* was the one who distracted you when she needed you. The one who thought that *Kyle* was a good idea."

"We've all had lapses when it comes to dating," he said. "It doesn't mean you should beat yourself up for it for the rest of your life on account of—"

He was interrupted by the sound of an old-fashioned landline ringing, jarringly loud inside the darkened house, despite the noise of the storm outside. As Giselle moved toward where the black corded phone was sitting on its own small table, he warned, "You might not want to do that. Those wires can conduct lightning."

"It'll be Claudette from up the mountain. She's the only one who ever calls on this line, and with this storm…"

Malcolm was surprised to hear the elderly widow was still living on her own in the rustic cabin farther up the mountain. She and her late husband had lived there full-time since Giselle and Kate had both been small. Though he'd never met her personally, Kate had sometimes dropped in to check on her grandmother's onetime friend or gift her a small care package of items she'd picked up from the pharmacy or grocery store in town.

Giselle lifted the receiver. "Claudette, are you all right?"

Even from where Malcolm stood, he caught the terrified shriek that had Giselle wincing and pulling the phone back from her ear.

"Please, I'm listening, and I have help right here with me to come if you need us." Giselle caught Malcolm's eye. "But I need to know exactly what's wrong. What's happening right now at your place?"

As the woman spoke, Giselle's face paled and her eyes grew rounder. "I need you to stop for a moment. Listen to me, please. *Let* him break into the garage. Forget about the Bronco. Just keep your doors locked and stay out of sight inside your cabin. I've just been told there's a dangerous criminal on the loose—and—Claudette, no—"

Giselle shook her head as her neighbor continued speaking. "That old SUV can be replaced, but you cannot—"

"Tell her I'll be right there. I'll borrow your car and head straight to her," Malcolm said, his heart a wild drumbeat in his ears to think that he was so close to finally stopping the man who'd inflicted so much pain on his family.

Though he dimly remembered what he'd told Giselle—

and what he'd promised *himself*—about calling the authorities rather than attempting to confront Markus on his own, Malcolm realized that, with another woman's life imminently at risk, there was no longer any question that he had to personally act.

"I'm coming with you," Giselle insisted, before once more speaking into the phone. "Did you hear that, Claudette? My Kate's fiancé—he's a dog handler with Search and Rescue—is coming with me. We're on our way. And no, this fugitive who's trying to break into your garage isn't there to bother your chickens, no matter how special they are. So please stop worrying about them and keep yourself safe right now."

Giselle frowning, nodded, before her expression softened. "No—you listen to me, *please*. I think it's wonderful that you have that rifle. But I just want you to hold onto it right where you are in case he tries breaking through your locked doors to get inside the house. Do not, under any circumstances, go outside with it—*Hello? Can you still hear me?*"

After tapping at the phone a few times, Giselle shook her head, tears in her eyes as she looked up at Malcolm. "I thought she'd just hung up, but the line's dead."

"Forget the phone," he told her. "We need to get over there, right now."

"Just let me get my bag and gun," she said over her shoulder as she hurried toward the mudroom to grab her boots and jacket as well.

"I'm not sure your coming is a great idea," he said. "Maybe you could stay and try contacting the authorities on your cell."

"I'm not sure if you know Claudette—"

"Only by reputation. Kate said she wasn't much on strangers, especially of the male persuasion."

Giselle nodded. "That's Claudette, all right. Only now, she's older, even harder of hearing, and just about impossible to reason with when something gets her riled. And she's plenty upset right now, seeing what she called 'some wet and filthy vagabond' trying to pry his way into her car shed."

"Did I hear you say she has a Bronco?" Malcolm picked up Pacer's harness.

"The thing's ancient, but it still runs great," Giselle balanced on one foot to shove the other into a boot. "My point, though, was that Claudette not only won't listen to a stranger in her current state of mind, she might even be a hazard. She keeps a .22 rifle to safeguard her chickens."

"She did seem pretty preoccupied with them," he said as he knelt down to get Pacer situated.

"She brings me eggs, so I hear a lot about those fancy poultry shows she used to take their ancestors to back when she got out more."

He rose and accepted his jacket as she passed it to him. "I guess everybody needs something to love to keep them going." He glanced down at Pacer, reminded anew of what a critical lifeline the bond between them had provided for him.

"Maybe," Giselle said. "But as far as Claudette goes, you'll need me with you to make sure she understands that you're there to help keep her and the things that she holds dear safe. Otherwise, she could decide you're just as dangerous as one of the hungry foxes or weasels she's always watching out for—and leave you just as dead as any bullet from Markus Acker's gun."

* * *

After running through the rain to her garage, Giselle climbed behind the wheel of her red Crosstrek as Malcolm loaded Pacer into the rear seat before getting in beside her.

As she strapped in and fired up the engine, she said, "Before Claudette started in about her chickens, she mentioned that since she keeps the shed locked, her Bronco's keys were in there, in the ignition."

"So in other words, if he does break in, he'll be gone in a flash," Malcolm reached inside the pocket of his jacket. "Let me try 9-1-1, see if we can get some backup to meet us up here. And maybe they can put up roadblocks to keep him from making it over to the interstate."

He turned on his phone as Giselle backed out of the garage. "No signal," he said as she started up the hill. "Mind if I try yours instead?"

She shook her head. "In all the rush, I'm afraid I left it back inside. That was stupid."

"It doesn't matter," Malcolm told her. "It'll more than likely be using the same cell tower as mine is. Storm's probably knocked out all service."

"So we're completely on our own," she said. As they turned onto the road, lightning pulsed overhead, and the heavy rain renewed its assault. "Just what we needed."

"If you need to stay inside the car at Claudette's, I'll certainly understand."

"I didn't come with you to hide." Hearing the sharpness in her own voice, Giselle blew out a breath. "I'm only nervous, that's all."

"Just try not to accidentally shoot anybody you don't mean to with that old revolver of yours," Malcolm warned.

"You don't have to worry about that." She slowed to make a sharp right. "After my grandfather passed away,

Grandma decided she didn't care for having a loaded weapon around the cabin."

Malcolm's head whipped around to stare at her. "Wait a second. Are you seriously telling me that gun—the same gun you *pointed* at me earlier—isn't even *loaded*?"

She shrugged. "Not the last time I checked. And I have no idea when I last saw that box of ammo."

"So you were just bluffing me before? Do you know how incredibly dangerous that is? How foolish, to threaten an unknown intruder the way you did me with a weapon when you're not even certain of its status? Which means, I'm sure, it hasn't been cleaned or tested since your grandfather, who's been gone for, what, fifteen years, at least?"

Irritated by the judgment in his voice, she blasted back, "There's no need to lose your mind about it. I only had the gun as a deterrent, that's all. I was never going to hurt anyone."

He shook his head. "But what if it hadn't been me, Giselle? What then? Because if Markus had seen the useless thing and perceived you as a threat, he would've shot you down without a moment's hesitation."

Feeling her face heat, she said, "You know, I've done just fine on my own up here for three years without you mansplaining my survival for me."

"If you can't see the difference between mansplaining and discussing reasonable precautions when we're on our way to confront a man who meets the textbook definition of a serial killer, you ought to be *really* grateful I'm here to point out the difference."

As the rain intensified, her grip on the wheel tightened. "When this is over, I hope you'll remind me to throw you and your ego a parade."

"This isn't about my ego. It's your total disregard for your own safety."

After flipping on her high-beam headlights, she pointed out a gap between a large pine tree and a boulder just ahead. "If you could quit talking about yourself for one minute, we're almost there."

Tapping the brakes, she turned left. An instant later, she shrieked as the Subaru came face-to-face with a far larger vehicle barreling directly toward them on the steep and narrow, deeply eroded drive as it slewed around a sharp curve.

When the thirty-year-old Bronco failed to slow, Giselle jerked the wheel to the right to avoid smashing into it head-on. But as deeply rutted as the drive was from years of prior rain events, the Crosstrek's right-hand wheels immediately ran up the side of the mud-and-stone cut.

As the Bronco blasted past them, she heard the shriek of metal as the side-view mirror was shorn off. But her startled gasp almost instantly gave way to the blood-freezing conviction that they would flip over as the Subaru's right side continued its climb.

"No, no, *no*!" Giselle cried out, before jerking the wheel back to the left. At the same instant, a portion of the rain-saturated slope collapsed beneath the vehicle's weight. Malcolm shouted in alarm at the same time as Pacer yelped from the rear seat.

Somehow, the Crosstrek skidded and bounced down on all four wheels before Giselle hit the brakes. By some miracle of physics she would never understand, the Subaru squelched to a stop in the low center of the drive, which had become a chute for the rainwater pouring down it.

"You—are you okay?" Malcolm asked, as she sat in stunned silence, shaking visibly.

"I—I'm fine, b-but—" she stammered, shaking her head before asking an incredulous, "—how on earth are we *alive*?!"

* * *

"We can waste time later debating over whether you're the world's best driver or its worst one," Malcolm said, his pumping heart still in his throat and his gut still somewhere on the floorboards. Relieved when a quick glance told him that Pacer, too, appeared unharmed, he returned his attention to Giselle. "For now, I'm more concerned with whether you saw which way Acker went after he left here."

She shook her head. "All I saw were the Bronco's headlights—and my life flashing before my eyes. But there's really only one way he could've gone. This road dead ends in less than thirty yards if you try to take it any higher. So he must be heading down the mountain—and back toward the state highway."

Realizing she was right, Malcolm nodded before he noticed the rising water level. "We need to get out of this gully quickly before the engine floods out and we end up drowning in this mud. But before we go after Acker, we have to make sure your neighbor's safe."

"You don't think he could've *taken* her?" Giselle asked, recovering from her shock enough to resume driving. "You didn't see her inside of the Bronco, did you?"

Malcolm thought back before shaking his head. "I couldn't see anything but headlights. But at this point, there's not much I'd put past him. Not even dragging an elderly woman to a couple of ATMs and forcing her to max out her daily withdrawals before he dumps her somewhere."

Giselle shuddered. "You don't think he'd—that he'd really kill her after taking her money, do you?"

Malcolm couldn't bring himself to say what he was thinking, so instead he deflected. "Let's just hope she listened to your excellent advice and stayed safe inside her house."

As they approached the front of a snug-looking cedar cabin with a steeply pitched green roof and matching shutters, Giselle pointed toward the open front door. "I hope that just means she ran to check her little flock after he took off with her Bronco."

"I'll head down and check the outbuildings," he said. "Meanwhile, why don't you go to the house first and call for her before you move in my direction? That way, if she's in there calling the authorities or maybe hiding somewhere upstairs, she'll hear a friendly voice and know it's safe to come out of hiding."

Though Giselle had at first looked poised to argue— perhaps about his idea of splitting up—she instead hesitated and then nodded. "I guess that makes sense. All right."

"Then I'll meet you and Pacer out in that little blue barn, where she keeps her chickens." She pointed out one of a pair of outbuildings a short distance behind the cabin, one of which—the weathered gray shed he presumed had held the Bronco, had its door standing wide open.

"All right. I'll start there," he said before bailing out of the passenger side. Once he'd unloaded Pacer, he looked back at Giselle over the roof of the Crosstrek. "Just be careful to announce yourself at every step, in case Claudette's inclined to shoot first and ask questions second."

Nodding, Giselle said, "As an armed male and a stranger, I'd definitely be more concerned about your safety than mine."

"I'll definitely keep that in mind."

As Pacer led him toward the two outbuildings, the dog's left ear—the only one he was able to raise at all—

sprang to attention, quivering at its tip before he gave a plaintive whine.

"What do you hear, boy?" Malcolm asked him, eyeing the large open door of the gray shed that must have been the outbuilding where the old Bronco had been stowed.

Sniffing the air, Pacer tugged him in that direction rather than toward the little blue barn. After a few steps forward, Malcolm paused and, taking his own advice, called and identified himself before adding: "Miss Claudette, I'm the friend Giselle mentioned on the phone. She's checking inside your house right now. We've come to help you. Can you hear me?"

After waiting in silence with the rain splashing down into growing puddles, he tried again. "Can anybody hear me?"

Once more, he heard no human answer.

Praying he would find her there, he broke into a run... and stopped, spotting a bloody handprint on the white trim of the blue door.

Chapter 5

Giselle was more than willing to run through heavy rain to meet Malcolm out at the barn after discovering the house was empty. But when she opened the door, flash after flash of lightning lit up the sky, and she gaped at the rare sight of hail clattering down, striking against the ground, the cabin, and the glass and sheet metal of her Subaru. Ranging from the diameter of dimes to quarters, the icy chunks bounced off every surface they struck and quickly began to accumulate in low spots.

She startled at a splintering sound, as a large window to the left of the doorway where she was standing cracked diagonally. When the swirling wind snapped off a pair of treetops in the yard and sucked them up into the sky, she fought to push the door closed for her own safety.

Worried that might not be enough to keep her safe, she then ducked inside the shelter of an interior bathroom— the cabin's one windowless room—question after question spinning through her mind. Had Malcolm found Claudette, and if so, what was her condition? And would they and Pacer all be safe from the storm's fury, perhaps inside the barn? She wondered, too, had what she'd just witnessed happening with those two treetops been the prelude to a tornado that would flatten everything around her— including both outbuildings and perhaps even this cabin?

But instead of the rushing, train-like sound so many news reports had led her to expect, the rattling of the hailstones and the howling of the winds died down over a course of several minutes that felt as long as hours. When she finally dared to peek outside again, she found that the lightning, too, had subsided.

Not surprised to find Claudette's landline still dead when she checked it, she headed back outside, where she felt a hot rush of relief to see both outbuildings and the trees nearest to them all remained undamaged. When her gaze strayed to her red Crosstrek, however, her jaw dropped, seeing that one of the treetops had come down across the SUV's now-mashed hood and shattered windshield. What sheet metal remained visible was a moonscape of hail damage.

"Wow..." Unnerved by the fact that she and Malcolm had been sitting in that vehicle only minutes before its destruction, she breathed a silent prayer that both he and Claudette were safe and pulled up her jacket's hood against the rain. Jogging toward the barn, she avoided low spots where some of hailstones had piled up and shouted, "Malcolm? Are you all right?"

He appeared in the doorway, his green eyes somber. "I'm fine—and relieved as hell to see that you're in one piece, too—"

She flung her arms around his neck, giving him a quick hug before she could think better of it. Withdrawing almost as swiftly, she said, "In a lot better shape than my poor car."

"Your car?" Sounding thoroughly distracted, he barely glanced in its direction.

She felt a quick jab of annoyance, imagining he'd been bothered by a hug that had been nothing but a reflex.

"Just look at the poor thing. It's pulverized," gesturing toward the Subaru, until something red against the white-trimmed blue doorframe caught the corner of her eye. "Wait—is that…is that *blood* right there?"

She turned enough to realize it wasn't a smudge so much as a…

Oh, no…

"I'm almost positive it is, so please don't touch that—" His palms rose. "Giselle, you should stay back. There's no need for you to see her."

"You mean Claudette's inside there? You mean she's—? She's *hurt*?" Giselle craned her neck to see past him. Surely, if her elderly neighbor was injured, she would need the re-assurance of a friendly face, someone she knew well to help her. "Please, let me go to her. She needs me."

Malcolm shook his head, his broad shoulders filling the doorway and Pacer whining near his feet. But Malcolm's voice was gentle as he laid one big hand on her upper arm. "I'm sorry, Giselle. Very sorry. But I'm afraid that she no longer does."

Beneath the weight of his hand, her shoulder quivered. "Then she's—you're saying that she's…?"

"Gone, I'm afraid. I'm so sorry."

"No. That can't be right." She shook her head emphatically, her throat too tight. "Please tell me you're—"

"I found her in here just before the hail started," he continued, his gaze regretful. "Judging from this handprint, I'm guessing she was shot confronting him at the shed before she ran inside here, injured. Then she fell and—and most likely bled out in front of her hens' enclosure."

"I—I wonder—do you think she suffered…?" Giselle's vision blurred at the thought of the neighbor she thought of as a last, tenuous link with her childhood dying such a cruel and lonely death.

Malcolm's strong arms closed around her. As he pulled her to his chest, her stomach flipped with the memory of the last time he had held her like this. Only that time, they had both been sobbing, their hearts both shattered beyond repair when they'd learned that Kate was gone.

Because you stopped to save me. Do you despise me for delaying you for those critical few minutes half as much as I've come to hate myself?

"I'm so sorry, Giselle." Malcolm stroked her shaking shoulders. "I can't say for certain, of course, but considering that it appears to be a chest wound and judging by how much blood is pooled around her, I believe she would have lost consciousness very quickly. So I can't think she was aware for more than a matter of seconds before—"

"I so hope that you're right," she said, grasping at that lifeline, "and that she didn't—she didn't have time to feel too much pain or be too frightened..."

Malcolm gave her a clean bandana from his pocket, which she used to wipe her tears. Peering over his shoulder, she caught a glimpse of her neighbor, lying prone, one frail arm thrown out before her in the straw. As Malcolm had warned Giselle, a shockingly large, deep-crimson circle had ponded around her chest and torso.

"Oh, no—no, Claudette," Giselle choked out, feeling something break inside her.

"Let's get you away from this." With a nod and a light touch, he directed her attention toward a wired enclosure, where a dozen hens crowned with the feathery white bonnets that marked their breed scratched and pecked about their enclosure looking for unclaimed morsels.

"That's it," he told her, his words as soothing as the

steadying hand he kept on her shoulder. "Keep watch over this peaceful little world that she created, that she loved. Not a sight she'd never want remembered."

"But she—I need to—"

"Shh. Right now, you don't *need* to do anything but keep on breathing," he said. "Right after the worst of the storm passed, I managed to get a couple of calls out, and help is on the way."

Her hand found Pacer, who had maneuvered himself to offer comfort. She stroked the shepherd mix's broad, warm head and thick ruff as she looked up at Malcolm. "The police are coming?"

"Police, an ambulance—and most likely more rescue people than we'll know what to do with," he assured her, his voice the one point of calm amid the maelstrom of emotion threatening to tear her into pieces.

"But what good can any of them possibly do at this point?" she asked, fresh tears streaming as the reality of the situation struck her. "They'll be as useless to her as they were for Kate."

"It's true, they won't be able to bring Claudette back at this point. You and I both know that no one has that power. But they'll do the same as Liam, Ajay, Fletcher, and so many others on the law enforcement joint task force have been working to do for my uncle, my mother, and all of Acker's other victims and bring her the justice she deserves. That, and to see that Acker's stopped before he gets the chance to add even more names to the list of lives that he's destroyed."

"He *has* to be stopped," she insisted, her red-rimmed eyes burning with the light of a fierce determination, "because it's absolutely clear that anyone who could do this kind of thing is nothing but pure evil. Evil in the flesh."

Chapter 6

Disturbed to see how pale Giselle was looking, Malcolm suggested that she wait inside Claudette's house, away from the body and out of the weather. But because he needed to be certain they wouldn't be disturbing a portion of the crime scene, he asked her, "You didn't find any signs in there of a break-in or a struggle inside, did you?"

"Everything looked neat enough in there," she said, "except the .22 rifle I mentioned earlier was missing from its rack. Did you notice, does she still have that with her?"

"I didn't see it out here. She could've dropped it by the shed when she was hit or somewhere near there. I'll take a look, but I'm betting we won't find it at all."

Giselle frowned. "Then you think Acker's taken it?"

"It's hard to imagine Markus would miss the chance to add another loaded weapon to his arsenal," Malcolm said grimly.

"As if he wasn't already dangerous enough."

"We can only hope this weather was as hard on his stolen ride as it was on yours." Malcolm nodded in the direction of the Crosstrek. "I'm afraid that if he makes it to the interstate, he's going to be a heck of a lot harder to catch than if they can keep him contained within this general area."

"I can't help fantasizing about this storm sending another of those flying trees down from the sky to squash him like a roach inside that stolen Bronco," Giselle said.

"I'd definitely spring for popcorn and two tickets to *that* movie," Malcolm said, though in his heart he knew that getting rid of someone as smart and adaptable as Acker was highly unlikely to be so simple.

"While I'm inside," Giselle said, "should I be looking for the Bronco's plate number or anything like that for the police?"

"That'll all be in the state's system, so they should be able to pull it up with their computers. But if Claudette has any next of kin—"

"I know there's no one local, but she did mention a niece on the East Coast that she was fond of."

"If you see an address book, maybe you can find this niece's contact information."

"Should I—should I—try to reach out and tell her that her aunt's...?" Giselle asked, running her hands through Pacer's fur.

"Oh, no." Taking her hand in his, he noticed how very cold it had gone. "Definitely leave the notification to the police. And before you worry about any of it, I want you to make yourself a cup of tea if Claudette has it. You still drink tea, don't you?"

She nodded.

"And why don't you take Pacer inside the house with you as well? Let him keep you company for a while," he suggested.

"You're sure you won't need him to work?"

"Not for a while, I don't think. Besides, he's been pretty much glued to you since you came out here." He glanced down at his dog, who was smiling in open-mouthed canine bliss as she rubbed his ear. "If I were the sensitive sort, I might have to dock his pay a biscuit or two for his disloyalty. Though I really can't fault him for his good taste."

"Thanks, Malcolm. As terrible as this is, it's a relief to have you to help me through it—especially after I practically chewed your head off earlier."

Her eyes brimmed with regret. But when she stopped petting Pacer to give Malcolm another quick embrace—the second time she'd done so—it took him by surprise. Reminding himself that they'd just survived an ordeal that would have shaken anyone to their foundations, he told himself that he had no business feeling any different about that hug than he would have had it come from any female friend or family member.

Except it wasn't what he felt at all, and it didn't sit well with him. Being anywhere near her didn't sit well, making him uncomfortable in ways he'd rather not delve into too deeply. But her expectant look reminded him she still awaited his response.

"So, neither of us was a pleasant surprise for the other today when I showed up on your doorstep," he acknowledged. "But moving past that, I'm seriously relieved to see you're safe and sound. I'm absolutely certain Markus came *right* past your cabin before he headed up to find your neighbor. He might've just as easily stopped and killed *you* for your SUV instead."

For one horrifying instant, he pictured her body lying in a pool of blood rather than Claudette's.

Laying a hand over her chest, Giselle drew a deep breath, a flush suffusing her face. "And once more I'm left knowing that my survival may have cost the life of someone I cared for."

"You can't blame yourself for things outside of your

control," he told her, only to see she'd stepped away to gesture toward the open barn doorway.

"Look at that," she said. "A break in the rain at last. Pacer and I had better run inside while we can manage it without getting soaked."

Noting how quickly she had changed the subject of the guilt she carried, he made a mental note to try again to talk to her about it another time. Nodding toward the darkening sky, he said, "Go on ahead, then. I'll check in with you soon."

She'd been inside only a few minutes when a familiar blue Jeep Wrangler Rubicon pulled up. Moments later, Ajay Wright jumped out. Though he was dressed for search and rescue fieldwork—and the weather—rather than in his police uniform, there was nothing informal about the intense expression on his face as he approached, with his SAR-trained yellow Lab, Pumpkin, trotting at his side.

Malcolm didn't look away, knowing he deserved the royal chewing out he was about to get for disobeying a directive issued for everyone's safety. But as Ajay drew nearer, he saw that the lines etched into his warm brown brow were those of concern rather than anger, and his grip, when he grasped Malcolm's forearm, was that of a friend, not an accuser.

"Before I see this body you've called in, I need to know if you're okay," Ajay said.

"I'll be just fine. I'm—"

"The minute I heard that half-baked story about you running off to see some girlfriend no one had never heard of, I knew damned well *exactly* the kind of stunt you'd pulled. I even knew the reason, considering how upset you were about my decision—a decision I made along with Liam Hill and the whole damn task force—to hold off on the search until we had both the conditions and the manpower in place to assure everybody's safety."

"I'm sorry," Malcolm told him. "Sorry I questioned your professional judgment and even sorrier I took off on my own to do this. But at the moment, I couldn't think of anything but Acker laughing at everything he's put my family through while he runs off to start his murderous cycle all over again someplace else."

Ajay regarded him, the intensity of his golden-brown gaze softening a fraction. "I've known you for quite some time now, and you've always been so reliable, so focused on doing the right thing for others, that it's easy to forget you're carrying some pretty heavy baggage of your own. It's only been, what, three-and-a-half years since your fiancée's passing, hasn't it? Maybe that, in combination with these latest losses—"

"Listen, Ajay, I know how close you and my sister are, but whatever Lizzy's telling you, I'm not looking for any excuses for my actions."

"It's a damned good thing," Ajay said bluntly. "Because there's *no* excuse good enough to make up for shutting off your GPS tracker and leaving me scared spitless I'd end up having to explain to the woman I love how I'd missed the signs her brother was about to go rogue and get his fool self killed."

Malcolm winced, realizing he shouldn't be surprised that his father had broadcast the news of Malcolm's "secret rendezvous" far and wide the second he was out of sight. Buck had been practically giddy since he and Malcolm's Aunt Jenny had found themselves in a relationship. After Jenny's husband Robert passed away a while back, she realized Buck was the person who had truly loved her for years. And it was only natural that Lizzy would have mentioned it to Ajay, especially considering Malcolm's recent—and very firm—insistence that he had zero interest in meeting one of her single friends for coffee *just to see how things might go.*

Nodding toward Giselle's wrecked Subaru, Malcolm said, "It's clear to me now that coming up here in this weather was the wrong move—and risking your safety by running off the way I did was a worse one, so whatever your decision, I'm prepared to accept the consequences."

"I'm glad to hear that, Malcolm, because until I feel confident that you're thinking like a team member again instead of a lone wolf with no regard for personal safety, your only involvement with SAR is to be at Crosswinds, assisting Sebastian and Della with that latest batch of pups that they're training."

Malcolm's pride stung at the thought of being relegated to puppy duty, of all things. The headstrong younger man he'd once been wanted to argue the decision, to shout at Ajay that he needed to continue his involvement with the hunt for his uncle's and his mother's murderer with one of the best trailing dogs on the team. But he saw Ajay watching him, waiting to see if he was really man enough to accept the consequences he'd more than earned without balking.

Nodding, Malcolm drew a deep breath. "Whatever you need from me is fine."

Ajay nodded. "*Good*, because right now, there's a victim deserving of my full attention and a task force I need to help coordinate so we can get this perpetrator into custody as soon as possible. Do we understand each other?"

"Absolutely, we do," Malcolm said, understanding that it could take some time to repair the damage he'd done to their relationship—if it could be repaired at all. But there was little time to worry over such things, as Ajay kept him busy answering questions about what had happened as he headed into the barn to do his initial assessment of the victim and scene.

When an SUV with law enforcement markings and an ambulance pulled up, Ajay poked his head outside again and told Malcolm, "While you're waiting, I want you to have the EMTs check out that hand I've noticed you've been keeping out of my sight."

"It'll be fine," Malcolm said, amazed that he had even noticed the bandage.

"No, Malcolm. You'll get yourself checked out, now," Ajay said, more firmly. "You're part of a team. And a team sees to members who are hurting so they'll be prepared to serve the mission together at some point in the future. Do we understand each other?"

"Absolutely," Malcolm answered, grateful that despite the hell he'd just put Ajay through, the man cared enough about his welfare to give him hope that what amounted to a suspension from real search-and-rescue work wouldn't last forever.

After getting his hand rewrapped by the EMT, who advised him to visit the emergency clinic in town for X-rays and further evaluation as soon as he was able, Malcolm spotted Giselle walking toward him, her eyes puffy and red-rimmed. Seeing him, Pacer trotted ahead of her to greet him.

"He started whining at the door when he spotted the other dog out here," she said by way of explanation.

"Probably figured he was missing out on some action," Malcolm said as he rubbed his dog's ears.

"He's not the only one," Giselle admitted as Ajay stepped out of the barn and joined them.

Malcolm was quick to launch into introductions. "Giselle Dowling, this is Lieutenant Ajay Wright. He's coordinating Owl Creek Search and Rescue and also co-directing the task force in charge of the manhunt for Markus Acker. Claudette Hogan was Giselle's family friend and neighbor."

"I'm so sorry we're meeting under such circumstances," Ajay told her. "My condolences on your loss."

"It doesn't—it doesn't seem possible it's real." Her voice thickened as she brought her hand to her mouth. "I keep hoping I'll wake up from this. But it's not a nightmare, is it?"

Malcolm laid a hand on her shoulder as Ajay said, "I can't change what's happened, I'm afraid, but I can promise you, my colleagues and I are already taking steps to bring the person responsible to justice. Liam Hill, my colleague from the FBI, is working out of our command post in Owl Creek, coordinating checkpoints along the only two routes leading out of this immediate area and putting out a statewide BOLO on the Bronco registered in your neighbor's name, just in case the suspect has somehow managed to slip past our net."

"Surely, you know you're chasing Markus Acker?" Giselle asked, sounding confused.

"We certainly believe that to be the case," Ajay said, "but since Malcolm tells me that neither of you saw him face-to-face, we don't yet have confirmation."

"Assuming it really *is* him, though," she said, clearly unwilling to consider any other possibility, "do you think it's likely he's already left the area?"

"What with all the downed trees around this elevation—" Ajay gestured toward the Subaru "—I have serious doubts about him getting very far. Even if he could escape, I have to suspect there's some reason he's been lingering close to this area so long in the first place."

"Like what?" Malcolm asked.

"The general thinking on the task force has been that he's holed up in some unoccupied ski cabin he's broken into, using it as an easy source of shelter and supplies. But either he's run low or something's forced him to move on for some reason. Or possibly he has some new plan in mind."

"Have you come up with any theories on what that might be?" Malcolm asked.

"Presuming he sticks with his usual M.O., he's going to need funding to reestablish his cult in a new location and start recruiting and fleecing some new converts. Or he may try to reconnect with past followers still willing to help him."

"Who could possibly want anything to do with him now?" Giselle asked. "Surely, everyone's seen on the news how he's been exposed as a swindler and a killer."

Ajay explained, "Acker had them so twisted inside-out with all that happy-family garbage he was selling them that at least some might still be vulnerable enough to fall for it again, regardless of how badly he abused them."

She shook her head. "I'm not sure whether that's more sad or sick."

"There's room enough for both, I'd say. We've been trying to reach out to as many as we can, offering them some incentives to give us a call instead of helping him in case he does reach out—everything from offers of counseling and job placement assistance to information about the reward fund that's been set up for anyone offering help resulting in Acker's apprehension."

"You really think one of those ex-cult types would rat out their former guru?" Malcolm asked him.

"Money talks," Ajay said. "Especially when it's paired with a firm reminder of the penalties for aiding and abetting someone fleeing multiple murder charges. Or maybe a dirty, desperate Markus Acker will have broken down too badly to lay on the same charm he once did with them."

Malcolm could picture the well-dressed, fit, articulate man—so used to adulation by his followers—now spitting mad at having been reduced by circumstances. "I can imagine that seeing him in that state could finally open some eyes."

"Which once again leaves him on the run, on his own and strapped for money. And with absolutely nothing to lose since he knows he'll never breathe air as a free man again if he's caught."

"Does this have anything to do with that text that Lizzy sent out last week warning everyone in the family that we should all take extra precautions until he's been captured?"

Ajay nodded. "I'm sure it does. I've warned her that with Acker on the move, this could be the most dangerous time for everyone in your family since he's already zeroed in on them as a potential source of wealth. Plus, there's a history between Marcus and the Coltons."

Malcolm felt an icy chill cleave through him as his thoughts went to his loved ones, from the oldest to the very youngest and most vulnerable members of his extended family. "You really think he'd have the guts to make another run at any of us at this point? With the task force closing in on him and everyone well aware by now what he's capable of, the idea seems almost suicidal."

"If he were a normal person, I'd tell you you're absolutely right," Ajay said, "but Acker's desperate—and enough of a narcissist to imagine he's capable of making one more end run around us."

"I'll get the word out about what's happened up here today," Malcolm said, "and make sure everyone in the family understands that he's definitely mobile as well."

"That's a good idea, but I need to review today's chain of events with both of you before you leave here for the ranch—or at least that's where I presume you'll be going, Malcolm."

"I'm hoping that we both will," Malcolm was quick to say, glancing at Giselle. "We have plenty of space for guests there, and with Markus armed and on the loose—"

She shook her head. "I wouldn't want to intrude on your family."

"Don't be ridiculous. You wouldn't be intruding," Malcolm told her. "And we both know there's no way that staying in your cabin is a reasonable option, especially now that you're cut off without transportation."

"You would be awfully vulnerable alone up here," Ajay agreed.

"And the phones have been in and out, too," Malcolm added. "So unless you'd rather contend with having Pacer and me camped out on your porch every single night for the duration to stand guard over you—"

She rolled her eyes at the suggestion. "That won't be necessary, Malcolm. I'll take advantage of your hospitality—but only until either Acker is in custody or I've had the chance to make arrangements for a rental car and lodging."

"For what it's worth," Ajay told her, "I think you've made a very wise decision."

"I'm not sure I had another choice," she said, "unless I wanted to deal with Malcolm and Pacer staking out my doorstep morning, noon, and night. I'd definitely never get any writing done then."

"So now we're pretending you were doing loads *without* me?" Malcolm fired back.

She sent a look in Malcolm's direction that convinced him to drop the subject.

After briefly excusing himself to speak to Fletcher and two other officers who'd arrived about evidence collection, Ajay returned and asked Malcolm and Giselle to join him inside of Claudette's cabin, where he planned to record their statements using his phone.

Once Ajay had asked the last of his questions, Giselle walked over to the kitchen counter, where she picked up an address book. Passing it to where he stood with Malcolm beside the small table where they'd all been seated, she said, "I found this earlier in Claudette's sewing room. Her niece's name is Lorna Hunnicutt. She lives in Massachusetts."

"So this Lorna is the only family?"

Giselle nodded. "Unless you count that little flock of hers. I know they're only chickens, but Claudette—she loved them."

Malcolm grabbed some tissues from a console adorned with poultry-themed trophies and photographs of a smiling, younger Claudette holding various chickens with long blue ribbons. Passing the box to Giselle, he said, "Don't you worry about those hens. If Ajay and the niece have no objections, my dad knows a nice retired couple who keep farm animals, mostly minis, around to keep their grandkids happy. I'm betting they'd love to add Claudette's little flock to their menagerie. That way, you'd never have to worry about them ending up in anybody's stewpot."

"I'd appreciate you seeing to that," Ajay said. "As soon as we're finished processing the scene, I'll give you a heads-up so you can come remove them from the property. In the meantime, I'll be sure they're taken care of."

"Thank you both so much," Giselle said. "And I can help you collect them later, Malcolm."

With her SUV undrivable, Ajay asked Malcolm for his truck keys and assigned a junior officer to retrieve the pickup from the trailhead where he'd spotted it earlier. Turning to Giselle, he added, "That way, you can make a quick stop by your place to pick up whatever you'll need for your stay at the ranch. I'd definitely like to see both of you off the road before full dark."

Malcolm and Giselle shared a look. In her eyes, he saw the realization that even on the run from the authorities, the armed and dangerous Markus Acker had the potential to pose a threat to them on these lonely, unlit roads.

A short time later, Ajay excused himself to step inside of Claudette's sewing room, where he said he planned to contact her niece.

Giselle shook her head as he closed the door behind him. "What a terrible part of his job that must be, notifying people with such awful news. I don't know how he does it."

"He's a good man," Malcolm told her, as he headed for the small living area with Giselle following. "He's been amazing for Lizzy, too."

"He's seeing your sister?" Giselle took a seat on a striped sofa draped with a fringed blanket. "Is it serious?"

Malcolm chose a sturdy-looking chair that faced her.

"I'm sure it is. They're great together. As hellacious as this past year has been, I can't tell you that no good has come of it. My cousin, Fletcher—you may have seen him outside—has come back to work as a detective here in town, and his sister Frannie—"

"Isn't she the one who's into books?" Despite her sadness, Giselle felt a smile tug at her lips. "I remember we had that in common."

Nodding, he said, "She owns Book Mark It, the local bookstore and café. You'd love the place. But she has another project going now as well." His green eyes warmed with pleasure. "She and her husband, Dante, are expecting their first child soon."

"I'm so glad to hear it," she said. "After your losses, Coltons deserve something to celebrate, and what could be more wonderful than welcoming a new life?"

"Is that—is that something you've ever imagined for yourself, having a family of your own someday?"

She was quick to shake her head. "Maybe at one time I thought that way, in some distant sort of future. But now?" The scoffing noise she made was tinged with bitterness. "How can I imagine moving on now, writing a new chapter of my story that Kate can't ever be a part of?"

Malcolm's forehead creased. "She'll always be a part of you. Of both of us. And I know she wouldn't want to see you stuck forever, holed up in that old cabin like some recluse."

"Is this your way of telling me that *you've* come unstuck, Malcolm?" she challenged. "That you're out there enjoying a healthy social life—or going out with any women since the accident?" Hoping she was wrong, she added. "Or maybe by this time you've moved on to something more serious? After all, it *has* been more than three years."

He shook his head, "No. I—no," he stammered. "And I can't imagine five years or ten or a lifetime making any difference. No one else will ever…could ever hope to compare to—"

"Malcolm," Ajay said, as he came down the hall, his phone in his hand.

"Did you reach Claudette's niece?" Giselle asked.

"I've left a message for her to call me, but I'm afraid that something else has come up." Once more, Ajay's attention turned to Malcolm. "It's about your truck, over at the trailhead. I've heard from the officer I sent to retrieve it from the scenic overlook where I spotted it parked earlier, above the lake."

"Was there some sort of problem?" Malcolm asked.

"She's telling me it's missing from the lot."

"The three-year-old silver RAM? You're sure you have her looking in the right spot?"

Ajay nodded, his expression grim. "I am—especially since she's just discovered Claudette Hogan's wrecked Bronco. Looks like Markus must've rolled it off the hillside into some heavy timber."

"Guess he figured it would be too hot, after murdering the owner," Malcolm said. "But why steal *my* truck?"

"Most likely, it was the only vehicle left up there in this weather. You didn't keep a magnetic key box on it, did you? In case of a lock-out?"

Malcolm sighed. "I thought I had it hidden well enough, but yeah. I lost my keys a couple of years back while I was out doing SAR work, and it turned out to be a huge, expensive hassle to replace them."

"Thought I remembered you mentioning something about that at one time," Ajay said. "Anyway, I'm sorry about your truck."

"Don't be. It's all on me, the way I figure—Claudette's death, the loss of my pickup. If I had only listened to you and waited until tomorrow to head out with the team, we could've counted on support from the whole task force, just the way you said."

Giselle shook her head before reaching out to touch his hand. "Claudette's death is a tragedy, but it happened because of Markus Acker's choices, Malcolm. Not yours or mine. He's the one who pulled that trigger."

"She's right about that," Ajay insisted. "And as furious as I've been with you all day—mostly because I couldn't quit worrying about breaking the news of your death to your family—your actions today may have kept us from losing whatever momentum we'd gained after that hiker called the tip line about spotting a man matching Acker's description in this vicinity. As much as I hate to admit it, you and I both know this kind of rain would have obliterated any scent trail. So let's not waste any more time or energy on self-recrimination. All right?"

With that, he offered Malcolm his right hand.

Malcolm hesitated. "I don't suppose this gets me out of puppy duty over at Crosswinds, does it?"

"I don't know, man. Does it change any part of that GPS-tracker stunt of yours?" Ajay asked. "And anyway, *who* doesn't like puppies?"

"*I* like puppies," Giselle murmured as she stroked Pacer's shoulder.

"That's not the issue, and you know it," Malcolm said as he shook Ajay's hand. "But I'll quit complaining and take my medicine."

Giselle felt a knot inside her loosen as some of the tension between the two men eased.

"And while you do," Ajay said, "All the members of the

task force and I will be doing every single thing possible to run Acker to ground and bring him in, I swear it. And if I have a single thing to say about it, we're going to do it before he has the chance to take another life."

Chapter 7

The stormy afternoon's gloom had given way to a deeper evening darkness by the time that Ajay was able to spare an officer to drive Giselle, Malcolm, and Pacer back to the ranch, following a brief stop at Giselle's cabin.

"Don't worry too much about forgetting something," Malcolm said as she looked through her closet. "We can always stop back tomorrow to pick up anything else you need."

But as she rode with him in the rear seat of the police SUV, however, she couldn't help picturing herself walking back inside of the blue barn, looking down at the blood-matted straw where she had last seen Claudette's body.

Giselle's stomach turned, her heart fluttering. She turned to hide her face, her shallow breaths steaming the police SUV's side window as light raindrops pattered down against it. Seeming to sense her mounting distress, Pacer, who was resting on the floorboard, shifted his position to lick and nuzzle her hand.

"You okay?" Malcolm asked her.

"Just thinking about having to return there," she said, her voice sounding thin and reedy in her own ears. "After what happened—what we saw inside."

"I know it's hard," Malcolm said, "but I want you to

try right now to focus on your breathing for me. Pay attention to letting the air out—all of it. That's good. Then allow yourself a moment before you fill your lungs again completely..."

For the next portion of their journey, he helped her center on that one thing: breathing, reminding her that she was safe with him. At first, she had a hard time focusing, worried that the officer transporting them might be listening and judging her for not doing a better job of holding herself together. Gradually, however, Malcolm's quiet, steady tone captured her full attention, until she felt the tension draining from her body.

Exhausted from all the nervous energy that had been coursing through her, she eventually found her eyes growing heavy as she threaded her fingers through the fur of Pacer's warm ruff. The next thing that she knew, Malcolm touched her elbow, waking her.

"I hate to disturb you," he said, "but we're just driving up to the ranch's main house and I didn't figure you'd like your first meeting with my father and anybody else who might be up this late to be slung over my shoulder while I hauled you inside like a sack of feed."

"Um, definitely not." Straightening, she yawned. "But you've probably forgotten, I *have* met your father. And most of your siblings and your cousins, too, at that big engagement cookout celebration your dad hosted for you and Kate here."

He smiled. "And that wasn't enough to scare you off?"

"Far from it," she said, remembering how she'd originally rolled her eyes at the idea of a family living surrounded by their crops and livestock in a home that Kate had described as a custom big red barn. "I was totally charmed. I remember how your sister had just finished updating the space. Everything was so fresh and modern."

"Lizzy hasn't lived out here on the ranch for some time, but she still loves nothing more than when Dad sets her loose with a budget and a mission to spruce things up and bring us up to date."

"It wasn't only your home, though, that impressed me. Everyone was so friendly and fun to be around that day." Giselle smiled at the memory. "And they all kept gushing about how excited they were to have my sister joining the family. I'm sure you remember how much they adored her…" She tipped her hand in an awkward gesture. "But that was Kate—wherever she went. She had an energy people were drawn to."

Nodding, he glanced out the window as they rolled up to the house, but not before she glimpsed the pain in his eyes at the reminder of the treasure he had lost.

Once they had both thanked the officer for taking the time to bring them here, Giselle and Malcolm headed for a side door, where someone had left a light on. With Pacer beside them, Malcolm carried his backpack over his shoulder while Giselle slung her tote and overnight bag over her arm and walked with him through what was now only a fine mist.

As they reached the sheltered porch, she stopped short, putting her bags down on a bench beside the porch. "Before we go inside and face your family—"

"It'll probably only be my dad at this hour, unless my aunt Jenny's visiting. They've been seeing each other for a while now."

"His brother's widow?" Wincing, she said. "Sorry—I know that came out sounding as if I'm judging, but I suppose it's only natural that they might comfort each other."

"Don't be sorry. It's definitely taken a little getting used to for a lot of people. But my aunt and uncle Robert hadn't really been close for years before his death, and Mama Jen and my dad... My siblings and I all grew up thinking of our aunt Jenny as a second mother, since she helped with us so much after our own mom ditched us. They genuinely care about each other and make each other very happy."

"Then that's all that really matters, isn't it?" Giselle said quickly. "And what I'd *wanted* to say—before I put my foot in my mouth, at least, was thank you, for helping me before."

"For helping you?" He shook his head.

"The way you helped me get a handle on my breathing in the police cruiser, slowing me down so I could catch hold of my emotions. It really—it made a difference for me."

He nodded. "I could tell by the way you dropped off right afterward. You were clearly so worn down by everything you'd been thinking and feeling, you didn't have enough energy left to stay awake."

"You've been there, too, haven't you?" she asked quietly.

He hesitated, studying her for a long moment before admitting, "All too often, especially in that first year or two after the accident. I'd have these—I guess you'd call them episodes, where I'd find myself right back there, living through what happened. But I expect you'd know something about those, too, considering that we were both there."

Her heart bumped at her sternum, her mouth drying in an instant. "I—I definitely do know. It's funny...how I used to...used to imagine that a person...would have to be asleep to have night terrors."

He nodded, their gazes coming together, holding. She saw the sadness in them and heard his hard swallow before he spoke again.

"Ranchers are doers. We aren't talkers. So I threw myself into the things that needed doing around here on the ranch. And then there was the SAR volunteer work and the training. But it wasn't helping, not enough…because the better part of me was still back out on that lake."

In her mind's eye, she saw the diamond pattern of the water sparkling. Pictured the red speedboat—the one that was never identified afterward, despite extensive efforts by investigators and the Colton family's offer of a large cash reward for information—racing for the towrope. Saw Kate's head turn, in that last split second, the white of her teeth flashing with a scream that Giselle's memory had mercifully muted…

"My father came across me one day," Malcolm told her, turning to peer into the mist-softened darkness, "out in the working barn, messing with my lariat sort of idly when I figured there was no one else around. Only somehow that loop ended up sailing up across the top of one of the rafters—"

"You weren't planning to…?" she asked, a bright line of alarm cutting through the past like the sharp corner of a razor dragged across soft flesh at the deadly image of the dangling noose that took shape in her mind.

He shook his head and then sighed. "I can't honestly tell you *what* I was thinking because I don't rightly remember. I only know that my dad says he saw a blankness in my eyes that day when he spotted me. It must've scared the devil out of him, because as allergic as he's been his whole life to talking seriously about things like a person's feelings or, worse yet, mental health, he made a bunch of calls and pulled some serious strings. Never mentioned a single word about it to any of my siblings, as far as I know, but he got me into some intensive sessions starting that very afternoon."

A warm tide of relief spilled through her. "So you got the help you needed?"

"I got some valuable first aid—and eventually, what you might call a sort of toolkit with some techniques to help me break myself free when I start to spiral. I won't lie and tell you that it's filled in the giant crater that day on the lake left in my heart. But so far, it's kept me right here with my family—and this guy—" He reached down, to rub his dog's ears, "where I'm needed."

"That has to be nice, to know there's someone who still needs you," she said.

"You have a hell of a lot more to offer than you imagine," he assured her.

She made a scoffing sound. "Thanks for the vote of confidence, but I'm not really sure what anybody'd want from a washed-up ghostwriter whose social skills have dried up with her income."

"Don't you worry, Giselle," he said, reaching out to touch the side of her arm. "I'm pretty sure I've got some ideas for you on that front."

"As much as I appreciate your trusting me with your story—and your tip about the breathing techniques—I'm not looking to be anybody's pity project," she told him as she jerked her arm away. "Especially not somebody who can't help but remind me of the worst moments of my life."

Malcolm tried to continue the conversation, but Giselle only shook her head. Before he could think of anything more to change her mind, Pacer lunged toward a rattling at the door a moment before it opened.

"I thought I heard voices out here," said Malcolm's father, who was—Malcolm was grateful to see—still dressed in a pair of jeans and sweatshirt, though his silver-tinged brown hair was mussed as if he'd been relaxing with some TV. Quickly raking it back into some semblance of order, Buck Colton—a tall and hearty-looking man who remained fit from years of ranch work—frowned at Malcolm, his deeply tanned face crinkling. "I didn't realize you'd be back tonight, son—or bringing home a guest."

"You remember Giselle Dowling, don't you, Dad?" asked Malcolm. "You met her a few years back, at the party for Kate's and my engage—"

His father speared him with a shocked look. "You're dating Kate's *sister*?"

"Dating?" Giselle erupted, shaking her head with her eyes flared in what looked like horror. "No! It's bad enough I'm being forced to—absolutely not."

Malcolm felt himself wince down to the subatomic level as he realized the misunderstanding was entirely his fault. "Listen, Dad, what I told you earlier, about visiting a woman I've been seeing in Boise for the weekend. That was actually just a cover story."

"A cover for what? Spill it, son."

"Why?" Malcolm asked irritably. "So you can blab it to the entire family, the way you told everyone that I was seeing someone after I asked you to keep it quiet?"

His father frowned and waved off his complaint. "Serves you right for getting an old man's hopes up, however you want to sugarcoat it. So, are you going to tell me what this is all about or not?"

"Pacer and I took a little trip on our own to the mountains above the lake," Malcolm explained, "to try to pick up Acker's trail before the storm could wash it out."

His father stiffened. "So you lied to me and went off on your own to risk your neck? Do you have any idea what it would do to me, or to this family, if you'd ended up getting yourself hurt or worse out there? I thought we'd been through this before and you were past this sort of nonsense."

"It's not anything like that, Dad. I promise you it isn't," Malcolm said, shaking his head as he held his father's gaze. "I had no intention of getting myself killed. I only wanted to finally put an end to this hold Markus Acker's had on our family once and for all."

"All on your own, instead of acting as part of a team, like anybody with some damned sense?"

Malcolm grimaced before waving off the criticism. "You can save the lecture about my impatience. I've already heard enough from Ajay. And Pacer and I *did* hit on Markus's trail, which we ended up following past the Dowlings' old family ski cabin, where I found Giselle living on her own."

For the first time, his father stopped and truly seemed to look at her. "That's odd. I understood that you've been out in California all this time. Writing those stories for the stars your sister was so proud of."

"I'm afraid I can't seem to make myself care about their dramas any longer," Giselle confessed, sounding defeated by the admission.

"Well, I never *could* see what was so interesting about them, so join the club," Buck said almost cheerfully before waving them both after him deeper into the entryway. "Why don't you come on inside with me? Could I get you something? A drink? A sandwich, or I've got a real nice lasagna that my Jenny brought by earlier. I could heat it up for you if you're up for a late dinner? If you don't mind my saying so, you two look like you've had quite the day."

Giselle started to demur, but Malcolm said, "I'll warm myself up some of that lasagna in a little bit, Dad, but I can make you something meat-free, Giselle. You do eat eggs, right? Or how about a cheese sandwich with some fresh lettuce and tomato?"

"As much as I appreciate the offer, I'm too exhausted to think about eating right now," she said, leading him to notice that she was looking somewhat pale. "Maybe just some water."

His father hurried off to the kitchen before returning with a full glass, sparkling with ice. Beckoning them both into the great room, he looked from her shaking hands, as she accepted his offering, to Malcolm, once they were all seated.

"Well, son?" his father asked, handing him a beer, the top already popped off. "You going to fill me in? Did you ever find any sign of Markus?"

"About the time I reached Giselle's place, the storm's full fury hit." Malcolm raised the temptingly cold beer before setting it down again on the table at his elbow without drinking any of it.

"Thank goodness you were someplace safe, at least," his father said before nodding toward Malcolm's bandaged hand. "But what happened there?"

"A minor fall. I'll go and get it looked at tomorrow. But unfortunately, after leaving Giselle's property, Acker encountered one of her older neighbors."

"Claudette Hogan," Giselle supplied, her voice thick

with emotion. "He—he murdered her. An old friend of my grandmother's…"

"I'm so sorry—and so damned furious. Forgive my language, but that sorry excuse for a man should have been put in prison—or put down like a mad dog—months ago." Malcolm's father leapt up from the recliner where he'd been seated, his big fists knotting in impotent frustration as he paced the room. "First, he took my brother, and then he—how many others have to die or have their lives turned upside-down before he's finally stopped?"

"I know, Dad. I know," Malcolm said, feeling utterly undone by his father's grief as he, too, stood. "It's why I had to try to find him. I couldn't bear to let it go on any longer. But now he's killed another woman, and he has my truck to get around in."

"Your truck?"

"It's my own fault, I'm afraid. But both Ajay and I agreed that there was no way Giselle should stay alone up there so close to where the murder took place, not knowing if Acker might still be holed up somewhere nearby for some reason."

"No, of course not," his father said, giving her a sympathetic look. "Heaven only knows we have plenty of extra room here."

"I won't impose on you long," she said. "In the morning, I'll start looking for someplace else to—"

"You couldn't impose if you wanted to, young lady," Buck Colton insisted, his rich voice resonating in the high-ceiled great-room. "As far as I'm concerned, you're practically family. You know, we all thought the world of Kate, and she'd tell anyone who'd listen about her little sister. She was so proud of you. You know that, don't you? Not just of what you did and the people you rubbed shoulders with, but who you are inside."

"Th-thank you for that." Rising from her seat, Giselle stared at him, her eyes shimmering with moisture.

Malcolm's father surprised him by going to her and, without a moment's hesitation, enfolding her in one of the same dad hugs he might have given Lizzy.

But Giselle stiffened in response, clearly unused to anyone making such an assumption about her state of mind. Before Malcolm could warn his dad to back off and give her space, however, she crumpled against him, responding exactly as his sister might have. And sure enough, his father signaled for Malcolm to pass over the box of tissues, reassuring her in that way of his that had so often made him and his siblings believe that, despite whatever seemingly impossible odds were stacked against them, tomorrow might somehow turn out to be a better day.

Chapter 8

Lying low didn't come easily for Markus Acker. By nature, he was a man who preferred getting out and interacting with his fellow humans, using the gifts he had been given, namely patience, intelligence, and cunning, to transform himself into whatever it took to convince the gullible to devote themselves body and soul—and bank accounts—to his needs.

Only upon the rarest of occasions, such as when his greed outstripped his caution, would Markus resort to riskier measures. Regrettably, in recent months, several such incidents had led to certain acts. Acts resulting in a string of deaths that law enforcement had eventually linked to him, just as he was certain that they soon would today's.

Markus didn't have it in him to regret the resulting fatalities themselves. After all, who was he to know how much longer any of the lives he'd terminated—he thought again of that frail-looking, pathetic woman, her hair more white than gray—would have lasted anyway, or whether any of his "victims" had been especially happy? What he *did* regret was that these so-called "murders" had forced him to abandon the comfortable life he'd worked so hard to build and hide out like some filthy desperado, sleeping in a musty cabin and surviving on old canned goods.

The thought was especially maddening since he'd been so close to reaching his very own Wilderness Chapel of Contemplation. Located on one of the small, wooded islands a short distance off the southern shoreline of Blackbird Lake, the spartan chapel was, by design, neither connected to the grid nor a place of creature comfort. Yet the moss-covered hillside structure was at least stocked with the basic necessities of life. And more importantly, Markus suspected that the last penitent he'd sent there—to contemplate the wisdom of questioning one of his directives—would still be waiting faithfully, completely unaware of recent events and eager for his chance to do whatever was necessary to once more regain favor...

But Markus had opted against that choice for now, fearing that the authorities might have somehow permeated the layers of false entities he'd used to hide his ownership and set up some sort of remote surveillance. Instead, he'd broken into a seemingly abandoned cabin, where he'd bided his time for two long weeks. He might have remained there for a little longer, but earlier that day, two powerfully built men wearing flannels, jeans, and work boots had shown up towing a trailer loaded with the kind of heavy equipment that made it clear they'd come to do extensive property cleanup. With his supplies dwindling and the two men looking too capable to risk taking on single-handedly, Markus had hurriedly shoved what he had into his backpack and slipped out the back way undetected in the hope of finding a better place to wait for the authorities to decide that he must have long since moved on already.

Yet even though he'd finally secured himself a decent vehicle, leaving the Owl Creek area wasn't something he was prepared to do. Instead, he had to find a way to recover what he rightfully had coming to him, what he desperately needed if he didn't want to waste years building himself back up from absolutely nothing.

He still felt hurt and angry, recalling the betrayal that had ended with Jessie Colton, who had vowed so many times that her true loyalty was to him rather than the wealthy family she had turned her back on. She'd even gone so far as to unwittingly assist him with a scheme to defraud them in the past. What he'd imagined to be his perfect control, however, had shattered the moment she'd chosen to catch one of the bullets he had meant for her daughter and her lover, who'd been scheming to bring down everything he'd spent years building.

His lingering rage over her betrayal, however, had little to do with any real attachment he'd felt for the woman he'd planned all along to abandon once she had served her purpose. Instead, he'd been furious to have been cut off from access to the small go-bag he'd hidden inside one of her most prized possessions, which contained not only the money he'd intended to use to escape the country, but his most precious asset as well. Unlike the poorer quality, easily discernable fake he'd had made for Jessie, his own nearly undetectable falsified passport was his only ticket to starting afresh in a civilized overseas destination. Once there, he would be free to access the offshore accounts where he'd put away the bulk of what he'd stolen from the trusting zealots who'd so foolishly signed over their investments, inheritances, and retirement accounts to his "ministry" over the years.

The real question was, how could he gain access to the home he and Jessie had once shared—*her* home—to retrieve the go-bag from the hiding place he was praying the authorities had missed in any search they may have conducted? Was it possible that his secret remained in place, just waiting for him to reclaim it—or could Jessie's heirs have already begun the process of removing their mother's old furnishings, perhaps inadvertently carrying out his treasure along with them?

Alarming as the thought was, Markus vowed to do whatever it took to find out—and gain the cooperation of any Colton that might be needed. After all, for a man already wanted for as many serious crimes as he was, why pause at something as inconsequential as kidnapping and another paltry murder?

As Malcolm stood drinking coffee at the kitchen counter the following morning, the phone in his back pocket started buzzing. Hoping for an update from Ajay or any one of his relations or SAR teammates who might be involved with the hunt for Acker, he frowned seeing Sebastian Cross's name flash across the screen.

It wasn't that Malcolm didn't have a great deal of respect for the founder of Crosswinds Training, where Malcolm had spent so much time putting the broken pieces of his shattered soul back together while learning about trailing with Pacer. Still, he'd hoped to have a few days' grace before Sebastian called in the puppy training chit that Ajay had evidently already handed to him.

Dredging up some semblance of manners, Malcolm mumbled a good morning and asked after Sebastian's fiancée Ruby—who was one of Malcolm's favorite cousins—and their infant son.

"Ruby's great, and Sawyer's an amazing kid," Sebastian said, boasting. "What a set of lungs that boy has, even at two a.m."

"I have to wonder if Ruby's as enthusiastic about that

part as you are," Malcolm said, grinning at the image of Sebastian, with his shaggy blond hair, lumberjack's build, and beard, as doting partner and father.

"She was *very* enthusiastic when I took him for a drive last night and let her get some extra shut-eye."

"I'll bet she was, especially when she had to get up early to open her vet clinic. So what can I do for you this morning?" As if Malcolm couldn't guess.

"Heard you and Pacer had a pretty rough day yesterday."

"So you've spoken to Ajay?"

"Lizzy called Ruby to warn her about Markus and give us an update," Sebastian said. "And then Ajay texted me something about you getting injured."

"I'm going to need to have my left hand x-rayed, but I doubt it'll slow me down much."

"I understand you had a brush with Acker, too. And lost your truck as well. Tough break," Sebastian said, sounding genuinely sympathetic.

Malcolm stalked toward a window overlooking the paddock where his big buckskin quarter horse, Sundance, grazed near the fence line next to a pinto mare named Ivy. "Not nearly as bad for me as the poor, innocent woman who caught Acker's bullet."

"I was sorry to hear that. Did you know her?"

"Not personally," Malcolm said, "but she was a friend and neighbor of Kate's and Giselle's. I ran into Giselle while Pacer and I were working the scent, and we—we discovered the victim together."

"I'm sorry," Sebastian told him. "I remember Giselle Dowling a little, back from when we went to school together—and I understand she's suffered a lot of losses over the years."

"Yeah. She's completely on her own now," Malcolm explained, "so she's staying at my family's ranch until it's safe for her to go back up to that cabin."

"Sounds like a really good idea until Acker's in custody. Your sister said she's warning everybody in the family that he's on the move in your truck."

"I'm glad to hear that Lizzy's got that covered," Malcolm said.

"So if you're feeling up to it later, with your hand and all," Sebastian said, "I was wondering if you might swing by Crosswinds this afternoon. I've got somebody here who wants to meet with you."

"Let me guess, there's a problem child among your current crop of pups who could use my special one-on-one attention."

"I'm definitely hoping you can help us salvage the time and training we've already put into this one, but I wouldn't call so early about just that."

Hearing something in his voice, Malcolm set his mug down on the counter. "What's going on, Sebastian? Have you heard something about the search for Markus that I haven't?"

"Nothing except that they're still looking high and low. It's something else. I almost hate to bring this up, with everything your family's had going on this past year, but I knew you wouldn't appreciate being blindsided."

Malcolm felt himself tense. "Come on and spit it out, man. Just tell me what's up."

"It's about that flyer you've had posted on the back bulletin board at Crosswinds these past few years—the one offering a reward for information on the red boat that caused the accident."

Recognizing the bitter taste of disappointment, Malcolm let him in on the reality he'd been living with for years now. "If someone's come to you with information, I need to warn you. I'm still getting calls on those flyers a few times a month. Some of the callers mean well, even when it turns out the boats they're describing aren't remotely similar to the one I had drawn up for that graphic we used. Others are just tragedy junkies who get some kind of sick pleasure trying to pry details about Kate's death out of me."

"Why didn't you tell anyone you've been dealing with that garbage? A few of us could've helped you screen the calls, saved you a whole lot of pain and aggravation—"

"This was my responsibility, my fiancée, and I wasn't about to pawn it off on anybody else. I couldn't," Malcolm explained. "What if I did and someone who hadn't been there missed some critical clue that I would've known was legit?"

"I see what you mean," Sebastian said. "Still, I'm sorry you've had to deal with clueless and insensitive callers."

"Those haven't been nearly as bad as the scammers, once word got out about the reward my family was offering. After that, so-called tips starting flooding in from everywhere—wild stories meant to cash in."

"That's terrible, but I'm positive that what I heard yesterday is no scammer," Sebastian told him. "Just hear me out."

"I'm listening."

"Have you met Kelsie over here yet? She's this teenager we've had working part-time at Crosswinds, mostly just kennel cleaning and dog-walking for the moment, but the kid's got aspirations."

"The girl with the reddish-blond hair," Malcolm said,

recalling a freckled face and friendly smile. "Seems like a good kid."

"She is, but the sorry excuse for a car she drives is broken down again this week, so she's been begging rides from family members. Her uncle stopped by yesterday afternoon to say hello and to thank me for giving her the job. Apparently, it's been a lot of help after a bad stretch she went through after losing her best friend to cancer last year."

"That's damned rough."

"It surely is. But anyway, the moment the uncle spotted your flyer hanging on our bulletin board, the guy did a double take and walked straight over to tap at it, saying he'd seen that boat that very day. A customer had trailered it to his shop. Did I mention Kelsie's uncle is a boat mechanic at a repair shop over in Hadley?" Sebastian said, naming a small town about thirty miles north of Blackbird Lake.

"You did not," Malcolm said, his mouth going bone dry.

"He told me this customer had bought the boat from a storage facility that auctioned the contents of a unit after the rent hadn't been paid in quite some time."

"So *that's* what happened to the boat," Malcolm blurted, his heart accelerating. "The son of a bitch driving it crossed the county line to put it into storage. To deliberately hide it because he absolutely *knew* that he'd sent the raft with Kate and Giselle on it flying."

"It sure as hell sounds that way to me," Sebastian said. "I want you to know Kelsie's uncle took the flyer and headed to the sheriff's office to report that the boat's in his shop now."

"Where's this shop exactly?" Malcolm asked.

"Do you think you should wait until you hear from the investigators, man? You wouldn't want to do anything to possibly compromise their investigation, would you? Or what if your showing up somehow tipped off the boat's original owners and led them to move it somewhere else—or maybe even try to do something more drastic like destroy it? You don't want to mess things up now, when we've got the first real lead we've had in more than three years."

With adrenaline's drumbeat in his skull, it was hard to think straight, but Malcolm heard some sense in what Sebastian was saying.

"No, I don't," Malcolm said, "but I won't sit around and wait forever for the sheriff's department investigators to pick up the phone and call me, either. I'm heading straight over there this morning to find out what they're doing to track down the men who were in the boat that day."

Sebastian waited a beat before saying, "You probably aren't going to want to hear this, but at the risk of hacking you off, I'm going to offer you a little friendly advice right now."

"If you're going to counsel patience, I've been waiting for more than three years already, watching that department kick the case from a retiring detective with one foot out the door, who could barely be bothered to check out the local marinas, to a rookie detective who started out sounding determined but eventually quit returning any of my calls."

"I can only imagine how frustrating that must have been."

"Frustrating's not the half of it," Malcolm said. "But I only made things worse when I tried asking Ajay to give Danvers, the detective working on the accident investigation, a call. You know, to offer any assistance that the Owl Creek police could give with the investigation."

"I take it that didn't help."

"Made things even worse, in fact," Malcolm explained. "The sheriff, apparently, is super-sensitive to jurisdictional boundaries. He didn't at all appreciate an outside agency trying to muscle in on his turf."

"I can't imagine how aggravating all this must have been," Sebastian said. "But still, for right now, I'd advise taking a couple of deep breaths and going to get your hand seen to. Then swing by here if you're up for it, and we can work on smoothing the rough edges off this wild bunch of puppies I've got—especially this wrecking ball of a ringleader who keeps getting everyone into trouble. You can even bring Giselle along if you'd like."

"Why do I get the feeling you're just trying to distract me?"

"Because you need to give this detective half a chance to check out this fresh lead before you go charging and put him on the defensive again. Otherwise, you and I both know the case may end up getting pushed back again—or maybe not happening at all."

"Fine. I'll give Detective Danvers *one* day," Malcolm agreed, seeing the sense of what he was saying. "But if I don't hear from him by tomorrow morning, then he's definitely going to have me breathing down his neck."

After carefully sticking to the most obscure back roads to navigate his way there, Markus passed by the late Jessie Colton's home several times to assure himself that all the neighbors and their children had left for work or school for the day. He was doubly grateful to spot no new signs on the house's front lawn boasting of a new security system, either, and best of all, no parked vehicles to give any indication that anyone might be present. Still, he remained wary, checking for any bowls and toys that might indicate the presence of a dog, which would require elimination. Once he'd satisfied himself that none was present, he hopped the solid stockade-style back fence from the next street over and then attempted to peer through several rear windows to get a look inside the house.

But it was little use, since someone had taken care to close every window covering, making it impossible to peer inside. Could it have been the authorities, after ripping out the false bottom panel he'd built up underneath his one-time lover's supposedly valuable antique Victrola record player?

Telling himself he was being paranoid, Markus went to the back door. Someone had replaced the old lock, making short work of Acker's plan to fish out the hidden spare key from its fake rock in the garden. Annoyed, he ended up smashing a rear window panel instead before carefully reaching for the latch inside and letting himself in that way.

For the first few minutes he stood listening, his blood rushing as he worried that he'd made so much noise, it was possible that someone he'd missed might have heard it and called in a report. Deciding his best chance would be to get in and out of the house quickly, he began to look around at cardboard boxes stacked around the kitchen counters. Most bore labels such as "Kitchen Utensils—Women's Shelter" or "Food Bank—Canned Goods," though someone had already removed the table and chairs from the small dinette area.

His gut churning, he headed for the family room. There, he spotted more boxes, where a sofa, television, and a pair of end tables had once been, though the leather recliner and coffee table remained in place. Praying that the Coltons hadn't given away the Victrola as well, he remembered how Jessie had always insisted the thing was practically an heirloom and assured himself that not even a family with Colton money would simply toss a valuable antique without a second thought. Still, he sprinted for the bedroom, his lungs burning with panic as he raced up the stairs…

Only to find the record player long gone…along with his traveling money and his precious passport.

Shouting with rage, he assured himself that he would make them *all* pay unless he could quickly find some way to retrieve it. And he would damned well see that they paid interest on the pain and suffering they'd cost him.

Dressed for the day in a pair of joggers and a casual turquoise top, Giselle followed the smell of coffee downstairs to find Malcolm in the kitchen a few minutes after eight, his back to her as he stood over a cutting board covered with fruit at the oversized kitchen island. But his knife was idle as he gazed out the nearest window—staring out into the middle distance. Probably brooding over whatever Markus Acker might be up to, Giselle imagined, or his own failure to find and stop the man before he'd killed again.

Deciding not to start the day by bringing up a sore subject, she simply greeted him. "Good morning."

Malcolm turned and smiled at her, freshly shaven and wearing a dark gray Henley and faded jeans that fit his tall, lean body all too well. "Morning. You're up a lot earlier than I expected. I always remember you sleeping in until all hours when you came to visit Kate."

"That was mostly because of our marathon late-night gab sessions." Giselle smiled wistfully, thinking she'd give anything to experience such bliss again. "Besides, after sleeping in that dark cave of my cabin bedroom for so long, that eastward-facing guest suite and this beautiful, bright sunshine definitely woke me up this morning."

"Guess I should've shown you how to close those automated curtains last night."

"And miss the sight of all those gorgeous horses and cows grazing and one of the cowboys riding out at dawn? No, thanks," she said, smiling.

Humor sparked in Malcolm's green eyes. "So you're into cowboys these days, are you?"

"Purely from an aesthetic standpoint, so don't get any weird ideas involving awkward introductions to your ranch's hired hands."

"We have a strict policy against the harassment of our employees anyway, miss," he told her with a tip of an imaginary Stetson, "so I'm afraid you're out of luck there."

When she laughed at his delivery, he said, "All kidding aside, I hope you're feeling a bit better this morning."

She nodded. "As unreal as everything that happened still seems, a shower and a good night's sleep certainly have me feeling a lot more human, thanks."

"You'll feel better still once we've gotten some caffeine and breakfast in you. Let me start the kettle for you first..." He walked over to the stove and turned on a burner underneath.

"Thanks."

"No problem. And I've been cutting up some apples and berries to go with the yogurt and muffins we had on hand, if that sounds like something you might like for breakfast. Or I could whip up a veggie omelet for you. It'd just take me a few minutes."

She raised a hand. "Honestly, Malcolm, I stopped listening after *muffins*. Although the fruit and tea sound good, too. Will your dad be joining us as well?"

"He's off breaking the news to Aunt Jenny in person about this latest murder. But the truth is, those two can barely seem to stay apart these days."

"And you're okay with this?"

"How could I not be? My brothers and my sister and I were all so little when our mother left us high and dry, but my father was the best single parent and role model you can imagine. And as much as I always liked Uncle Robert, Mama Jen deserved a man who truly appreciated her. Someone who'd never dream of sneaking around behind her back with her selfish sister..."

"Are you telling me that your uncle Robert and your mom were...*involved* back in the day?" Giselle made a face at the idea of such a horrible betrayal.

Malcolm nodded. "We've only recently learned that after my mother left my family, she moved to a nearby town and secretly gave birth to two children fathered by my uncle."

"So you're telling me that you and your cousins have a couple of half-siblings that you knew nothing about? Have you had any contact?"

"We *did* meet after Uncle Robert's death—and to everyone's surprise, both Nate and Sarah are amazing people. We now consider them our sister and brother and look forward to getting to know them even better."

"That's wonderful, and I'm very happy your father and your aunt have each other to help them cope with whatever feelings that must've brought up."

"So am I, but enough with the family history for now. What kind of tea would you like?" He showed her several boxes from a cupboard.

"Ooh, that Irish breakfast tea, please," she said, "maybe with a little honey in it, if you have some."

He pulled out a bag and dropped it in a mug for her before pouring the steaming water over it. "You've got it. I'll just finish putting the fruit onto our breakfast tray, and we can sit right here and eat at these barstools if you're okay with casual dining. Otherwise, we can go into the dining—"

"Oh, please," Giselle said. "After eating on my own in my cabin for the better part of three years. I'd happily have my breakfast sitting on the floor."

"I'm sure Pacer would be *very* enthusiastic about that idea." Malcolm nodded toward the dog, who had planted himself in the spot with the best view of the food Malcolm had been preparing. "But if you want a real shot at your muffin, I'd definitely suggest the counter."

Giselle hadn't been eating long before she noticed that Malcolm was mainly just sipping at his coffee while barely picking at his food.

"When I came out here," she said, "I couldn't help noticing how worried you looked. And now—" She gestured to his nearly untouched plate. "This isn't like you. Has that hand gotten worse this morning?"

"It's definitely bruised and swollen enough that I still plan on going to the Express Medical Clinic to get it checked out, but after keeping it wrapped and elevated and icing it off and on last night, the pain's not bad at all."

"So what's bothering you, then?" She shook her head. "You haven't gotten bad news, have you? Acker hasn't hurt anyone else, has he?"

"No, thank goodness it's not that. But I've had a couple of calls before you got up, starting with my cousin, Fletcher Colton."

"I remember you mentioning he was at Claudette's yesterday." She shook her head. "But I don't believe I've actually met him."

"He was with the Boise Police Department back around the time Kate and I became engaged, so you probably wouldn't have run into him back in the day, either. That's a shame because he's a great guy. Practically another brother to me."

"I've heard you say the same about more than one of your cousins, you know—except for the women, who are all 'practically sisters,'" she teased.

"We did all grow up thick as thieves," he admitted, "but that doesn't make it any less true. But getting back to Fletcher, he came home from Boise last year and was hired on by the Owl Creek PD as lead detective. I'm not sure how he pulled that off, considering that his father was one of Acker's victims, but somehow, Fletcher talked his way onto the joint task force."

"He sounds like one very determined person."

"He's definitely that when he sets his sights on a goal," Malcolm agreed. "And right now, nothing's more important to him than hunting down the man who's caused our family so much pain, which—" He drew an audible breath before grimacing "—he's told me in no uncertain terms I'm to leave to the professionals from now on so they won't end up having to waste their time running to my rescue."

Giselle couldn't help but smile. "I'm liking him already. So did he share any updates on what's going on with the search for Acker?"

Malcolm nodded. "Unfortunately, there's been no sign

of either him or my stolen truck so far, so they figure he's most likely found himself another vacation place to break into in the area."

"Or is it possible that Acker's gone back to wherever he might've been hiding before he headed toward my place earlier?" she asked. "After all, he did manage to hang out someplace for two weeks undetected, so it must have been pretty well hidden."

"I'm sure the task force will be considering all possibilities. They've put a statewide BOLO out on my truck, alerting every law enforcement agency that the driver's armed and dangerous. They're also bringing in extra manpower for door-to-door checks of as many properties in the general area as they can."

"I only hope the searchers stay safe," she said.

"That makes two of us," Malcolm agreed. "But as Fletcher reminded me, this is what law enforcement trains for, so now's the time for us to sit back and leave them to it."

Peering at him curiously, Giselle said, "You mentioned that you'd gotten more than one call. Was the other anything important?"

"I...ah...it was just Sebastian Cross, the owner of Crosswinds, wondering when I could come help out with that litter he's been training."

"I didn't realize that's Sebastian's place. I remember him from back in high school," she said, momentarily distracted from his hesitation by old memories. "He was a good guy, from what I can recall."

"Still is—and part of the family now, too, since he's engaged to my cousin, Ruby. They have a baby boy as well."

"Is there anyone in or around Owl Creek your family *doesn't* claim as a relation?" she asked. "At this rate, you'll need to book the football stadium for your family reunions."

Laughing he said, "I'm sure it seems that way at times. And anyway, Sebastian remembered you as well. In fact, he mentioned that you'd be welcome to come with me today if you'd like, while we work with the puppies."

"That sounds like fun, thanks," she said, flashing a quick smile before zeroing in on his odd behavior. "But I can't help suspecting that's not what has you sitting here brooding over a plateful of delicious food.... Is there something else, Malcolm?"

"Don't you think I have enough to worry about, between Markus being out there doing heaven knows what in my truck and my status with the SAR team now being in question?" He frowned, his gaze avoiding hers. "Add to that, my aching hand, and maybe I've got more on my mind than eating."

"You're sure there wasn't something else? Something it might help to talk out?" she said, unable to recall the last time she'd seen him so grumpy. "Because, if you're conflicted about hosting me here like this, without Kate around to act as a buffer..."

Tossing his unused napkin over his food like a white flag, he stood to stare down at her. "Why on earth would you think that? I invited you here, didn't I?"

"Yes, but you probably felt obligated because of the circumstances. But now, perhaps, it feels awkward."

"The only thing that's awkward is you picking apart my eating habits," he insisted. "I'm *fine* with having you around. Stay as long as you like."

She felt her brows rise. "And I thought *my* social skills were rusty."

"You're absolutely..." He gusted out a sigh. "You're

right. I'm being an idiot—not to mention a terrible host. I didn't mean to make you feel unwelcome."

"So why *did* you, then?" she demanded.

He drew an audible breath. "Because about an hour ago, I found out that someone might have found the boat."

She blinked reflexively. "What boat? Wait. You don't mean the…?"

"The *red* boat," he said, pausing to let the significance sink in. "It hasn't been confirmed yet, but apparently, it's been hidden away for years, inside a storage container north of the county line. After the bill went unpaid for some time, however, it was purchased by a bidder who took it to a marina for a tune-up. The boat mechanic ran across one of my flyers and reported it last night."

"The boat that killed Kate…" Giselle's mouth went so dry, she could barely get the words out. "Why didn't you tell me right away?"

He shook his head. "I'm still trying to wrap my brain around it. Plus, Sebastian—he's the one who told me—talked me into promising to give the sheriff's department detective on the case some time to investigate before immediately jumping down their throats and demanding information."

"That—that actually makes sense," she said. "But this—don't you see what this could mean? We could actually end up learning who the driver was—maybe even seeing him charged with leaving the scene—or even—"

"Don't, please. This was exactly why I didn't want to tell you." Malcolm shook his head. "I didn't want to get you too excited for something that might never happen."

"What do you mean, *too* excited?" She stared at him. "This could be it, Malcolm. What I've dreamed about forever—justice for my sister."

"The only real justice would be in giving her—and all of us—our lives back."

"Believe me, I'm as painfully aware of that as you are," she said. "But I can't—*we* can't—have that, so we'll have to focus on seeing the person responsible for hitting us held accountable for the damage he did. Making him face up to what he cost us after slithering away and hiding for all these years."

"Then we'll do our very best to move the authorities in that direction. But don't be shocked if we encounter some major disappointments along the way."

"Considering what we've both lived through during the past few years," Giselle said, "disappointments are nothing we can't handle. Especially now that we have real hope that someone might finally be named, in a court of law, the responsible party in Kate's death. Someone who can shoulder a portion of the blame we've been spending these past few years heaping on ourselves."

Chapter 9

Later that morning, as they waited for his X-rays to be read at the minor emergency center, Malcolm peered over at Giselle, who was wrapping up yet another phone call with a representative from her insurance company, and wondered if she'd been right. Had it only been the sheriff department's failure to name anyone who might be legally held accountable that had left each of them trapped in a prison of self-blame for so long?

Malcolm had to admit that, for a long time, he'd harbored resentment against Giselle as well for bringing along her useless boyfriend Kyle on that visit, especially after she'd returned to her life as if nothing had happened. Realizing now how incredibly wrong he'd been about that, however, made it impossible to hold onto any trace of that anger any longer. Instead, he felt only compassion—along with a tenderness he'd never seen coming and a bone-deep desire to protect her from further pain.

Easy there, he thought, warning himself that whatever he was feeling was less about Giselle herself—as beautiful, bright, and appealing as she was—than the many small ways in which she reminded him of her sister. *You're only missing Kate, that's all.* And as for why his thoughts kept returning to the way it had felt to hold and comfort

Giselle, or how he couldn't quit thinking about those two quick squeezes she had given him, he vowed that the last thing he was going to do was embarrass her—or disgrace himself—by treating her as a substitute for the only woman that he wanted.

He waited for her to finish her call before asking, "Any news about your car?"

She nodded. "They're going to need me to go back to take a bunch of photos from all different angles for their app and then input the vehicle identification number. But according to the person I spoke to, as soon as I've done that, the process should go quite smoothly, and I should receive a payout for the claim—assuming they decide the vehicle is totaled."

"Considering what it looked like, I can't imagine any other outcome."

"The woman on the phone said that if my description was even close to accurate, she had no doubt I'd have my payout in four to six weeks."

"I guess you'll need to start thinking about a replacement vehicle, then."

"Oh, joy," she said grimly. "Car shopping."

"That bad, eh?"

She rolled her eyes. "You try doing it while female. Some of those salespeople are still living in the Stone Age. Last time, I ended up going through four dealerships before I finally found one who deserved my business."

"I could go with you this time to run interference," he said. "I actually kind of enjoy the whole horse-trading aspect."

"As much as I appreciate the offer," she said, splashes of color coming to her cheeks, "what does cowering behind some random man teach these people about how to earn the business of all the women who are coming in there to make their own financial decisions?"

"So I'm some random man now?" he asked, biting back a smile as he called her on it.

"Not to me you aren't, but as far as those jokers are concerned," she said before frowning and shaking her head. "The point is, I'd rather walk out on those who refuse to treat me with respect or give me what my research has told me is a fair price. Then I'll call their managers and let them know exactly why they've lost my business after I've closed a deal elsewhere."

"It's good to hear you sounding like yourself again," he said honestly.

She shook her head. "How do you mean?"

"Yesterday, I have to admit you had me worried. Worried you'd forgotten how to stand up and fight for the kind of life that you deserve."

"I believe it's possible that I had, at least a little," she conceded, her expression growing somber. "But sitting in that cabin blaming myself for everything and beating my head against the wall hasn't changed anything in more than three years, so maybe it's time I tried a new approach."

Before he could offer to help in any way he could, she turned her head toward the sound of approaching footsteps. Dr. Herrera, who'd examined him earlier, was back, looking eager to discuss Malcolm's imaging results.

Giselle rose, saying, "I'll give you two some privacy."

"You're fine staying," Malcolm said. Turning to look at the older woman to make sure that she'd heard, he added, "I take it you have the report back on my hand?"

Dr. Herrera nodded. "The news is just as I suspected.

You have a fracture near the knuckle with some ligament involvement."

"Is that serious?" he asked.

"An orthopedist will need to monitor your healing and see that you complete the correct exercises to restore full mobility, but I don't see any reason to believe you shouldn't have a complete recovery."

"That's good to hear." Malcolm felt relief wash over him.

"Meanwhile, I'm going to give you an immobilizer splint that will protect your fingers, hand, and wrist, so you should be able to stay active, with some reasonable care," she said. "I'm also sending you home with printed instructions for managing any pain and swelling, along with a prescription for a painkiller to have available should you need it."

A short time later, they left the clinic, his left hand feeling stiff and awkward—but reasonably comfortable—inside of the well-padded splint.

After a quick stop by the pharmacy to drop off his prescription—though he suspected he might not end up needing anything stronger than the over-the-counter medication he'd been using so far—Malcolm climbed back behind the wheel of a dark-blue pickup that bore white door decals marking it as ranch property. "What do you think? Shall we run up to take those photos of your SUV so we can get the clock ticking on your insurance claim?"

"Do you think it's safe to go back up there?" she asked.

"I can't imagine Acker having any reason to return there, of all places, since he'd have to figure law enforcement would be thickest around a place where he committed a murder only yesterday."

"I suppose that's true," she said, still sounding uncertain. "I'll go ahead and text Ajay, though, just to make sure they've finished processing any evidence." Malcolm pulled out his cell.

When Ajay didn't immediately respond, Malcolm told himself not to take it personally. "He's probably swamped right now—or maybe even catching a few hours of shut-eye if he ended up working through the night."

"The pictures can wait for now. Let's distract ourselves with something else, then," Giselle suggested before her blue eyes brightened. "I vote for puppies."

He couldn't help but smile. "Why am I not surprised?"

"I mean, unless you're not feeling up to it…with your poor hand…" she added.

"I'm fine, and I'll tell you what. I'll make you a deal. How about we grab a quick lunch first at one of these places around here?"

"I could go for a veggie burger," she said, "but only if you'll let me steal half of your fries."

"You've got yourself a deal." He smiled, recalling how Kate would often say the same thing. "Afterward, we'll grab my prescription and then drive out to Crosswinds. That way, we'll already be most of the way to the lake, if Ajay gives us the go-ahead on the photos."

"Either way, I'll get to hang out with some *puppies*," Giselle practically sang, "so consider me all-in."

Located on a beautiful, fenced property overlooking the mountains along a private road that bore his family's name, Sebastian Cross's Crosswinds Training facility consisted of a neatly painted kennel building, along with outdoor training and play areas. After saying hello to Malcolm, the tall and bearded Sebastian turned a welcoming smile on Giselle. "It's great seeing you again after all these years. My fiancée is one of your biggest fans."

Assuming he was merely being polite, Giselle nodded. "That's kind of her to say."

"Seriously. I'm not just blowing smoke here," Sebastian said, brushing longish, dark-blond hair from his eyes. "If I could talk you into signing one of her copies that I managed to sneak off her bookshelf before you leave today, it would earn me some very serious rewards."

Giselle flashed a smile. "Anything for the man who controls access to the puppies."

Malcolm chuckled. "I tried telling her we're here to work with them and not just to play and cuddle."

"Come on, Mal," Sebastian scolded him. "You know we always turn them out ahead of their training session to blow off a bit of steam before we get them started so they can give us their full focus. A few minutes of fun surely isn't going to determine which of our potential future detection dogs will make the cut."

"Sure, make *me* out to be the bad guy," Malcolm said. "But don't complain when she's lining them up for belly rubs and using her phone to order them all matching sweaters. She's already got my Pacer half-convinced to forget about the search-and-rescue business and start a new life as her personal lapdog."

Sebastian laughed. "There's not a chance in the world you could ever keep that workaholic dog of yours from trailing."

"You talked about the puppies making the cut," Giselle said to Sebastian. "Do you mean to say that not all of them can be taught to do what they're bred for?"

"They can all be *taught*, but unfortunately, not every one of them will necessarily have the temperament or develop their skills sufficiently to measure up to our professional standards."

"So then what happens to them?" she asked, hoping they didn't end up in some scary animal shelter.

"Since they've already had so much training time invested in them to get to the point where they are, we first reach out to other programs where we feel their individual skills and energies might be a good fit. For example, right now, out of the litter of eight we're working with, I see three that probably won't be suitable for scent detection."

"That many?" she asked.

"Considering how high Crosswinds' standards are, a pass rate of greater than fifty percent would be exceptional," Malcolm assured her.

Nodding in agreement, Sebastian explained, "Two of the others have qualities that I believe could make them excellent candidates to become service dogs for the hearing impaired, so I'm going to have them evaluated by a partner program to see if they'd be interested in continuing their training."

"And the third?"

When Sebastian hesitated, Malcolm said, "They can't all be rock stars."

"But if anybody can keep this hot mess of a puppy from washing out completely, I have faith that Malcolm here can help me do it," Sebastian told her. "This guy's definitely the Goofball Puppy Whisperer."

Looking around, she asked, "So when do I get to meet these pups? Those aren't any of them, are they?" She pointed out a trio of fawn to reddish-brown colored dogs with a shepherd look to them who were romping and wrestling around one fenced area.

"Oh, no. Those big fellows—they're Belgian Malinois—are just having a little free time after their last training session. Let me go put them up. Then I'll bring out the Puppy Pack."

"Sounds good," Malcolm said, turning to Giselle as Sebastian walked off and whistled for the big dogs, who instantly responded to his signal.

"Wow," she said. "Those dogs are beautiful, but a little intimidating when they turn and run straight toward a person."

"They're a little intense for the average person but amazingly driven and focused when they're given a job to do," he said. "But don't worry. The puppies we'll be working with are a whole lot smaller."

"I assumed they'd be larger breeds as well, like these dogs or Pacer."

"Most people think of big dogs when they imagine working dogs," Malcolm said. "But in some cases, there are advantages to using smaller, less intimidating breeds in public-facing settings like airports and other transportation hubs. What really matters is that the animal is highly responsive to training and has a great nose. That's why, in this particular instance, Sebastian decided to try—"

"Oh, my goodness!" she laughed as a wagging, low-to-the-ground tricolor blur of motion raced and tumbled over each other as they entered the play area. Just about the cutest blur of motion she had ever seen. "Are those..." She leaned forward, trying to focus on the flopping, reddish-brown ears "...beagle babies?"

As he led her toward the gate so they could step into the enclosure, he said, "They're a little older than they look—about five months now—because they're on the smaller side, even for beagles. And wait'll you get a load of the runt. Livewire that she is, she's extra-tiny."

"So which one is she?" Giselle asked as Malcolm

opened the gate and quickly ushered her inside before stepping in behind her and closing off the potential escape route.

It turned out to be a good thing that he moved quickly, because the moment the pups noticed their arrival, they stampeded in Giselle and Malcolm's direction, their tails wagging and their small brown faces split with adorable white blazes and happy beagle grins.

Laughing as she bent to greet them, Giselle offered pets and sweet talk in equal measure and noticed that Malcolm, too, could not resist the young dogs' joyous greetings. But after briefly indulging them, Malcolm began asking them to sit in a semicircle around him, praising them lavishly as first two of the pups, then five, and finally all seven obeyed his verbal command.

"Good dogs, every one of you," he told them. "So where's your naughty sister?"

"I've given the wrecking ball a few minutes of one-on-one. Now let's see what you can do with her," called Sebastian from outside of the gate. A moment later a red-and-white-colored puppy charged in. Despite the fact that she was only two-thirds the size of the smallest of the other pups, she moved as if it she had been supercharged, a snapping, yapping dervish of pure energy who leapt onto the backs of or plowed into one sibling after another.

The result was pandemonium, as the puppies immediately forgot the humans and turned their attention to defending themselves against the onslaught. Clearly realizing that his only hope was in corralling the troublemaker, Malcolm used a firm voice to command, "Scarlett, *sit*," slapping the side of his leg in an attempt to garner her attention.

When she paid him no heed, he ducked down as she

raced past and reached to scoop her up. He nearly had her, but the splint on his left hand made him awkward enough that she was able to wriggle free and stir up her littermates once more.

Still at the gate, Sebastian began removing the other pups singly and in pairs, giving Malcolm a chance to focus on the disruptive element and motion for Giselle to step to one side. As the overly excited Scarlett continued to feed off the energy she'd set into motion, Giselle wondered how the pup might respond to the opposite approach.

As Sebastian removed the last of the other puppies, Giselle sat down on the ground, drawing her knees up and casually draping her arms around her bent legs. Immediately intrigued, Scarlett came racing toward her barking.

"Good instinct," Malcolm called over. "But now, *don't* give her attention. No pets, no voice, no eye contact. Not until she chills out and shows us the calm energy we're after."

It took at least twenty minutes, by Giselle's reckoning, a period during which she repeatedly, gently deflected the pup's repeated attempts to engage her with nips and yips and pitiful whining. When she started with the play bows, flattening her white forelegs to the ground while wriggling her behind in the air and imploring with a pair of liquid brown eyes, Giselle felt her resolve weaken.

"Look at her," she said, deciding Malcolm was being a little too hard-hearted. "She's only a baby who needs love and understanding."

"Hold your position," he advised, "please. I know she's pulling out all the stops, but trust me, what she needs even more than coddling is to make the connection between calm, settled energy and achieving the kind of bond she really longs for. Otherwise, she's not only facing being bounced out of the scent dog training program here but an altogether uncertain future."

"What do you mean?"

"I mean that whether it's in some sort of working environment or even a pet home, nobody wants the kind of dog who constantly creates disruptions, much less bites, scratches, and jumps onto people and other animals in order to get her way. And Sebastian's absolutely committed to making certain that no animal that comes into his program ever ends up with an unhappy outcome."

Giselle nodded, steeling her resolve. "All right, then. You've convinced me."

"Don't worry," Malcolm said. "Under all that beagle stubbornness, I'm convinced that there's a very bright mind working. Since she seems particularly interested in you—it's not unusual for dogs to be especially drawn to women—and what she's doing isn't working, I'm betting she'll come up with the solution pretty soon. Either that, or finally wear herself out."

Sure enough, it was only a few minutes later that Scarlett heaved a long-suffering sigh and plopped herself down a few inches from Giselle's leg, panting rapidly.

"Can I pet her *now*?" Giselle asked.

"Give her just a little while longer to relax," Malcolm said. "Otherwise, she'll just jump back up and hype herself up again."

When the panting finally stopped and Scarlett closed her eyes, Malcolm quietly instructed, "Now, try to keep everything as low-key as you can. Your voice, your movements, and especially your touch, because we don't want to overstimulate her. Try speaking to her first and then maybe allowing the side of your leg to come into contact with her shoulder."

Giselle did as he suggested and felt something inside her unfurl as, instead of jumping up and biting at her hands or running around wildly, Scarlett slowly raised a foreleg, clearly indicating her hopes that Giselle might favor her with a scratch.

Instead of giving in, Giselle said softly, "You really *want* to be a good girl, don't you? You just happen to be wired a little differently, aren't you?"

Scarlett slowly lowered her leg, seeming content to simply watch Giselle's mouth as she spoke.

Taking this as a step in the right direction, Giselle reached out to stroke her blaze-marked head and shoulder a few times, her heart melting when the whip-like white-tipped tail began to slowly wag.

Malcolm smiled. "*Very* well done. Now, let's find out if she remembers anything of the basics that her puppy raiser and Sebastian have tried to teach her."

They continued working with her for a session that seemed to fly, a period during which Scarlett continued to gravitate toward Giselle, following a few, but not nearly all the commands Malcolm suggested. With Malcolm, however, she did far worse, no matter how soothingly he tried to speak or how he attempted to lower himself to her level.

When Sebastian came back to ask for his assessment, Malcolm gestured toward the young dog, who was calmly maintaining a sit position and allowing Giselle to stroke her head.

"I think there's a great dog behind all her outbursts," he said, "but maybe not a working dog. I'm not sure she'll ever have that kind of discipline and focus. She could still have a wonderful life as a loving pet if she can learn to control her impulses, though."

When Sebastian nodded, Malcolm continued, "Scarlett

needs intensive one-on-one work—preferably with Della, since her response to Giselle makes it clear she'll do far better with a female trainer."

"I've noticed, too, that she does better in sessions with Della," Sebastian said, "but as busy as we are right now around here, I'm afraid that extensive one-on-one time with only her isn't really feasible. Not when I have a target date to finish training the rest of the litter—*if* I can keep Scarlett from undoing all our hard work."

Malcolm shook his head. "Maybe the best thing you can do then is remove her from the premises. Let me take her to the ranch with me."

"I thought you said that she needed a female trainer."

Tipping a hand toward Giselle and Scarlett, Malcolm said, "I realize she's no Della, but look at her. The woman's clearly a born puppy whisperer. And with a little guidance from me…"

"What's this?" asked Giselle, her blue eyes wide and her expression dubious as she looked up sharply. "Just what is it you're getting me into, Malcolm?"

Grinning, he assured her, "I promise you, you'll thank me later."

"But just in case you don't," Sebastian said, "can I get you to sign that book for Ruby *before* you leave with your new charge?"

Chapter 10

As Malcolm carried the kennel and other supplies Sebastian was sending with them to the pickup, he glanced over at Giselle, who was having difficulty getting Scarlett to walk correctly on the leash without leaping up and biting it or rolling onto her back and kicking her feet every which way.

"I know she's a handful," he said, "but try not to give her enough slack to let her get away with that. If you shorten up your lead—"

"I'll *try*," Giselle said.

Distracted by movement from across the lot, Scarlett threw her head back and gave a single *barroo* of a bark, greeting the slim, teenaged girl who came running toward them with a bag of kibble in her arms, her long, strawberry-blond braid bouncing along her back.

"Sebastian asked me to let you know you should continue feeding her this special puppy formula," Kelsie said as Scarlett's entire red-and-white body wagged in excitement to see her. "And, I know this is going to sound silly—"

Glancing at Malcolm, the girl blushed so deeply that her freckles appeared to vanish "—since I've seen you here before and know that you probably know more than

I ever will about training dogs like her, but she really seems to like it when I sing to her."

Giselle smiled warmly. "It makes perfect sense to me and helps to explain why she likes females so much. You've been giving her extra attention, haven't you?"

Kelsie nodded at her. "After I overheard Sebastian and Della talking about how she might be an early cut from the program, I was afraid something bad might happen to her, so whenever I could, I rushed to finish up my regular duties and pulled her out to try to see if loving on her a little extra might help. That wasn't the wrong thing, was it? I didn't end up messing her up so she's being perma-nently kicked out of Crosswinds, did I? Because I love what I do here, but if I hurt Scarlett, I'll tell Sebastian right now that I'm quitting."

"Hold on—please," Malcolm urged her. "I'm sure Se-bastian and Della would both be glad to hear you've taken some initiative, although I'd suggest that you try talking to one of them about *how* they'd like you to reinforce what it is they're doing next time. I know that Sebastian in par-ticular has mentioned thinking that you have potential for working with the dogs."

"Really?" she asked, her brown eyes shining. "You're not just saying that to be nice?"

Meeting her gaze directly, he said, "I promise I'd never lie about something so important. Here, let me put up this crate and take that dog food off your hands."

"Let me get that," Giselle said, nodding to indicate his hand in its brace before stepping in to help him fold down the truck's rear seat and place the crate and food inside.

"That's not necessary, but—"

"No, I've got it," she insisted, passing him Scarlett's lead. While Giselle loaded the wiggly pup a couple of minutes later, Kelsie lingered outside the truck for a moment, her expression serious.

"Is there something else?" he asked her.

She nervously fiddled with the frizzed end of her braid, her expression serious. "I just wanted to tell you I'm really sorry, Mr. Colton. Sorry if my uncle Larry finding that red boat brought up a lot of bad memories for you. I know—I know how bad it hurts losing someone important to you, and I..." She sniffled. "I wanted you to know I'm thinking about you and the family and all, because it *really* stinks."

"Yes, it very much does," said Giselle, who had reappeared beside him. "Kate Dowling was my big sister... and I'm very sorry to hear you've suffered a recent loss as well."

"Oh, wow. That's rough. And, thanks," Kelsie said.

"And thank *you* and especially your uncle," Malcolm insisted, "for coming forward with the information he has. I can't tell you what a relief it is to have some hope after all this time that the case might finally be solved."

Kelsie nodded. "I really hope it works out. Um, my uncle says that if you want to get the straight scoop, to go ahead and call him." She passed Malcolm a business card featuring a boat overlaid with the image of a wrench and a couple of incidental grimy thumbprints. Printed below the name Larry Willets was the name, address, and phone number of Creekside Marine in Hadley along with the promise of *honest work at a fair price.* "He said that anything he tells the cops, you deserve to know as well."

"That's very..." Malcolm hesitated a beat before deciding on the right word. "I appreciate the offer." He slipped the card into his wallet before they said goodbye to Kelsie after promising to take good care of Scarlett at the ranch.

Once he and Giselle had the pup loaded and themselves in the truck as well, Malcolm pulled his cell from his pocket to see if Ajay had gotten around to responding to his earlier text message.

Nodding toward Kelsie, who was heading back inside the kennel, Giselle said, "Her uncle sounds like a pretty good guy—especially because I know how hard it's been getting any information out of the sheriff's office. I've barely been able to get the detective assigned to Kate's case to return any of my calls these past couple of years, either, and believe me, it hasn't been for lack of trying."

Malcolm lowered his phone. "Part of that may be my fault." He told her about asking Ajay to offer police support with the investigation and the sheriff taking immediate offense.

"Sounds like someone's awfully territorial," she said.

"Yeah. But I'm afraid my actions may've really messed things up there."

She grimaced, shaking her head before reaching out to touch his arm. "But if there's one thing we should both know by now, it's that second-guessing our past choices changes nothing. As of today, we finally have a fresh lead. *And* someone who's offered to discuss it with us, whether or not the authorities choose to play nice."

"We need to keep in mind, though, this boat mechanic's not necessarily offering his help out of the goodness of his heart," Malcolm warned her.

She shook her head. "I don't understand what you mean."

"I *mean* that Mr. *Honest Work for a Fair Price* has seen my flyer. The one promising a reward for information leading to the arrest of the responsible party," Malcolm said pointedly.

"So what if he has?" She shrugged. "You haven't de-cided that you don't want to pay it now, have you? Because if the money's an issue, I'll be glad to pitch in—or even foot the bill myself, if that's the sticking point. Justice for Kate would be worth anything."

Shaking his head, he said, "The money is not the issue. It's the ugly lies, the sick scams. You have no idea how many I've fielded. Dozens of them—Hundreds, maybe, some of them so twisted and revolting that I thank God you've been spared them."

"Wait, what do you mean?"

He made a face. "Suffice it to say that once the wrong crowd decides it might be profitable to exploit someone's family tragedy, they can be disgustingly inventive when it comes to cruelty."

"Oh, Malcolm, that's *terrible*," Giselle said, her voice faltering.

"It's all right. I've gotten used to—"

"You should never have had to. It's absolutely *not* right for a bunch of creeps and losers to treat any grieving per-son, especially someone as kind and courageous as you are, like that," she insisted, a fierceness sparking in her blue eyes that made her more beautiful than ever. "So I take it you're not going to reach out to Kelsie's uncle, are you?"

He shook his head. "Let's give Detective Danvers a rea-sonable chance to look into who put this boat into storage and see if he can track down the culprit first."

"I understand your concerns about maybe being scammed again. Truly I do," she said, even as a note of impatience crept into her voice. "But as far as I can tell, that guy hasn't exactly been a ball of fire up to this point."

"True, which is why I was very tempted to go get up in

his face right away myself and demand that he actually *do* something. But this may be the first solid lead he's gotten on the case, so Sebastian's right. We need to at least give him half a chance to run with it before we do something that might end up putting him and the whole department back on the defensive."

She frowned before blowing out a breath. "I guess I can see the sense in that. But we've already been waiting *so* long. *Kate's* been waiting...for any kind of justice."

Seeing the tears clumping her beautiful, long lashes and hearing the all too familiar anguish in her voice, Malcolm couldn't resist the impulse to reach over to catch her hand in his. Giving it a squeeze, he pulled it to his mouth and tenderly placed a kiss atop her knuckles. "Kate's at peace now, Giselle. And I believe she'd want us to try to somehow find the same."

She blinked hard, avoiding eye contact as she stiffly withdrew her hand before scooting back over and buckling herself into her seatbelt. After an awkward silence, she said in a strained voice, "So, are we heading straight back to the ranch now? Or should we see if we can get those photos of my SUV first, while we're this close to the mountains?"

Realizing how uncomfortable he'd clearly made her, he mentally kicked himself for getting so personal with her. What the hell had he been thinking, kissing her hand like some cut-rate Romeo? Would she imagine he hoped to take advantage of the situation—or worse yet, that he was thinking of her as some sort of *replacement* for the sister she was still grieving every bit as much as he was?

Sick with regret, he allowed the awkward change of subject drop and quickly checked his messages. "Ajay says his team's finished at Claudette's, so we're welcome to go over there and get those pictures. We can look in on the chickens, too, but one of my brothers and I will come back later to get them, after my dad's spoken to the folks I have in mind to adopt them."

"That sounds perfect, thanks," she said as he put the truck into gear and pulled out of the lot.

"And I'm sure Scarlett won't mind taking a little detour up there," Malcolm said. "We'll try to keep the trip as short as possible."

"Believe me, after what happened yesterday, I'm in no mood to linger."

"If it makes you feel any safer," Malcolm said, "when he spoke to me earlier, Fletcher made me promise that I wouldn't drive around unarmed until the task force has Acker in custody."

"Let's hope they're closing in on him as we speak—a good, safe distance from where we'll be," she said as Malcolm turned in the direction of the mountains.

As they reached the recreational area, they passed several marked law enforcement units from various agencies before they were stopped at a checkpoint where two state police officers briefly asked their destination while subtly peeking inside the vehicle through their lowered window.

Once they'd continued on their way, Giselle said, "Maybe we should've waited to drive up here. All I can think of right now is driving up to Claudette's yesterday in the rain, almost running into Acker head-on—and that awful scene in the barn…"

"Would you prefer I turn around?" Malcolm asked her. "If you want, I could take you back to the ranch and drive out later, or even tomorrow to take some photos for you. Just tell me what you need, and we could transfer them to your phone."

She sighed and shook her head. "As nice as it is of you to make the offer, we're almost there now. And in spite of the awful memories, I can't imagine anyplace less likely for Markus to return to, so let's just go and get this over with."

"If you're sure…"

"I am," she said, sounding determined.

"Then we'll get our errands taken care of and be on our way back home in no time. After that, you'll have nothing to worry about but getting Scarlett settled in and shopping for your next set of wheels," he said, hoping to redirect her thoughts.

"Have you thought about another vehicle for yourself?" she asked.

"To tell you the truth, it hadn't even occurred to me. I suppose I'll need to report the truck's theft to my insurance company as well."

"I'm crossing my fingers that you'll get lucky, and the police will find it soon, and in one piece."

As they reached Claudette's property, he steered carefully to avoid the ruts left by the emergency vehicles that had come through since yesterday. "I appreciate the thought, but honestly, I'd trade that truck and a whole lot more if I could only know that Markus Acker could never hurt anyone again."

"As my grandmother would've put it, 'from your lips to God's ears,'" Giselle responded, her words so solemn that they might have been a prayer.

Once Malcolm had parked the truck, he headed off to see to the chickens while Giselle went to the wrecked Subaru, her phone already in hand as she prepared to deal with her insurance. By the time he spotted her slipping the phone back inside her pocket about ten minutes later, Malcolm had finished up in the barn and was walking Scarlett on her lead outside the structure, where he'd been allowing her to sniff after small creatures among the debris blown down by the storm.

"Chickens seem okay?" Giselle asked as she walked over to join them.

"As far as I can tell, they're doing just fine. At least, they're eating and drinking—and I even spied a few fresh eggs in their nest boxes."

"Claudette would be so relieved they weren't too traumatized by—by everything they witnessed yesterday."

Since Malcolm had never given much thought to the emotional range of poultry, he was relieved when Scarlett introduced a change of subject, straining at her collar and barking when something rustled in the underbrush.

Pointing out a squirrel running up a tree trunk, he told the pup, "You keep that up, and I'm sure that pesky fuzzball will surrender."

As Scarlett settled, her tail wagging, Giselle smiled. "She seems so much more relaxed out here than she was at the kennel. Inclined to settle down when you speak to her."

"Probably overstimulated at Crosswinds, considering the amount of activity and all her siblings to distract her. I have the feeling she's going to flourish in a more natural environment where less is happening."

"Enough to eventually get back on track to become a working dog?"

"I don't see it for her, since those environments would hold so many more distractions."

"So what'll happen to her?"

"There are always people willing to take on dogs who've been given extensive basic training, even if they didn't score high enough to make the grade as professional K-9s. Sebastian has a list of prescreened potential pet adopters interested in career-change dogs. Some of those folks have been waiting to get one of Crosswinds' program candidates for years."

"Oh, I see," she said. "Then I guess I'd better be extra careful with her—not that I wasn't always going to be, of course."

He shook his head. "I don't understand."

She shrugged. "Not to let myself get too attached, I mean. She really *is* adorable, and I was kind of thinking, if she were about to become homeless, maybe I would volunteer...since we seem to get along so well. But it was a silly idea. Please forget that I said anything."

"There's nothing silly about it," he said. "It's obvious that you're even more in love with dogs than Kate was."

"I'm sure she told you about the spaniels our grandparents had back when we were growing up. They were the sweetest."

He nodded. "She did. And I'm sure you'd make an incredibly devoted owner. We could always talk to Sebastian about getting you signed up for his wait list. I'd been thinking of suggesting it to you myself, almost from the moment I saw how you were with Pacer." *And how untethered and unhappy you seemed on your own, up at the cabin. Just the way that I was.* But he knew better than to voice that thought.

"I don't know," she said, shaking her head. "Like you mentioned before, that could take years, and who knows where I might be by then or what I might be doing for work and whether it will involve the kind of extensive travel I did while I was ghostwriting for celebrities?"

"Do you really see yourself going back to that profession? Would you even want to?"

"I'd definitely like to go back into some kind of writing. But not the kind I did before—if anyone would even have me after Nico finally ticked me off enough that I deleted scores of hours of recorded interviews and destroyed hundreds of pages of work product."

Catching something in her voice, Malcolm abruptly stopped walking Scarlett to turn and fix a serious look on her. "What exactly did he *do* to you? Because Kate shared some of the stories you told her over the years about wild celebrity behavior you've put up with."

Shaking her head, she said, "To be fair, most of my clients were absolute dreams to work with. Some of them still send me gifts from time to time and reach out to see how I am—even after hearing how my agent dropped me."

"But there *were* definitely a few jerks mixed in there," he reminded her.

"The word 'jerk' doesn't begin to touch on Nico's conduct," she admitted.

"So I ask again," Malcolm said, "what did this guy do—other than trashing your career?"

"Actually, *I* did that part all on my own."

"But why? Tell me, did he…touch you, Giselle?" At the thought of it, Malcolm wanted to track down the musician, cut through his phalanx of steroid-pumped bodyguards, and knock the sneering grin off that famous face of his for daring to cause her a moment's grief.

But once more, she shook her head. "Not me, no. He limited his gross behavior around me to allowing his male parts to hang out of his silk robe while I was interviewing him about his disgusting exploits, no matter how many times I asked him to cover himself or walked out of the room on his exhibitionism. Which, I have to tell you, was not nearly as impressive as he seems to imagine."

"That still doesn't make it right."

"*He's* not right," she said. "But anybody who hasn't been in a cave for the past ten years knows this guy's greatest joy in life, probably even greater than creating music, comes out of shocking and outraging people. Besides, I'd beaten out a *lot* of other ghostwriters to get this gig and was going to be very well compensated for my labor—so I was willing to overlook a certain level of discomfort, the way that everyone always ends up excusing Nico."

"So what was it then that finally pushed you over the edge?" Malcolm had to know.

She heaved a sigh. "There had been this big mentorship competition for young musicians, and the girl who won it was only fifteen. And a very *young* fifteen, if you know what I'm saying, like it was obvious that she'd been pretty sheltered. Still, she was unbelievably gifted in her own right, someone I'd bet anything will make a huge splash in the industry with her ability to spin out these original songs that have a person leaning in to catch not only every note but every breath between them."

"Don't tell me he was flashing his 'assets' around her as well," Malcolm said.

"At first, it seemed like he was actually behaving better. But Cami Carlson—that's the girl's name—idolized him to such a huge extent, his attention was like a drug to her. And I could see that he—that utter piece of filth—meant to take advantage of that beautiful, sweet child."

Malcolm's contempt for the man went white-hot. "Didn't she have a parent with her, watching over, someone you could warn?"

"If you could call him that. I know that stage mothers get a bad rap, but this 'manager-daddy'—" She angrily sketched out air quotes with her fingers "—had nothing but dollar signs where his protective instincts should've been. When I tried to have a private word with him, he only accused me of being jealous and told me not to do anything to sabotage his daughter's shot at making it big."

"Some father." Malcolm made a scoffing sound. "So what about Nico? Did you confront him?"

"I went to his handlers first to see if maybe I could generate some interest in getting them to run interference. But all those little toadies did was rat me out to the man himself. Predictably, Nico came absolutely unglued, shouting at the top of his lungs and throwing things—he smashed his second-best guitar that day—while accusing me of violating his trust to undermine him with his team and Cami's father. He was completely out of control, saying he had no idea how he could trust me with his story any longer."

Seeing the tears in her eyes, Malcolm asked, "Were you frightened of him, physically?"

"I was far more frightened by how close I came to begging for his forgiveness. To saying whatever it took to save my job—and the career I'd work so hard to build—to placate that vile piece of filth. And I might have done it, too, the way that everybody always has for him, if I hadn't spotted Cami leaving his bedroom at that moment, wrapped in nothing but a sheet."

His stomach turned. "That poor kid. So what did you do?"

"What else? I went with the nuclear option. I left that night and reported what I'd seen to investigators at the local police department. But, in the end, nothing happened, with Cami and her father denying it and everyone from Nico's camp calling me a disgruntled ex-employee—a woman half-deranged by grief for her drowned sister—and threatening to sue me into oblivion if I ever breathed a word of it in public."

"Those sons of—" He ground his teeth in frustration. "No wonder you destroyed the damned work product."

"I *had* to," she insisted. "Otherwise, they could've re-edited and used what I'd done to make that—that disgusting *pedophile* out to be some rules-flaunting rock 'n' roll hero for the ages. And I knew that Nico would never have the patience to sit through all those hours of interviews with anyone else again."

"That was damned brave of you," Malcolm said, looking at her with renewed admiration, "facing down a monster like that."

"It all would've been for nothing if I hadn't tracked down Cami's mother—who actually *does* care about her child's welfare, thank goodness."

"So I take it she had something to say about her daughter's 'opportunity'?" Malcolm asked.

"Apparently, she showed up on site, immediately realized Cami was lying about what she was getting out of her mentorship and told the girl she could come back in a few years and teach Nico a few lessons of her own about being a *real* professional in the industry. The kind of lessons she wouldn't have to learn on her back."

"Glad to hear that mama came through," he said.

Giselle nodded. "Then she packed up Cami into her minivan and drove away, leaving her husband with his jaw unhinged—along with the news that she was filing for divorce and full custody of his meal ticket. And she'd hired a real shark of a lawyer."

Stepping in closer, Malcolm laid a hand on Giselle's shoulder and looked her in the eyes, "I hope you realize that what you did *saved* that girl, whether or not she appreciated it at the moment."

"Considering the horrible names she called me, she most definitely did *not*," Giselle insisted. "But let's hope that three years maturity, her mother's influence, and going viral this past year with the song she recorded for the soundtrack of that blockbuster movie have shifted her perspective. It may've taken her longer than she'd hoped, but she's definitely made it to the bigtime now."

"Well, whether or not Cami *ever* appreciates the sacrifice you made for her—and how amazing you really are—I certainly do," he told her. "Maybe for the first time ever."

"Thanks for the reminder," she said. "Living up here in these mountains…" Closing her eyes for a moment, she lifted her face toward the azure dome of the sky and took a deep breath "… I'd almost forgotten that there was anything to me at all other than the things I've failed at."

Seized by an undeniable impulse, he took a step closer to pull her into his arms. But instead of pushing away, as he'd more than half expected, she squeezed him tightly back, as if she was holding on to him for dear life.

"When I'm listening to you, I don't hear *any* kind of failure, Giselle," he insisted. "I hear a beautiful, bold, and compassionate woman who's handled more grief than anybody ever should have, completely without support. But you have my word that that part of your life's all over now."

She pulled back enough to look up at him, her eyes damp with tears. An instant later, she was pushing herself up onto her toes and pulling his head down toward hers.

Draping her arms over his shoulders, she sealed her lips to his. The shock of their contact shook him to his foundations, barriers he'd imagined built to withstand eternity collapsing like sandcastles overtaken by the tide. In that moment, he was overwhelmed with an awareness of her trembling eagerness, with the heat surging through him as they stood entwined together, with the pulsing roar of his own blood rushing through his body.

Needing more of her, he deepened the kiss, forgetting where he was and why, only hours before, he had sworn never to do this very thing when he'd recognized the first stirrings of a powerful attraction to her.

All too abruptly, she broke off the kiss, leaving him bereft until she caught his gaze with a shy, sidelong glance and captured his hand in hers. When she guided it to her chest, her lips drifting to his neck, he cupped the softness of her breast and squeezed it, his mind filling with temptations, each more erotic than the next.

He had no idea how far things might have gone right there, but an angry yap of protest and a hard tug at his lower leg finally drew his attention, causing him to look down at Scarlett, who had managed to wrap her lead around his ankles. Frustrated with her inability to free herself, she was growing frantic, chewing at the lead itself.

Drawing a deep breath, he said to Giselle, "Let me— I'm sorry, but I need to take care of this. She's pretty upset."

As he bent to gently pull the portion of the lead she'd been chewing from her mouth, he reassured the pup, "There you go, Scarlett. Sorry I messed up and forgot about you down there for a few minutes."

"No, *I'm* the one who's messed up," Giselle insisted, looking deeply shaken. "*Really* messed up, standing right out here in front of all of creation trying to seduce my sister's fiancé where my friend was murdered only yesterday. What kind of monster even *does* a thing like that?"

"Not a monster, Giselle. A human being," he said gently, "with a perfectly natural need for connection." He picked up Scarlett, who seemed to need the reassurance of an ear scratch, and, on instinct, offered her to Giselle. "Or just a woman who's sensed that I'm finally seeing who you really are—for the first time ever. Or maybe it's you who's changed."

"I've changed, all right," she said, voice shaking, "if I've turned into the kind of woman who could jump from spending all my energy trying to figure out how to *honor* the sister who died in my place three years ago to the person who would make a move on her fiancé the first chance I get."

Too upset to take the pup, she turned and rushed back toward the pickup, leaving him one last glimpse of her tear-stained face.

Chapter 11

Markus Acker's gut turned to ice water when he saw sunlight gleaming off an approaching vehicle's windshield through the screen of trees that shielded his stolen truck from view. He was already on edge, worried that the two workmen who had evidently packed up after yesterday's storm hit would soon return to collect the tools and trailer they'd left behind outside his previous hideout—and even more anxious after hearing what had sounded like police sirens in the vicinity earlier.

If he'd had any choice in the matter, he never would have risked returning here, so close to the scene of the killing he'd committed. But this morning, he'd discovered, in a moment that still broke him out in a cold sweat to think of, that the little notepad he kept, containing all of his offshore account information, was missing.

With sickening clarity, it had come to him that it must have somehow fallen from his backpack when he'd been rummaging for a flashlight or his multi-tool when he'd first broken into the pitch-black cabin.

Immediately realizing that without the notepad, he'd be permanently cut off from his substantial nest egg, he'd had no choice but to return for it, no matter the risk— or who he had to kill to get it. When he'd discovered the property unoccupied and the notebook exactly where he'd expected it might be, he'd broken down for the first time in his long ordeal, sobbing with relief. But that relief had been tempered with a desperation to get away before he could be discovered.

As he eased slightly forward now, Markus saw that the vehicle he'd spotted wasn't law enforcement as he'd feared. But the dark-blue pickup did bear some sort of white logo on the driver's side door—a logo he realized with a start as it came closer—belonged to the Colton Ranch.

As the truck passed Markus's position, he struggled to get a good look at the vehicle's occupants. A glare prevented him from making out the passenger, but behind the wheel he glimpsed a dark-haired male in his mid-thirties.

"A damned Colton—has to be," he said aloud. But could this one lead him to the Victrola that held the go-bag containing his money and the ever-so-precious passport?

He decided that for now, he would attempt to follow and keep watch on the truck from a safe distance, to get a better idea of who he might be dealing with and whether he and his companion might somehow be taken by surprise. As Markus slowly pulled out, he hung well back. He needed time to come up with a solid plan for ending his time as a fugitive from justice—a plan that he admitted to himself might very well end with at least one additional Colton in the cemetery.

As Giselle and Malcolm left the recreational area, silence crowded into the space between them, crowded into the space inside of Giselle's lungs until, finally, she felt she'd die if she didn't shatter its suffocating spell.

"Once we get back to the ranch," she finally told him, "I'll start making calls. Line up a rental car for starters.

Then I'll find another place to stay until this manhunt's over, because I can't be with you at the ranch any longer. I'm sorry, but… I need some space right now to wrap my head around what happened. And to make absolute certain that I *never* make the same mistake again."

Malcolm glanced her way, his Colton-green eyes both sad and thoughtful. "I'm sorry to tell you this, Giselle— and even sorrier if I somehow misread your intentions when you kissed me—but as far as I'm concerned, it was the furthest thing from a mistake I can imagine. For the first time in forever, I feel like some part me that's been all bent up and off-kilter has finally dropped back into its track again and started running smooth and easy."

"But don't you understand? It wasn't *me* that you were thinking of. It couldn't have been."

"Hold on, please," he said. "Just give me a chance to finish speaking, and I won't ask any more of you. I swear it."

She leaned back against the headrest, pinching the bridge of her nose against an encroaching headache, before deciding she owed him at least that much. "Go on."

"I was thinking of *you* and you alone—the woman who'd risked her career, and possibly even her physical safety, with that entitled child predator you were working with on behalf of the well-being of a young girl. It's *you* I've been seeing in a new light—but I can also see the way this is tearing you apart, too." He paused a moment before adding, "And I won't allow that. I can't."

Confused, she said, "I'm not sure what you think you're going to do to stop it."

"How about taking a giant step backward in our relationship and forgetting about what happened today? Being the friend you obviously need instead of trying to become something it's clear that you can't handle?" he asked, a suggestion that took her utterly aback.

Before she could tell him that there was no way she could forget something as cataclysmic as that kiss had felt, he rushed to speak again, sounding almost desperate. "And let's definitely forget, too, the part about you heading off someplace you wouldn't be able to take Scarlett. Because we both know the ranch is the best place for you to build the kind of bond with her that I believe would truly benefit you both. Plus, to be a little selfish here, it'd keep me from losing touch with you again...maybe forever this time. Because I feel like, even aside from what just happened, there's something between us—a connection that's worth preserving. Don't you?"

As one of the two vehicles she'd noticed a distance behind them came up rapidly on their rear bumper, Malcolm slowed and waved the car's driver, who was clearly in a hurry, past them.

"We—we certainly both loved Kate," she agreed. "But part of loving her, for me, means understanding boundaries. Especially those that would amount to a betrayal of her memory."

She jerked her head, startled when the phone Malcolm had left in the console started ringing.

Malcolm frowned down at the screen. "I'm sorry. But this is Kelsie's uncle."

"You should see what he wants," she said, wondering why the finder of the red boat would be calling Malcolm.

Malcolm pulled over onto the wooded shoulder and made sure that she saw him hit the speakerphone icon before he connected. "This is Malcolm Colton."

"Larry Willets over at Creekside Marine, up the way

in Hadley. Got your number over at Crosswinds when I dropped my niece off. You know Kelsie, I understand?"

"Terrific kid. Hard worker," Malcolm said, the set of his jaw saying he hadn't yet decided whether the same could be said of her relation. "I'm told that you stopped by the sheriff's office yesterday—or maybe it was this morning? About a boat that showed up at your shop."

"Is that what you heard?" Willets asked him, before his tone and volume abruptly changed, rising to a level of hostility that had Giselle's stomach pitching. "That what *you* told somebody, Colton? Because I *don't* like being threatened. And I especially don't appreciate it when my family's brought into the mix."

"Threatened?" Malcolm's bewilderment was unmistakable. "Who on earth's been threatening you?"

"I figured maybe you could be the one to tell me, since Sebastian said that, other than you, he hasn't mentioned our conversation to another living soul. Yet whoever this fella is callin' my shop over here from a blocked number, disguisin' his voice and threatening me by name, sayin' he'll come after me and that niece of mine if I say another word to anybody in a uniform."

"First of all," Malcolm said, "I can't imagine why you'd think I of all people would want to threaten you for giving me the best damned news I've had in ages. Do you know how long I've been trying to drum up information on that boat you've got there—assuming it's the right one?"

"It *has* to be," Willets said. "Why else would the fact that it's suddenly turned up cause this kind of trouble? And whatever you had printed on that flyer, how am I to know that really wasn't all for show? Maybe you didn't really *want* the damned thing found in the first place?

Who's to say you weren't even somehow involved in this whole thing from the get-go?"

"What the actual—?" Malcolm demanded, his volume rising as he jerked forward in his seatbelt harness so abruptly that it snapped tight. "Are you honestly suggesting *I* had something to do with hiding that boat myself—or with my fiancée's *death*? Because I haven't found a need to go and physically stomp a mud hole in a man in my entire adult life, but for either one of those two lies, I'm of a mind to make an exception right this minute. And I promise you, you won't have to wonder for a second who's doing the stomping or worry about anybody in your family, either. Just what's left of you when I'm finished rearranging your skeletal structure. You hear me?"

Giselle sat frozen in the seat beside him, shaken to realize that the same Malcolm whom Kate had once joked was so even-tempered that he was impossible to pick a fight with had absolutely meant his threat of violence.

"So you're saying that it *wasn't* you, callin' me this mornin'?" Willets stammered over the phone.

"Glad you're finally putting two-and-two together," Malcolm said dryly. "But in case you have some further issue, I have a woman friend right next to me—my late fiancée's *sister*—who can verify that I've been with her all morning and haven't touched my phone. And if that's not good enough, you can—"

"No, no. I have to believe that that wasn't the reaction of a guilty man. And for what it's worth, I'm sorry," Willets said. "I was wound up pretty tight myself, on account of that caller bringin' Kelsie into his threats. I have to say, I prefer your brand of intimidation." With a low chuckle, he added. "The part about rearrangin' my skeletal structure was a nice touch, by the way. I'll have to remember that one in the future."

To Giselle's surprise, Malcolm laughed at that. "Feel free. I stole that one from my younger brother—or maybe it was one of my cousins. So I take it that you visited with Detective Danvers last night?"

"He'd left for the day already. But there was this lady sitting next to his desk there, dark-haired lady with a real nice set of—"

"Just get on with it," Malcolm said, cutting an apologetic look toward Giselle, who rolled her eyes in response.

"Anyway, she said her name was Rudolph. You know, like the reindeer?"

Giselle presumed that he meant Detective Danvers' partner, Ariana Rodolfo. Over the past couple of years, Giselle had gotten through to her on a few occasions and found her to be refreshingly honest, at least, about the realities of her sister's case.

"I assure you," she'd confided, her voice steeped with regret, "it's not for lack of effort put in. I was assigned to take a fresh look at all the cold cases and personally ran down every lead imaginable after I first came on with this department. But at a certain point, you run out of leads to explore. Out of everything except newer cases, each one with its own victim, along with family members desperate for answers."

"So my sister's file gets shut back inside a drawer somewhere, or wherever it is things go to be forgotten?" Giselle had accused, her pain and frustration spilling over into what she'd understood, even at the time, was pointless anger.

"I won't forget her," Detective Rodolfo had insisted. And though that vow was far more than she had ever gotten out of Detective Danvers, Giselle had been too frustrated to thank her or even to say goodbye before abruptly disconnecting.

"Rudolf-o, Rudolph—same difference," Larry Willets said now, responding to Malcolm's correction on his pronunciation of the detective's name over the speakerphone. "Whatever her name, she seemed pretty interested as she took my information and copied the photos I'd brought of the boat from my phone."

"What photos were those?" Malcolm asked him.

"She especially seemed keen on the ones where you could see where somebody'd scraped off the registration and the Hull ID numbers. Trailer tags were missing, too."

"So you're saying there's no way to trace this speedboat back to its original owner?"

"I'm sayin' that was damned well somebody's *intention*. Except they missed that scrap of paper I pulled out from between a couple of the seat cushions this morning," Willets boasted. "And who knows. Maybe the deputies'll come up with more, once they tow the boat off and take it into evidence this afternoon."

At the mention of that slip of paper, Malcolm's eyes had gone wide, finding Giselle's at the same moment that she reached over to squeeze his arm.

"So what, exactly, was on that paper?" Malcolm asked him, making what Giselle could tell was an effort to disguise his level of interest.

"Hard to say. Might've been a receipt or bill of sale at one time," Willets said, "but the thing's in such rough shape—like maybe it had been water-damaged and then dried all crumpled. When I tried to straighten it to take a picture with my cell phone, it started falling apart."

"Could you—would you mind sending me that cell phone photo you took of it?"

"No offense, Colton, but yeah, I would. If I had the sense I was born with, I wouldn't have run my mouth to you about it in the first place. You know, considerin' I still don't know who called to threaten me. If neither you nor Sebastian mentioned that I went to the cops to anybody—"

"What about your niece?" Malcolm asked him. "Kelsie could've said something to a friend, who brought it up to the wrong person."

"Now you're accusin' Kelsie of making trouble?"

"I'm sure she would never intentionally do that, but kids do talk. Or maybe someone from the sheriff's department mentioned this break in the case while in a coffee shop or somewhere else where it could've been overheard by someone with ties to whoever wanted that boat to stay hidden—"

"Listen, I've gotta go now. My boss—the boss is signaling for me to get back to workin' for a living."

"Is everything all right there, Mr. Willets?" Malcolm asked him, the concern in his voice telling Giselle he'd picked up on the same sudden tension she'd heard come into the mechanic's voice.

"Uh...yeah, sure, right as rain," Willets said. "See you tonight at dinner, darlin'."

The call disconnected, and Malcolm turned to look at her, his face lined with a mixture of confusion and concern. "You heard that, too, right? The strain in his voice? And what he just called me?"

"I'd swear he sounded scared," she said, goosebumps rising along her arms. "That man's in some kind of trouble. Should we call 9-1-1?"

"And tell them what, exactly? That we got spooked by

Willets's tone—or that a boat mechanic called me 'dar-lin'?"

Giselle made a face. "I see your point. But what else is there? Try calling him back?"

"I seriously doubt he'd answer." Malcolm checked his mirrors before putting the truck into gear and pulling back onto the road. "We can get there in about twenty minutes, if I step on the gas. Meanwhile, you need to try calling Detective Rodolfo, or maybe Danvers."

She gave an irritated huff. "That guy ignores my calls on a good day."

"Whoever you can reach is fine, as long as it's some-one that'll help stop this new evidence from possibly dis-appearing—and maybe keep Willets alive."

After leaving a voicemail and two frantic texts when Ariana Rodolfo didn't answer, Giselle decided to try one more time before giving up the effort.

On this attempt, however, the sheriff's department deputy detective finally picked up. "I'm seriously begin-ning to regret ever giving you my cell number," she said, sounding unmistakably irritated. "When I don't answer you, it's because I'm *busy*. It's definitely not because I want my phone blown up with a bunch of messages and texts about some supposed 'life or death' drama while I'm running down an important lead."

"But I meant the 'life or death' part *literally*! I'm almost positive that someone's just walked into Creekside Marine to silence Larry Willets," Giselle said, desperate to finally be heard. "I just heard him tell Malcolm Colton over the phone that he's received multiple threats this morning re-lated to speaking to you regarding the red boat someone brought into his shop."

"Oh, he reached out to *you* to say that, did he? Instead of, say, calling the sheriff's department?" Rodolfo sounded more suspicious than she did alarmed.

"He seemed to have some crazy idea that maybe Malcolm wouldn't *want* the boat found for some reason, not that it made a lot of sense to me," Giselle said. "But once Malcolm set him straight, he—"

"Went on to try his hand at whatever new game he's decided to try out?" the detective suggested. "I have Detective Danvers here with me right now, Ms. Dowling. I want you to know that at this very moment he's calling Mr. Willets to put your mind at ease. But while my partner's reaching out, let me inform you that Mr. Willets has a—a history with law enforcement that's given us both some reason to wonder if his story might not be exactly what he's representing."

"I'm sorry—what are you saying?" Giselle asked, cutting a quick glance toward Malcolm and wishing that she'd thought, as he had earlier, to put the call on speaker.

"He was a guest of the county a couple of times where he lived prior to this one about fifteen years back," the detective said. "Theft of materials from a jobsite where he worked and what looks to have been a bar fight…"

"Just because he did a little jail time during his younger years doesn't mean he's not entitled to protection now, though, does it?" Giselle asked her. "Because I'm telling you, this guy sounded terrified to both of us. And he said he'd found something that sounded like it might be written evidence, way down in the boat's seat cushions."

"Hold on just a second, could you?" Rodolfo said before muting the call.

While waiting for her to come back on the line, Giselle said to Malcolm, "I'm on hold, but it kind of sounds like she thinks Willets could be playing us. Apparently, the guy's had a couple of jail stints in his past. Nothing major-sounding, but…"

"Maybe she got a cop's gut feeling that something wasn't right when he came in to report the boat to her yesterday." Malcolm sounded a great deal less certain of the situation himself.

Before Giselle could respond, Rodolfo came back on the line. "Willets isn't answering the cell number he gave me," she said, "and Detective Danvers wasn't able to raise anyone at the main number for Creekside Marine, either. But at the moment, the two of us are right in the middle of following up on a time-sensitive lead related to this same case, so he's calling over to dispatch in Hobarth County—since Hadley's outside our jurisdiction—to send a unit to do a welfare check as soon as they have a deputy available."

"Right away, then?" Giselle pressed, unable to forget the fear she'd heard in the boat mechanic's voice.

"I'm sure they'll get to it as soon as they're able," the deputy answered carefully, "depending on their manpower situation."

"Which means that Willets could be a dead man by the time anybody bothers," Giselle said, her mind filling with images of Claudette lying face down in a pool of blood.

"Or more likely," Rodolfo countered, "he might instead be sitting around wondering why we weren't gullible enough to cross county lines to come running in response to that tempting bait he's dangled."

"I'm sure that, as someone in law enforcement," Giselle said, "you must find it aggravating, even embarrassing, to go running in response to people's cries for help, only to find that you've been manipulated for whatever reason.

But let me tell you how *I* felt yesterday when my neighbor called me for help and we *didn't* make it to her before she fell victim to a murderous fugitive from justice. A man still on the run today."

"I'm terribly sorry you were affected by that tragedy," the detective said, sounding genuinely regretful. "Of course, we're well aware of yesterday's homicide in the ski resort area and the ongoing manhunt, but I see no reason why Markus Acker would have any interest in either Larry Willets or a boat that may have been involved in your sister's death more than three years ago. Do *you*, Ms. Dowling?"

"I'm not trying to say this *is* in any way connected," Giselle said. "I only meant that I can't bear the idea of arriving too late to help again and possibly finding another body. Can't you understand that?"

Detective Rodolfo paused for a beat before demanding, "Wait a second. Are you telling me that you're on your way over to Creekside Marine right now?"

"Yes, Malcolm and I are heading over there together," Giselle said, glancing over to see him focused on the curving county road that tightly hugged a tree-clad hillside. The same route that she had for so long gone out of her way to avoid since it ran so close to the lake. Realizing it was far too late to turn around now—even if she knew that any dread she felt about the view soon to open up below them was worth the extra time a detour would add to their route—she fought back her nausea.

"I'll tell you what," Detective Rodolfo said over the roaring in Giselle's ears. "I'll make sure we communicate the urgency of this situation and ask, as a matter of professional courtesy, that a deputy be sent out to check on Mr. Willets right away. In the meantime, I need the two of you to turn around and go home—or *anywhere* but the vicinity of Creekside Marine in Hadley. Do you understand me?"

"I do, but—" Giselle began as they rounded the curve and the vast blue expanse of Blackbird Lake stole the breath from her lungs. Though the only signs of life were the silhouettes of a few birds bobbing on the sparkling blue surface about seventy yards below, Giselle's memory supplied a vivid summer scene alive with canoes and kayaks, anglers fishing in the shallows, personal watercraft, and swimmers in life jackets. And a pair of happy blond sisters—the one with far longer hair wearing a borrowed, deep purple bikini—laughing together aboard an inflatable raft being towed toward an unstoppable disaster.

"Ms. Dowling, are you still there?" the detective repeated, her voice floating in as if from a vast distance. "If you can hear me, please confirm that you're listening to reason here, for your own safety, if nothing else."

"Our—our *safety*?" Giselle stammered, blinking away the threat of tears as the past evaporated. "So you think I could be right about Larry Willets possibly being in danger?"

"Giselle?" Malcolm said, his forehead lined with worry as he glanced her way.

She gestured for him to wait a moment as the detective continued speaking.

"I'm certainly not ruling out the possibility," Rodolfo said, "any more than I am that you could be walking into some sort of shakedown he's cooked up looking for a reward for his assistance. Just give Hobarth County's deputy the chance to find out, and I promise you, as soon as possible, I'll personally get back to you and Mr. Colton with a full update on what's happening."

In the background of the call, Giselle heard what sounded like Detective Danvers urgently reminding his partner, *"We can't wait any longer—not if we hope to catch up with this suspect today."*

Coming back on the line, Rodolfo said, "I really have to go now, but we'll be in touch."

Once the detective ended the call, Giselle told Malcolm, "We need to get off this road and turn around. Detective Rodolfo doesn't want us going anywhere near Willets."

"Because she doesn't trust him?" Malcolm asked, switching on his right turn indicator to leave the road.

"She seemed uncertain whether he's trying to set us up or might really be in trouble. But whichever it is, I'm sure she'd rather have a deputy figure it out than have two civilians walk into the middle of it," Giselle said, feeling suddenly off-kilter as the turnoff narrowed, leading them down out of the mountains and closer to the lake. "But she—she d-did—she promised to keep us informed on whatever's ha-happening…"

"You haven't been this close to the water *since*, have you?" he asked gently as they rolled up to a stop sign.

She shook her head, her throat too tight to speak, her chest filled with the nearness of the lake whose presence she felt in her tingling nerve endings but could no longer see, thanks to the angle of the road and the screen of trees, partly leafed out with spring greenery, across the street.

As he waited for a couple of vehicles to come through the intersection, Malcolm said, "It really got to me, too, the first time I came this close. Let me turn the truck around up in this little park over to the right here. Then, I promise you, we'll get back on the road to the ranch again. Sound good to you?"

"The—the ranch will be fine for now," she managed, her breath catching as he pulled out and began driving toward a small park. Not the same park where the rescuers had brought an unresponsive Kate to continue attempting to resuscitate her shockingly pale and inert form. That had been miles to the north, near the edge of the ski basin. But at her first glimpse of the railings along the sidewalk, the benches, and even the empty parking spaces in front of a walkway along the lakeshore, Giselle cried out, their similar design elements sending her spiraling back to that desperate August day.

"Please stop! I have to—" She clawed to remove her seatbelt as a hot ball of nausea rose inside her, her awareness crowded with the inescapable images, the sounds and smells and textures surrounding the unimaginable price of her own survival.

Malcolm hit the brakes. "Are you all—"

But she was already flinging the door open and exiting the pickup. She only made it a few steps before her stomach made good on its threat.

After she was finished, she moved away and started walking. Feeling too raw to face conversation, she headed for the sidewalk, thinking that if she could just stand there for a minute and look out at the water, maybe she could find the peace and contentment she'd once felt each time she'd gazed out across its surface.

Yet she lasted only seconds before she had to turn away, screwing her eyes shut against the horrific images that assaulted her, one after another until her tears flowed freely. Eventually, she heard approaching footsteps, followed by the sound of Scarlett's whimpering before Malcolm softly shushed her.

"Not right now, girl," he gently told the pup. "She needs a little space. And how about some of this water bottle?"

Nodding, Giselle did her best to wipe away her tears, more than a little embarrassed by her meltdown but needing to rinse her mouth too much to turn down the offer.

"Here you go." He handed her both the container and a few of the fast-food napkins from the truck. "I figured maybe you could use these, too."

"Thanks," she said. "I—I'm sorry to have behaved like that. It's just that—sometimes I'm right back there. Trapped beneath the surface. Or in the boat, watching you do CPR before the first responders got there…"

She began to turn toward the low rumble of another vehicle pulling into the parking lot, but the engine shut down before coming any closer, and Malcolm was already shaking his head in response to what she'd said.

"If there's one person on the planet you *never* have to explain to, it's definitely me," he told her, his own expression haunted. "After what happened, I got rid of my own boat as fast as I could—practically gave the thing away because I couldn't bear the thought of ever having anyone else's life in my hands that way again."

Giselle cracked open the cap of the bottle she was holding. "For the first full year I lived in the cabin, I kept the big picture window covered because I couldn't even bear looking out at the lake from that distance. If the darkness hadn't gotten to me, I'd probably still have it covered up." Holding up the water bottle, she added, "Excuse me for a moment, please."

Walking away from him, she cleaned herself up as best she could. After depositing the sodden napkins in a nearby trashcan, she came back to see Scarlett wagging her tail as she stared up her, her sweet brown eyes pleading for attention.

Giselle knelt down to cuddle her and then surprised herself by laughing as she fended off the pup's attempts to cover her with kisses. Grinning, Giselle said, "Okay, now. That's enough. Blech, let's keep that floppy ear out of my mouth, too!"

Smiling, Malcolm offered his right hand and helped her back to her feet while keeping a firm grip on the leash. "She could definitely use some work on her manners..."

"No doubt about that, but at least she's got me laughing again, even here. So maybe you were right, about my needing her."

"It *has* been known to happen. My being right, that is," he said. "If you just give me the chance."

Catching a low rumble in his voice that put her to mind of the sort of shared intimacies she had no business thinking of, she stole a peek at him. And the look he slanted down at her had her all too aware of how close they were standing. In his eyes, she saw a depth of feeling she had never once glimpsed in any of the men she'd dated. In that moment she knew, with a certainty she could never recall feeling in her life, that if there was ever anything she needed—whether it was next week or twenty years from now—he would always be the one person she could pick up the phone to call.

When he stepped back, opening a respectful space between them, she knew as well that he was also the one man who would never ask anything of her in return.

At the thought, she realized it was the reason that once all of this was over, she needed to permanently lose Malcolm Colton's number. Because keeping in contact with a man she knew had feelings for her that she could never

allow herself to reciprocate—no matter what some trai-
torous corner of her heart might want—would be not only
wrong but unkind, and he'd already lost enough to the
cruel waters of this lake.

From somewhere not too far off, she heard the solid
chunk of a vehicle's door closing. In nearly any other setting, such a normally innocuous sound—a sound she'd
heard in parking lots thousands of times in her life before—would have gone unnoticed. But this time, a pin-
prick of alarm pierced her awareness.

A split-second later, she found herself spinning around,
as her mind clicked onto a detail that hadn't registered
on a conscious level. The vehicle she'd spotted out of the
corner of her eye when she had turned to wipe her face
a couple of minutes earlier had not been just any vehicle,
but a silver pickup matching the description of Malcolm's
missing truck.

On turning, however, the first thing she caught sight
of was not the pickup, parked about thirty yards away,
but instead the middle-aged man in a hooded gray jacket
who'd left it and was sprinting toward them, both hands
rising together as he aimed a—

"Gun! Behind you!" she shrieked, her cry so loud that
a phalanx of ducks floating on the water nearby took to
the air, quacking in alarm.

"Get down!" Malcolm shouted as he scooped up Scarlett—who gave a startled yelp—and, rather than following his advice to her, raced for the cab of the ranch truck
they'd been driving.

Having dropped flat to her stomach, Giselle stared in
disbelief, certain for one shocking moment that the very
man she'd been so certain she could count on was about
to drive off and leave her to what had to be Markus Acker.

But before she could recover, Malcolm burst back out of the pickup. Only this time, instead of the beagle, he was holding his pistol in his uninjured hand.

And unlike the man she assumed to be Acker, Malcolm didn't hesitate an instant before squeezing off three shots in quick succession.

With a shout of either surprise or pain, Acker swerved abruptly and then fell to the ground—perhaps only tripping in his haste, considering how quickly he rolled and sprang back to his feet. He'd clearly thought better of his charge, however, for he turned tail and made for the stolen pickup.

Malcolm, who'd been aiming to fire again, lowered his weapon, grimacing in her direction. "I may not have the stomach to shoot a man in the back, but I can't just let him get away. You coming, or should I call someone to come pick you up?"

She ran to the passenger door and flung it open, clambering inside to find Scarlett standing on the front passenger-side floorboard, shaking.

"It's all right, girl," Giselle said, bending low to try to soothe her as she pulled herself into the seat and Malcolm dropped the truck into reverse. "She's really frightened, Malcolm. Should I hold her in my lap to calm her?"

"No, try to keep her on the floor for now," he said, "and keep your head low if you can, too, because I have no idea what he's going to do when I go after him."

"Should I call 9-1-1, or would you rather try to reach Ajay?"

"Nine-one-one will be quicker, but you'd better buckle up first. Looks like he's on the move."

Giselle sat up to fasten her lap and shoulder harness, glancing nervously in the direction of the silver pickup as it snapped into place. As the silver truck started rolling, Malcolm backed out and then hit the gas, running the four-wheel-drive ranch truck over a concrete bumper through a grassy border between the parking lot and an area containing playground equipment.

Rattled by the rough ride—and the realization that instead of following from a safe distance as she'd expected, Malcolm was trying to cut off Acker's escape from the lot—Giselle sat bolt upright to brace herself. "Are you trying to get us killed? *Wait—*"

She snapped her jaw shut as the silver RAM braked hard and an arm was thrust out through its window. Not only an arm but a long, straight shape that she didn't recognize until the first bullet pierced their windshield and foam exploded from the headrest right beside her neck.

Chapter 12

If Malcolm lived to be a hundred, he knew that he would never forget the abject terror of Giselle's scream. Sick with the certainty that she'd been struck, he wrenched the wheel to the right, causing the truck's back end to spin around, exposing himself to danger but protecting her from the next shots he heard thwacking against sheet metal on his side.

Desperate to get them out of range, he mashed down on the accelerator. As the pickup leapt forward, the side window right behind him shattered, prompting an even shriller cry from Giselle.

A moment later, the silver RAM squealed out of the lot, prompting a screech of tires and the blare of a horn from what Malcolm saw was a large school bus full of what looked to be elementary children whose driver had been forced to brake hard to avoid a collision.

As desperately as Malcolm wanted to give chase, the sight of those kids, along with the sound of Giselle's sobbing, drove home the dangers of continuing to escalate this situation instead of calling in the professional law enforcement officers who were trained to deal with it with a reasonable degree of safety. With Giselle's earlier question—*Are you trying to get us killed?*—still ringing in his ears, he looked over at her, meaning to reassure her that he'd come to his senses.

That was when he saw the blood staining her sleeve, deep-red blood oozing out from beneath her right hand where she had it clasped over her upper left arm.

Heart dropping, he blurted, "You—you're hit?! Oh, Giselle! Oh, no. This is all my—I'm so sorry."

"Is—is there a—a cloth? A rag or towel or something I—can…" She looked around frantically.

Putting the truck in park, Malcolm got out and went around to her side but forced himself to check the back seat first, looking for any sort of cloth she could use to put direct pressure on the wound.

Not finding anything suitable, he peeled off his jacket and then stripped off his long-sleeved T-shirt. He wadded it up before opening her door. "Best I could do," he said, thrusting it at her.

Pale as Giselle was, her tear-stained blue eyes widened at the sight of his bare chest. "I—um—what're you—"

"Press this against your wound," he said, sparing a glance at Scarlett, who was crouched trembling on the floorboard but appeared physically unharmed. "But first, can you let me take a quick look."

Giselle was shaking as she nodded mutely and lifted her right hand off her blood-soaked upper left sleeve. He grimaced, seeing the slash-like tear in the fabric above a two-inch gouge across the surface of her flesh. Blood flowed from it unabated, but when he pulled her forward—causing her to cry out in pain, he was relieved beyond measure not to see a larger exit wound hidden on the rear side of her body.

As he leaned her back again, he said, "I'm sorry for moving you. I'm sure you're hurting. And I need you to keep as much pressure on it as you can stand," he said. "But the good news is, it looks like a graze wound, so I'm almost positive there's no bullet in you."

"*Good* news? You know what, Malcolm?" she shouted, angry tears streaming from her red-rimmed eyes. "Markus Acker, the man who *murdered* my friend only yesterday, just left one bullet in my headrest and another slicing through my flesh! Because *you* totally lost sight of everything except your need to take down the man who's hurt your family!"

The truth of her words hit him like a gut punch. "You're absolutely right, and I'm so sorry you're hurt. But I need to call 9-1-1 now, to get help on the way for you and report what's happened so the *right* people can catch Acker."

Even as Giselle was lighting into Malcolm, she suspected she wasn't being fair, not when she'd willingly chosen to join him in the truck after he'd told her he was going after Markus. But with adrenaline shuddering through her system, the sight and smell and stickiness of her own blood turning her stomach to an oily pool, and her arm pulsating with an electric-hot pain, she couldn't keep the anger from her voice.

By the time he'd finished with his call and then placed Scarlett in her kennel after giving the pup some gentle reassurance, Giselle turned to Malcolm as he climbed back behind the wheel. "Sorry I yelled at you," she said, her own voice soundly oddly distant to her. "I'm just—I'm a little freaked out, that's all."

"As you have every right to be. And you're hardly the first person I've upset lately with my actions where Markus is concerned." Looking stricken, he shook his head. "I don't like letting down the people I care for like this, and knowing that I've gotten you injured—"

"I'm—I'll be just…fine once I…" she began, meaning to reassure him she was okay. Or trying to before a wave of fatigue swamped her, and oily black blobs began to crowd into her vision.

"Hey there. You still with me?" Malcolm asked her, an urgency firming his voice as his hand squeezed her forearm.

She realized only then that her eyes had rolled back and closed as she leaned back against the headrest. She only wanted to shut out the sight of the blood for a few moments. To eclipse the memory of how it had the power to form small lakes when spilled from its proper vessel.

"Giselle," Malcolm repeated, fear piercing his voice this time. "Giselle, *please*. You have to—"

"Ow!" she said, her eyes flaring wide when he applied firm pressure to the wound on her upper arm. "That *hurts*, Malcolm!"

"Sorry if that's painful," he told her, though what she saw written in his face as he slowly came into focus looked more like relief than regret. "But after you passed out, I had to apply pressure to help control the blood loss. If that bullet nicked a major vessel… Wait a minute. Are those sirens?"

Straining, she nodded. "Yes, I think so." She wasn't sure she did, though, over the roaring in her ears.

"Let's cross our fingers that at least one will be the EMTs. You aren't hurting anywhere else, are you? Any other place I might have missed?"

She shook her head, an act she instantly regretted as the truck's interior did a slow spin around her. "No, but…"

She closed her eyes to stop the carousel.

"But what? Please talk to me," he pressed.

"I'm probably…" she murmured, but her voice strengthened as she put together the pieces of the puzzle. "Have them—have them check my blood…when they transport me…"

"*What* about your blood, Giselle? Is there something—can you look at me a moment, tell me—is there some kind of medical condition you haven't mentioned to me?"

Hearing the panic in his voice, she fought to open her eyes again, to try to alleviate his worry. "N-not that big a—" A wave of nausea. "Check the hemo—"

"You're not telling me that you're a bleeder, are you? That you have hemophilia?"

She tried to tell him that he had it wrong, that the last thing she intended to do was to die here, so near the same lake that had claimed her sister. But before she could explain, the roaring in her ears merged with the black blobs and she sank into unconsciousness once more.

Despite the number of task-force-affiliated law enforcement personnel who'd been entering and exiting the small park, Malcolm's full attention was glued to the receding ambulance. Though Giselle had been conscious and speaking to the EMTs when she had been loaded and no sirens had been switched on, he had a leaden lump in his gut nonetheless watching the flashing emergency lights as the unit headed off toward the nearest hospital in Conners, a somewhat larger community about a forty-minute drive from Owl Creek.

"I understand how worried you must be," said Owl Creek PD's lead detective, Fletcher Colton. With his athletic build, dark brown hair, and green eyes, he bore more than a passing resemblance to Malcolm himself, though the recent Boise transplant was a few years younger and had a squarer jaw and broader forehead. "But I've seen enough gunshot wounds in my career to tell you what the EMTs won't. She's going to be okay."

"She might've seemed a whole lot better before they took off, but after watching her pass out twice already…" Malcolm shook his head, zipping his jacket a little higher since he'd given his shirt up to stanch Giselle's wound. "I've answered enough questions for the moment. As soon as Greg makes it here to give this pup a lift back to the ranch for me, I need to get to the hospital to make sure they run tests on Giselle's blood. And make certain she doesn't take another bad turn."

When he started digging in his pocket for his truck keys, Scarlett tilted her head to look up at him from the end of her lead.

Fletcher laid a hand on his shoulder. "Sorry, Malcolm, but I can't let you go anywhere quite yet. For one thing, I don't want to answer to Ajay about why I didn't finish getting your truck processed for evidence. And anyway, if you haven't noticed, your left rear tire's flat."

Malcolm looked over and cursed, seeing that one of Acker's bullets must have punctured it. "I can have it changed in no time."

"You can hold on until we're finished here. Then I promise you, I'll take you over to Conners myself, where you'll see they've been busy checking her bloodwork and stitching up that little graze wound so she'll be ready to go home with you again in no time."

As much as Malcolm wanted to believe the cousin he'd known all his life, he couldn't stop picturing the way Giselle's face had gone slack when she'd passed out on him that second time. "You aren't just saying what I want to hear now, are you? Telling me whatever it takes to get me to continue willingly answering more questions for your investigation?"

Fletcher clasped his arm. "You're family first, Mal, not some stranger—or a suspect. I swear to you, I'd *never* do that. And especially not on this lake, of all places."

Pulling away, Malcolm starting walking, Scarlett trotting at his heels. Raking his hand through the disordered mess of his slightly longer hair, he strode to the railing and knotted his hands around the sun-warmed metal. When he heard Fletcher walk up behind him, Malcolm screwed his eyes shut against the images resurfacing from the past.

Instead of pushing him again with more of his damned questions, Fletcher appeared content to bide his time and give Malcolm a chance to pull himself together. When Malcolm looked around again, he saw his detective cousin squatting down, sitting on the backs of a pair of well-shined shoes, to rub Scarlett's floppy red ears and play with her a little.

Noticing Malcolm's regard, Fletcher asked, "So who's this cutie? New little sister for Pacer, maybe? I can see she's definitely not one of Kiki's charges."

Malcolm shook his head, knowing that since Fletcher's partner, Kiki Shelton, was a puppy-raiser for Crosswinds, the couple had the inside track on many of the young dogs that Sebastian and Della took into training. "She came to Sebastian via an out-of-state puppy raiser for potential airport sniffer dogs. But she's a—"

"Ouch—watch it there, Miss Mouthy." Wincing, Fletcher gently pried a pair of determined jaws open to extricate his fingers from the sharp puppy teeth that had clamped down on them. Looking up at Malcolm, Fletcher said, "Sorry to interrupt."

"That's fine—and a perfect illustration of the problem. Scarlett's a little homework training project from Sebastian," Malcolm said. "She's been something of a wild child around the kennel—but she's taken a real shine to Giselle."

"From what I've observed, she's not the only one." Fletcher rubbed at his fingers. "You've been spending time with Giselle, I take it?"

When Malcolm gave him a hard look, Fletcher patted the pup once more before standing again to look his cousin in the eye. "Whatever your relationship, I promise you, I'll be the last person to pass any kind of judgment."

"I never intended to see her again, much less drag her into this Markus nightmare. But running into her again—it's brought up so many...complicated feelings. Feelings I can't afford to let take hold." Malcolm grimaced, shaking his head at the impossibility of the attraction. "And right now, we have bigger worries. And not only Markus Acker."

Fletcher frowned and shook his head. "What are you trying to say?"

"We found out just this morning that the boat responsible for the accident three years ago—the boat that killed Kate—may have turned up. At least there's good reason to believe so."

"You're serious?"

Malcolm nodded before briefly explaining how the boat had been purchased out of storage and taken to a marine mechanic in Hadley, who claimed to have found information. "Detective Rodolfo from the sheriff's department's checking out the story he tried to sell me about someone possibly threatening him about it, but she didn't seem so sure this guy was on the up-and-up. Apparently, the mechanic has a sketchy record."

"What was *your* take on the guy?" Fletcher asked.

Malcolm shrugged. "I can't tell at this point whether he's in serious danger after finding evidence or he's really some kind of grifter with an agenda. But I'm afraid that after all the attempted scams and shakedowns, I wouldn't believe an honest person by this time."

Fletcher shook his head. "I tried to tell you years ago that putting up a big reward for information and trying to vet the calls yourself was a terrible idea."

"You and Max both did." Only now did Malcolm realize what an idiot he'd been to ignore the advice of both a seasoned detective and an ex-FBI special agent. "But at the time, I couldn't see any other way."

"For what it's worth, I probably would've done the same in your shoes, in spite of knowing better from my professional experience."

Malcolm shrugged. "Apparently, when it comes down to love, all the reason in the world flies straight out the window, the way it did when Markus Acker, of all people, came charging at us out of nowhere, aiming his gun straight at us."

"On the *exact* day you heard that this boat had turned up…" Fletcher's forehead creased as he frowned.

"You sound skeptical about the timing," Malcolm said, "but that boat vanished more than three years ago."

"Yes…less than a year after Markus moved to Idaho and established the Ever After Church in Conners."

Malcolm felt a wave of nausea assail him. "You aren't implying, are you, that the former Reverend Acker—or whatever it was he was calling himself back when he was scamming people into signing over all their assets and their free will to him—could've had some possible connection to the accident?"

"I'm not necessarily suggesting—"

"You're thinking he might have been the person *driving* that red ski boat on that afternoon in August, aren't you?"

Raising his palms, Fletcher cautioned, "Let's hold up a minute there, Malcolm. That's *way* too big a leap to make at this point."

"But if Acker *was* responsible for Kate's death, in addition to injuring Giselle the way he did just now, don't you see, there's no way I can possibly stay out of this."

"Seriously, Malcolm. Do you hear yourself? You're letting your emotions regarding Acker overwhelm your judgment."

"We already know for certain that he was responsible for the deaths of your father and my mother, and he just shot Giselle right in front of me, so why the hell wouldn't I?"

"I see your point," Fletcher said, "but I wouldn't be allowed within ten miles of this task force if my professional detachment were ever called into question. And as I was saying, if you start off certain you already *know* your investigation's endpoint, you'll accept only evidence that backs up that hypothesis and ask only the kind of questions that could possibly take you there. That sort of tunnel vision results in a lot of terrible police work."

Malcolm forced himself to take a breath to consider what Fletcher was suggesting. "So you're saying we have to stay open to the possibility that the boat's turning up at this particular juncture has nothing to do with Markus?"

"It could certainly be coincidental. Or maybe Acker was nowhere near the scene of the accident itself but had some involvement with the cover-up of the boat's location later, or of its mysterious reappearance at this time. Or maybe he's somehow tied to this boat mechanic's possible attempt to scam you. We just don't have enough information to know at this point."

"I don't understand," Malcolm said. "If Acker *is* somehow tangled up with the call I received from the boat mechanic, what would be his point? And would that have any bearing on why he showed up pointing a gun at me today?

"*Now* you're sounding like someone with real detective potential." Fletcher added a smile. "Or at least I'd say that if I didn't figure you'd pulverize Acker before you ever had the patience to pry the answers to any of those questions out of that slippery charlatan."

A darker-haired man in his mid-thirties jogged over, a slim six-footer with a trim beard wearing a navy polo beneath his Owl Creek PD jacket. "Sorry to interrupt," he said.

"You're fine," Fletcher told him before glancing toward his rancher cousin. "Malcolm, you remember Archer McKenzie? His Las Vegas PD experience and the fact that he's a real wiz, especially when it comes to evidence processing, has been incredibly helpful."

Malcolm and Archer shook hands, both men nodding.

"Sure. Hannah's introduced us," Malcolm answered, referring to Fletcher's widowed sister, who seemed happier than she'd been in ages since she'd gotten together with the Nevada transplant.

"Speaking of evidence," Archer said, looking at Fletcher, "I wanted to let you know the presumptive test on the dark stains you marked over here were positive."

Fletcher glanced back in the direction toward the parking lot. "So those are definitely bloodstains?"

Remembering the information he'd provided earlier, Malcolm felt his pulse accelerate. "Are you saying—you don't mean you've found blood over where I showed you

Acker dropped and rolled after I shot at him? I could've sworn I missed him." He ran those chaotic few moments of the shoot-out back through his mind.

"Perhaps not," Fletcher allowed.

"I still have to run another test to confirm the blood is human," Archer qualified. "Then, if that one's positive, I'll cross-match it to a known sample from Ms. Dowling to eliminate her as the source."

Fletcher explained, "We don't want to take a chance of letting a defense attorney get him off on any procedural errors once we take him into custody. But I do think it's very possible you left Markus Acker something to remember you by—maybe even an injury serious enough to force him to seek help."

"If I did happen to hit him," Malcolm said, "I damned well hope he's finally getting a good taste of the pain he's cost so many others."

"I'll leave the worrying over retribution to a higher power," Fletcher said. "All I want right now is to get him off the streets before he can destroy any other lives."

"Of course, I understand that." Malcolm admired Fletcher's composure but doubted he would share it if he'd just seen Kiki hauled off in the back of an ambulance.

"I've already sent out alerts with Acker's photo and description to every hospital and clinic within a hundred miles."

Archer nodded his approval. "That warning could save some lives—but are you sure you don't want to expand the radius even farther?"

"I could, just out of an abundance of caution, but the task force is fairly certain that won't be necessary," Fletcher told them, "because *something's* clearly holding him in this area, whether there's something he desperately needs or worse yet, some revenge fantasy he's cooked up against members of our family."

"That's a chilling thought." Malcolm winced, thinking of his father and the aunt he thought of as a second mother, his siblings, half-siblings, and cousins, not to mention their partners and even the little ones who should never have to think about such evil.

"One I pray I'm wrong about," Fletcher said. "But with the possibility of his being injured, too—"

"You're saying that I might've made things even worse?" Malcolm asked.

"Worse, better—it's impossible to say what might set off a ticking time bomb." Fletcher gazed out over the lake's wind-troubled waters. "Or who exactly it could end up going off on in the end."

Chapter 13

In the emergency department exam room where Giselle had been left to rest with a bag of intravenous fluids, she cracked open an eyelid and breathed a sigh of relief at the sight of Malcolm.

"Thank goodness it's you," she said, fumbling to raise the head of her bed. "I was scared half to death it would be a technician out for yet another blood sample. It's a wonder I have anything left for them to take by this time."

"No more needles here, I promise," he said, eyeing the fresh bandage now covering the graze wound on her upper arm. "Just a guy who's relieved as hell to see your color back and hear you sounding more like yourself."

When he bent to kiss her cheek, she couldn't resist the impulse to give him an awkward hug.

He returned it, his voice going rough when he said "Giselle," and squeezing her in return, hard enough that she understood how deeply she must have scared him at the park earlier.

Closing her eyes, she leaned her head against his shoulder, relief flowing through her to be in the strong arms of a man she knew she could always trust to look out for her interests—a man she knew she would always care about as well.

"I'm so glad you came," she said, telling herself that it was perfectly appropriate to embrace a good friend—even a male friend she'd once kissed, in a moment of poor judgment that could never be repeated—as she pulled away. "When I asked the nurse to watch for you and let you back here if you showed up, I wasn't sure if—"

"I would've been here a heck of a lot sooner, but there were a lot of questions that needed answering to assist in the search."

"Of course," she said, immediately understanding that the manhunt had to be the number one priority, before anyone else could be hurt. "Any new updates yet on—"

"Before we get into any of that, I have to know how you are. What did they say about your wound? And are they going to admit you?"

"Admit me? Not for this," she said, shaking her head as she gestured toward her bandage. "All it needed was some cleaning and a little surgical adhesive. Shallow as it was, the doctor says it should be fully healed within a couple of weeks and not even leave much of a scar."

"That's wonderful. But you're sounding awfully nonchalant for someone who went lights-out on me more than once." He cast a worried look toward her IV bag. "I don't mean to pry, but you did mention something about your blood. And I was afraid that—I was just *afraid*. For you."

"I get that," she said, "and I'm really sorry. This bag's only hydration, just to perk me up a little."

"Graze wound or not, you don't need to apologize for being *shot*," he said, sounding offended by the idea of it. "The shock alone, I'd imagine, would be enough to—"

"That wasn't what had me fainting," she said, frowning. "And I'm sure I had you imagining all sorts of terrible things with what I said about blood testing, but I promise you, it's nothing dire. Only my own negligence."

He shook his head. "I don't understand."

"Of course you wouldn't," she scoffed. "Not when I'm being cryptic. What I suspected—and turned out to be right about—was that I might be anemic again. It happens to some younger women, especially around their...their monthly cycles." She reminded herself that they were both grown adults and basic biological functions were nothing to be shy about discussing. "According to the doctor, my hemoglobin was low because I haven't been doing the greatest job getting enough iron in my diet."

"This has happened to you before, then? The passing out from not taking care of yourself properly? Because I'm totally prepared to reintroduce you to the joys of steaks and burgers. Or at least to chicken and fish, if the vegetarian lifestyle's not cutting it for you."

"Thanks, but no thanks," she said, having lost her taste for meat years before. "I've been given a supplement for the short-term to move the needle in the right direction. But in the long run, there are *plenty* of outstanding meat-free options that'll keep me in top form. I just need to remember that cooking for myself is no excuse not to pay attention to what's healthy."

"No, it definitely isn't," he said, "especially when I've tasted the evidence of what a fantastic cook you are when you put in the effort. But I think I understand. When you're alone the way you have been, it must be tough motivating yourself to do things that feel like they're solely for your own benefit. I know that during the past few years, there were a lot of days when, if I hadn't had family, Pacer, or ranch and SAR obligations to motivate me, I'm not sure I ever would've made it out of bed."

She avoided his gaze, not wanting him to get an inkling how often she had fought that very battle.

"Hey," he said, the tips of his fingers brushing her jaw, "I hope you know that I would never judge you. I only want you to be healthy and happy."

"I *have* been taking steps toward the healthy part. Doing some weight work and trail running to build my muscle tone and stamina. Trying to get back into scratch meal prepping for myself the way I was when you came by the cabin," she said. "All I have to do is stay motivated to keep it up."

"That's an excellent start, and for the time being, I want you to consider me a partner in that effort."

"I don't need a babysitter, Malcolm," she said.

"That's great, because I'm in the middle of a full-blown crisis and don't have the bandwidth to babysit anybody while I'm working to keep my family safe from whatever Markus's next move might be. What I *can* be, though, is the kind of friend who'll have your back—especially if you'll help to keep an eye on mine."

"Sounds more than fair to me," she said. "Earlier, though, you put me off when I asked you about Markus. Please tell me there's been some good news about the search for him."

"It looks like I may have clipped him during the shoot-out," Malcolm told her. "There was enough blood found where he fell after I fired on him that an alert's been sent out to medical facilities. And while Fletcher was driving me over here, he got word about a possible sighting of my truck on the road to Owl Creek. Ajay's got everyone he has on it, even air support from the state."

Excitement zinged through her. "Do you think they might really have him this time?"

"For my family's sake—and the safety of the whole community—I hope they do. Especially after finding Claudette yesterday and watching you get hurt today."

"But I wasn't his real target, was I? It definitely looked to me like his attention was focused on you."

"Fletcher had the same thought when we talked about it."

"You don't think he was aware it was you before tracking him with Pacer, do you?" she asked. "Maybe he could've been watching you through a pair of binoculars on the mountain and seen the two of you and then decided you were a particular threat."

"That's not a half-bad theory," Malcolm said, "but I'm fairly sure Pacer and I didn't come nearly that close to him, especially with yesterday's poor visibility. And anyway, he would've been more focused on my K-9 as the threat instead of me personally."

"We passed him in the Crosstrek, as well," she said, "but it was awfully quick, and the visibility was awful."

"If we couldn't see him, I can't imagine he got a good look at either of us."

Shaking her head, Giselle asked, "What then?"

"Fletcher figured Acker might've spotted that Colton Ranch logo on the truck I was driving today and assumed I was one of the members of the same family that's been causing him so much grief lately."

"Oh, poor him," she said sarcastically. "Sounds like he only has himself to blame for whatever troubles he's run into, considering his scheme to kill your uncle and rob the Coltons blind."

"I don't imagine that the concept of fairness has ever figured into Markus Acker's thinking," Malcolm said.

"I suppose it comes with the territory when you're a

homicidal narcissist with cult members willing to treat you like some sort of god on earth," she said.

"I need to tell you," Malcolm said. "Fletcher has a theory that Acker's crimes against our family may go back even farther than we ever imagined."

"What do you mean?" she asked.

He turned a somber look on her. "Before I tell you, you need to understand that this is only a very tentative working theory. The red boat's turning up right now could be exactly what it seems to be—a very lucky break after years of frustration in finding—"

"Wait. What are you—?" She shook her head, desperately trying to keep up with his change of subject. "You aren't saying that in some way, *Markus Acker* of all people could be—that he might have something to do with the—the *accident*?"

For the third time that day, black spots edged her vision. This time, however, Giselle fought them back, in spite of the nausea threatening to overwhelm her.

"I don't know *how* he might be involved," Malcolm said, "or if he has anything at all do with—"

"Murdering my sister," she said flatly.

His face blanching, he nodded. "Or helping somehow with the cover-up or even using the bait of the boat this morning, along with Kelsie's uncle Larry at the marina, to try to lure us—or probably just me—out where he could ambush me on my own. I'm only sorry you happened to be with me. If I'd had the faintest idea that I might've been being played—"

"Let's not either of us waste another second apologizing for things that weren't our fault. Now, I should try calling Detective Rodolfo," Giselle said. "We need to find out whatever happened to Larry Willets at Creekside Marine. We have to know whether he's tied up with Markus somehow or if instead he's one more of Acker's victims."

Nodding his agreement, Malcolm said, "Fletcher's out in the lobby trying to reach one of the sheriff's department detectives right now. Meanwhile, we should—"

He was interrupted as the emergency physician who had treated her earlier returned to talk about sending her home.

"I don't mind if my friend hears this," Giselle said, certain that whatever the doctor had to say would take only a few minutes.

"She'll be staying with me for at least the next few days," Malcolm said, darting a look her way that brooked no argument on the subject, "so the more I know about how to assist with her recovery, the better."

A leanly built, middle-aged man in navy scrubs and thick, dark hair streaked with silver, Dr. Avila glanced curiously at Malcolm's immobilized left hand and forearm but asked no questions before nodding. Returning his attention to Giselle, the doctor reviewed her wound care. After emphasizing the importance of her staying close to home for several days, he advised her to follow up with her family doctor for further care.

"I don't exactly have one in the area," she admitted. "It's been a few years since I've felt the need to go in for anything beyond some recent vaccinations at the mobile clinic."

"Well, then it sounds like high time that you found yourself someone. Do you need a list of possibilities?"

"I'll ask around," she said vaguely.

"I'll make sure she gets in to see Dr. Beecham," Malcolm put in.

"Cynthia Beecham?" Dr. Avila asked, brightening.

"My wife swears by her. Good choice, but I hear it can be tough for a new patient to get appointments."

"I have an inside track there." Malcolm smiled. "My aunt's one of her nurses and works there a couple of days a week."

"That's perfect, then," the doctor said before going on to hand Giselle a thick sheaf of printed papers.

"I'm a vegetarian as well," he said, "so I've included some suggestions for plant-based iron sources, since a lot of people find food sources easier to tolerate than the supplements."

"Thank you." Giselle said as the nurse who'd come in while Dr. Avila was talking unhooked her IV. "But I'm actually feeling so much better now. And I'm already quite aware of what I should be doing. I only need to make a point to actually do it."

"The fluids, painkillers, and rest you've had here may have given you the false impression that you're completely back to normal, but you've still suffered a serious physical and emotional trauma," Dr. Avila countered.

"You said yourself that the graze wound on my arm was minor," she argued, feeling impatient to get this over with.

"While the injury shouldn't leave you with any long-term damage, your system was quite depleted. And it can be more upsetting than you might realize, once you've had the chance to process that someone's committed a potentially homicidal act of violence against you."

"I haven't—I haven't really thought about that," Giselle said.

"But you likely will, so I've included among your papers contact information for a victims' advocate who can connect you with resources such as counseling or—"

"As much as I appreciate all you've done, I don't need naps and I don't need to chat about my feelings," she insisted, ignoring the look that Malcolm gave her. "I just need out of here, so I can get myself prepared."

"Prepared in what way?" Dr. Avila asked her.

"Prepared to make certain that the next time I encounter Markus Acker, *I'm* not the one who ends up in your ER."

Chapter 14

Malcolm wasn't certain which he found more disturbing, the thought that Giselle might be too passive to take measures to protect her own life or the idea that she might be actively looking forward to another violent confrontation with an unhinged killer. Between Claudette's murder and the shoot-out, she had reason enough to be upset, but he suspected the real trigger for her uncharacteristic outburst may have been his own suggestion that Acker could have been involved in Kate's death.

Noticing the alarmed look on the physician's face, Malcolm quickly explained, "The last couple of days have been an emotional roller coaster for both of us. But right now, the only things we're looking at doing are getting home where we can regroup, have a good meal, and meet up again with a certain puppy I know will be very happy to see you."

"Poor Scarlett. Is she all right?" Giselle asked, her expression turning anxious. "I'd forgotten all about her."

"She's fine. No need to worry. My brother Greg showed up with a change of clothes for me and then took her back to the ranch to hang out with his kids and Briony."

"Thank goodness."

Once Giselle had changed back into street clothes—with the exception of a scrub top one of the nurses had found for her to replace her own blood-soaked shirt—she and Malcolm were escorted back into the waiting area, where they were told Detective Fletcher Colton was waiting to see them.

"Do you see him anywhere?" Malcolm asked Giselle.

"I don't think so," she said, scanning the room, which was crowded with a variety of individuals, some holding ice packs to bandaged heads or towels to bleeding body parts. Another leaned over a trashcan, his greenish hue indicating the possibility that he might at any moment fill it, and a particularly alarming-sounding woman tried—and failed—to cover the sound of her deeply phlegmy coughs.

"Whoa," Malcolm said quietly, sticking out an arm to prevent Giselle from moving any farther into germ central.

"I'm with you on that," Giselle whispered.

"There's Fletcher outside," Malcolm said, gesturing toward a window, where his cousin stood near the edge of the parking lot, talking on his cell phone in the shade of a maple tree.

Spotting Malcolm inside, Fletcher waved, imploring the two of them to come outside to meet him. They quickly found an exit and left the emergency department.

"That was a good call, finding yourself a patch of green grass and fresh air," Malcolm told him. "Giselle, this is my cous—"

"I'm Detective Fletcher Colton." Fletcher offered her a hand after tucking his phone back inside his pocket. "We met briefly earlier right before you were loaded into the ambulance, but I don't expect you to—"

"It's a bit of a blur," she admitted, "but I do remember speaking to you."

"I hope you're feeling better now."

"Oh, definitely. Thanks for asking," she said. "But I

was hoping we might be able to get some information from you."

"I know this isn't anything to do with the task force's investigation," Malcolm elaborated, "but we were both wondering if you'd heard anything from the sheriffs' department about whether they found Larry Willets safe at the marina?"

Fletcher nodded. "I was just giving an update on the two of you to Detective Rodolfo, since she reached out when she heard about what happened. She also asked me to let you know that Willets voluntarily came in to her office to answer some additional questions and turn in a piece of evidence that he claimed to have collected from the boat before it was taken in for further processing."

"So he wasn't harmed at all?"

"Didn't sound that way," Fletcher said. "But I got the impression from our conversation they're trying to figure out how he fits in with the other suspects they've identified."

"What do you mean, the *other* suspects?" Giselle blurted, beating Malcolm to the punch.

"I should probably let someone from the sheriff's department explain that to you."

"Don't do that to us." Malcolm looked his cousin directly in the eye, "especially since you and I both know there's no telling how long it might take for someone else to get back to us in person."

Clearly uncomfortable with the situation, Fletcher allowed his gaze to drift to Giselle.

"Please," she said. "After everything we've gone through, don't you believe we've at the very least earned the right not to be treated like small children? Or be bounced around from voicemail to voicemail for hours or days while we wait for answers?"

After a moment's hesitation, Fletcher sighed. "I guess you have at that, both of you. So, this morning, Deputy Rodolfo and her partner tracked down the couple who previously owned the facility where the boat was stored before it was sold to its present owners. The hope was that one or both of them might remember something more helpful than the phony name and address listed on the paperwork they filled out more than three years ago."

"And they hit pay dirt, I take it?" Malcolm asked.

"The husband seems to have been the one who helped them. He didn't recall anything helpful, but it turns out his wife remembered that one of the two *boys*, as she called them, was the red-haired son of someone she'd gone to school with. They dug out an old high school yearbook and came up with a woman's name, and from there they ended up setting up a—"

"So you're saying that they've *arrested* them?" Giselle all but shouted, her eyes wide.

"They've identified two men, both of them mid-twenties," Fletcher said. "Twenty and twenty-one that summer and only about a week out from heading back to the dorm at Boise State for the fall term."

"You mean they were—they were damned *kids*?" Malcolm burst out.

"Adults, in the law's eyes," Fletcher pointed out. "But we still don't—"

"Who the hell are they?" Malcolm demanded.

"Do they have them in jail yet?" Giselle asked at the same time.

"These suspects, at this point, have no idea the deputies are even aware of any such boat accident," Fletcher said.

"For all they know, the sheriff's department may simply want to speak to them about their unpaid storage bill."

Malcolm frowned and shook his head. "They'd have to be pretty idiotic to voluntarily go in for a conversation about their 'missing boat' when they've been hiding it all this time following a fatality accident."

"You'd think so, wouldn't you?" said Fletcher. "But you'd be absolutely shocked at how many people will respond to exactly such an invitation—not so much because they aren't worried about what the authorities might know but because they've had a whole lot of time to sweat over what might happen to the lives they've been building since their original crime took place. The crime that they've long since begun to hope that people have forgotten about by this point since no one's caught onto it for this long."

"No one's forgotten a thing," Malcolm angrily insisted. "At least *we* never will."

"It's impossible," Giselle added, slipping her arm through his, "when the nightmares are always *right there*, just waiting for you to let your guard down."

Though the sadness of her statement hit hard, Malcolm felt something of a kinship in the way they stood together, lending each other strength in their shared trauma. Even if some part of him, a part that had stubbornly taken root and refused to be tamped down inside him, wished they might share more.

Fletcher nodded his agreement. "Of course, no one's forgotten Kate's death, for all their wishful thinking. But they'll be dying to find out what, if anything, the sheriff's department really knows and desperate for any chance to put their worried minds at ease."

"So what do *we* do now?" Giselle asked.

"Let me take you two back to the ranch," Fletcher said,

"where both of you can get some much-needed rest and do some healing while we all wait to hear the outcome of these interviews and whether Acker's been arrested."

"You sound almost like you're expecting some news on that at any moment," Malcolm said hopefully. "I mean on Markus."

"Maybe it's because we got a credible tip on a sighting and location, still in your truck," Fletcher told them. "Or maybe I'm just thinking that no fugitive's luck can hold forever. But whether it takes minutes, hours, days, or weeks, they eventually always slip up, especially when they're under this much pressure—and if he's in pain, as the blood we found at the scene of the shoot-out seems to indicate, that only pushes the chances even higher that we'll soon be celebrating an arrest."

"As far as Acker's concerned, we've all had our hopes dashed more than once," Malcolm reminded him. "But exactly where is it that he was spotted?"

Looking him directly in the eye, Fletcher's voice turned firmly official. "In answer to that question, all I'm going to tell you is that I don't expect to hear another word about you going off on your own, doing anymore freelancing with Pacer. Or with anyone else, either, for that matter." He looked pointedly at Giselle. "Do we all understand each other?"

Recalling the hail of bullets that had not only grazed Giselle's arm but punctured the headrest so close to her neck and struck his own side of the pickup, Malcolm said, "I hear you, Fletcher, but I'll remind you, Acker was the one who came for *me* today and not vice versa. And if he comes again, I promise you, he's going to find me more than ready to protect myself and anyone who happens to be with me."

"Trust me," Fletcher said, "Acker's got enough to worry about avoiding the dragnet that's tightening around him right now to be trying to follow you two to a ranch where he's bound to run into one of any number of Coltons or hired hands who'll all be on the lookout for him."

"We've got everyone on high alert and putting the house's new deadbolts to good use."

"Good. So quit feeling like you need to do law enforcement's job for us and try to take it easy for a little while, both of you."

Exhausted, hungry, and in pain, Markus Acker sat inside the idling pickup on a dusty back road two days later, knowing he was nearly out of options. After that freaking Colton cowboy had jumped out of his pickup and shot off a significant chunk of his damned upper *ear*, he'd wanted nothing more than to hunt down and kill the bastard for the insult—not only for the bloody injury he'd inflicted, but for permanently marring an appearance Acker had always taken so much pride in. Not only was the wound agonizing and disgusting, it would make him all too easily identifiable once it was discovered. Seeing his own reflection in the mirror now, gaunt and filthy, dressed in ragged clothes and with thick gauze peeping out from beneath the oversized stocking cap he wore in an attempt to conceal his clumsy efforts with the truck's first aid kit, he felt disgusted, diminished from the man he'd been before he'd been forced into hiding. The man whose followers had practically seen him as a god.

What he would do to have them all back, hanging on his every word as they competed for new ways to better please him. But by now, that had been ruined—most of his people likely turned against him as surely as Jessie the

Betrayer. Yet he wondered if there might be one, at least, whom he might trust now, even at his lowest—one so blindly loyal that Markus, who had never had nor wanted his own children, had granted the younger man the extreme privilege of allowing him to call him Father. Just as he had, in private, when he'd needed something especially dubious, referred to his acolyte as Son.

He would do so again today, he decided, should his follower remain in the Wilderness Chapel of Contemplation, where he'd been sent only days before the meltdown that had led to the downfall of the Ever After Church. He could only hope that in the aftermath, no one had given a moment's thought to the nearly-silent acolyte who—it was just possible—remained there, completely isolated from all news from the outside world.

And completely open to performing one last, vital service to the man he considered the closest thing he still had to a father on this earth.

Over the course of the three days following the shooting, Giselle struggled to heed both Fletcher's and the ER doctor's advice to focus on her recovery. Malcolm tried to keep things as low-key as possible, taking her for easy strolls, helping her fix healthy meals, and working to keep various family members from overwhelming them with visits to check to see how they were faring, since word of their ordeal had spread.

Soon the two of them fell into a routine of sorts, with Giselle's favorite part being Scarlett's training sessions, repeated in brief intervals three times daily to suit the pup's short attention span. Except for one morning, when a brief but heavy shower forced them to improvise indoors, she and Malcolm—and often Pacer, modeling his most dignified, grown-up-dog behavior—worked in a grassy outdoor paddock, with an expansive view of the mountains in the distance—more often used for training horses. With the excitable pup always on the lookout for opportunities to dart off snapping at some insect, bark her lungs out at any ranch hand who happened to ride past, or race over to roll in some smelly pile that would neces-sitate a struggle to get her in the bathtub later, Giselle couldn't afford to let her attention wander for so much as a split second.

Still, she found their efforts rewarding—even fun, since there was no way to spend any amount of time try-ing to outsmart the ornery Scarlett without laughing at her antics. The diversion served as welcome relief from the time she spent worrying over whether the Coltons would ever again be safe from worries over Markus Acker, who had somehow managed to disappear again.

Somehow, though, she was even more bothered by the sheriff's department's failure to make the swift arrest that she and Malcolm had both hoped for. Not long after the ranch truck was returned—its formerly flat tire changed—the prior day, Detective Rodolfo had come by the ranch for an in-person chat. She'd been quick to inform them that so far, they'd found no reason to believe that Larry Willets had been involved in any conspiracy involving the boat, its storage, or its reappearance at this time.

"Now that the threatening calls from that blocked num-ber he claimed to have received have stopped, he actu-ally appears interested in wanting to help solve the crime himself," she'd said, sounding equal parts amused and annoyed by this development. "That's just what we need around here, another wannabe true-crime podcaster."

Afterward, Rodolfo had spoken of the two suspects

who'd rented the storage unit where the boat had been abandoned. The first had come into the sheriff's office with a story about how he and his friend were working at a lakeside marina one hot summer day when they were paid cash to trailer the red speedboat across county lines and store it under a name and address—both of which had turned out to be fictitious—scribbled on a scrap of paper. After he'd insisted that he'd had no knowledge of the boat's involvement in any accident, the detectives' questions had grown more pointed.

"At that point," Rodolfo told them, "he told us to direct all further inquiries to his lawyer and walked out on us."

"And you just let him?" Giselle blurted.

"We'd gotten what we were getting from him for the moment."

"What about the other one?" Malcolm had asked next.

Rodolfo shook her head. "I'm afraid the news is worse there. It turns out the other kid, the red-haired one the storage facility woman had recognized, was reported missing by his parents, just a few months after the boat accident, after leaving his dorm at Boise State and never showing up back home."

"Missing?" Malcolm blurted.

Rodolfo nodded. "Apparently, he'd had some significant issues during the early weeks of the semester. Disruptive outbursts in his classes—when he bothered showing up—tearing up his dorm room. But the last straw was when he jumped on the hood of a commuter's car in the parking lot and started shouting all kinds of nonsense at the driver."

"Had he always had these kinds of issues?" Malcolm asked. "Or was he using something that anybody knew of?"

"From what I've gathered, this was way out of character. This kid liked to party some, but he was on track to graduate with honors," Rodolfo told them. "He managed to disappear without a trace—but not before draining every penny from a family trust he'd gained access to after turning twenty-one. So we know he wasn't *completely* out of his mind…"

"You *have* to get that first guy talking," Giselle said. "I'll bet he knows what his friend was really running from."

"I'm sorry," Rodolfo told them. "We've tried everything we're able to. We've even been discussing an immunity deal with the DA, where we would agree to let Suspect One off for his role in hiding the boat if he'll only give up the real owner. But what if we sign off on something like that, and then it turns out that he's been lying about his true role in the accident? We certainly don't want to absolve him of the threat of prosecution if he's actually the one guilty of intoxication manslaughter…"

As Giselle and Malcolm walked back toward the house now, with the dogs trotting beside them, Giselle shook her head. "Sorry. You were saying something? I'm afraid I was off chasing butterflies in Scarlett-land or something."

He smiled at her. "I was just saying you had that worried look on your face again," he said. "I thought we'd agreed we were going to take the afternoon off from fretting over police business so we could go test-drive some possible new wheels for you."

"Can you honestly say you haven't been doing some worrying of your own?" she asked, unwilling to be sidetracked into another conversation about the pros and cons of various models. "I've caught you looking distracted more than a few times, especially since Rodolfo told us about those two guys."

Rather than denying it, Malcolm removed his cowboy hat to rake his fingers through his hair. "If only we could've talked her into giving us their names … I'm sure I could've at least talked to that one who clammed up and personally persuaded him to come clean with what he knows."

She cast a sidelong glance in his direction. "I'm not so sure I'd trust you not to resort to methods that would end up getting you into serious trouble, if you ever got that close."

He snorted, smiling wryly. "So you think of me as the menacing sort?"

She stopped walking to face him, recalling all the times she'd seen him affectionately scratching Pacer behind the ears, scooping up Scarlett for a cuddle, or taking a couple of carrots or apples to the fence line to handfeed them to Sundance and his pinto pasture-mate, Ivy, while he stroked the horses' strong necks.

"Normally, I think that any kind of violence goes against your very nature," she said honestly. "But I know how painful it is to finally get this close yet still not have any concrete answers. I heard it in your voice the other day when you were on the phone with Willets threatening to, how was it you put it? Something about rearranging his bones?"

Turning toward her, Malcolm snorted. "I hope you don't believe I'd have really done any serious damage. I'm not that kind of person."

"Says the man who whipped out a pistol and started blasting away at Acker before I could react to what was going on back at that park."

"Yes, and he *still* nearly managed to come close to killing you. I've been having nightmares ever since about turning my head to see you bleeding—and that bullet hole right by your neck."

Seeing him grimace, she laid a hand on his arm. "Hey, I understand. And I didn't mean to give you grief for saving both our lives. You did what you had to—and what *I* certainly would have been no help with—especially since we figured out that the gun in my bag wasn't even loaded."

"We can change that, if you'd like," he told her. "But I wouldn't feel comfortable arming you without giving you some serious training, both in safety and basic marksmanship."

She thought about it carefully, recalling how angrily she'd spoken at the hospital about never again wanting to be taken by surprise. But when her thoughts turned to guns, a deep-seated discomfort rose up in her, one that had her shaking her head. "I know how tough I talked before, and at the time I really meant it. But I'm not sure I could really pull a trigger. I mean—it seems so simple, the idea of him or one of us. But sometimes, the bullets don't go where they're intended, do they? So often I'll watch the news, and I'll see where one's ended up in a toddler sleeping in his crib across the street or an old man shaving at his bathroom mirror. And then, in the blink of an eye, not only the lives of the person struck, but every single person who loved them are changed forever, sometimes destroyed, and I can't help think about how our hearts were crushed, our souls stamped into splinters when Kate was taken from us…"

Seeing how intently he was staring at her, she shook her head. "You're probably thinking you'd expect no less than this kind of cosmic touchy-feely weirdness from someone who can't even eat anything that had a mama."

"Do you *really* want to know what I was thinking?"

"I'll probably regret saying so, but I've always been way too curious for my own good," she said, raising her brows expectantly.

"I was thinking, Giselle Dowling," he said, speaking with a quiet sincerity that made her lean in to listen to him more closely, "that your soul is as beautiful as the rest of you, and I hope you won't ever let the ugliness that exists in this world change you."

"It's not that I'm not flattered—sincerely—but you should know as well as anybody, this world dulls everybody's colors." She dropped her gaze, remembering the vibrant enthusiasm of the optimistic, often sassy younger woman she had once been. Perhaps, she realized, her gaze dropping to Scarlett as the pup jumped to the limits of her leash at Pacer, waving her paws and flashing white teeth in an attempt to lure him into playful combat, it was her nostalgia for the version of herself lost to the lake that had drawn her to the sweet and silly little beagle.

"I'm pretty sure there's an entire rainbow still inside you," Malcolm told her. "All you have to do is give yourself permission to let it shine again."

She looked up into the face of a man she'd grown to deeply care for, allowing a sigh to slip free as she did…

And wincing when Malcolm immediately reacted, asking, "What was that for? Am I embarrassing you, talking rainbows instead of barbed wire and billy goats like the simple rancher you've always had me pegged for?"

She shook her head, her shoulders shaking.

"What's so funny?" he asked.

"Only the idea that anyone who's ever had more than the briefest of encounters with you imagining you as a *simple* anything," she said. "What I was embarrassed about, honestly, was the thought of all the years I wasted

hanging with a crowd who never saw anything in me beyond the long, blond hair, the trendy fashions, and whatever celebrity cache they imagined might've rubbed off
on me from my work."

"I'm sure you had your share of fun running around
town spending money and looking like a million bucks."

"What *passed* for fun, you mean." She shrugged, since
even the memories of those days had lost their luster after
her so-called friends had dropped her. "But the thing is,
I doubt that any of those people, including the couple of
men I was foolish enough to trust with my heart—ever
really saw me. Not the way a rancher does who has not a
single thing in common with me except the worst day of
our lives."

"I'm pretty sure you're wrong on that count," he said.
"We both loved the same woman, a woman who lived
for both of us."

"I miss her *so* much." Giselle balled her fists, her heart
breaking open with the memory of what it had been like
to have someone in the world who had loved her so completely, someone who had been there for her from the moment of her birth. "I miss my family, Malcolm."

"I know you do," he told her, gathering her in his arms
and letting her lay her head against his chest as the tears
began to fall. "But I've got you right now. I've got you
for as long as you need a pair of arms to hold you up."

As Malcolm stroked her back and supported her, he
fervently wished that there was something—anything—
more that he could do to ease her anguish. He thought
about how effortlessly his dad—who always seemed to
know the right things to say around his aunt and sister—
had set Giselle at ease that first night he'd brought her to

the ranch by assuring her that she was practically family. But he was smart enough to understand that being welcomed as an honorary Colton could in no way make up for her personal losses.

Stepping back from him, Giselle wiped her eyes with a tissue she pulled from the front pocket of her jeans. "Thanks for that, but I'm so sorry. I shouldn't be—"

"It's fine," he was quick to say as they both, by unspoken agreement, began walking back toward the house. "I'm sure this business with the boat turning up has brought things back for you, the same as it has for me."

She looked up to study him intently. "Are you—are you doing okay, Malcolm? This hasn't dredged up any of those feelings, like you had before…back when your father saw you…" Her glance strayed toward the working barn.

He shook his head. "I won't say it's been pleasant, but having my family, my work, even distractions like this little dynamo here help." He nodded his head toward Scarlett, who was entertaining herself flipping around a spindly stick she'd picked up somewhere while Pacer watched her with a look of mild interest. "They've given me a lot more to focus on. But I do appreciate your asking about that time. Even my dad mostly likes to pretend that nothing ever happened—because it didn't, really."

"But it might have."

He hesitated for a long time before admitting, "Yeah. I'll own that. Just like I'll own up to the fact that what I was dealing with for quite some time was clinical depression. Millions of people do."

Having given her that opening, he gave her the invitation of his silence to speak about her own lost years.

But after an awkward silence, she said only, "I'm really glad you talked to someone."

"Talking to the right person's good. And there're other things as well, things that help a lot of people," he said. "If you're ever interested in—in discussing—"

"If you're trying to bring this around to me," she said, "I'd really rather not get into that now, Malcolm."

"Sure thing," he said, wondering why she couldn't draw a line between supporting him for getting the help he had needed and considering that such a thing might be a viable option for herself. But he'd heard that warning shading her tone, the one that told him that it was time to back off and give the seed he'd planted a chance to take root if it would.

They made it within about twenty feet of the house's back deck when Giselle lurched, saying, "Whoops, *Scarlett*!" as the pup—darting after a leaf blown by a puff of wind—tangled beneath her feet.

Malcolm grabbed at Giselle's arm but caught air as she plunged forward with a yelp before sprawling in an undignified-looking heap in a patch of grass.

"You all right down there?" he asked, amazed she'd been able to contort her body into such a position—with her shoulders down and her knees folded beneath her—to avoid squashing the beagle.

"Just *fabulous*," Giselle said, trying to push herself up to a kneeling position while at the same time fending off Scarlett's attempts to cover her face with kisses.

Malcolm knew he shouldn't have laughed, but Giselle's chagrin, combined with the small canine tornado's delirious joy at the chaos she had wrought, had him chuckling, even as he reached down to grab the pup and offered Giselle a hand up.

"Sorry I was too slow to catch you," he said, "but let

me take this one off your hands for now. And maybe from now on."

"Wait—what do you mean?" she asked.

"I mean, you've been a really good sport these past few days, but it's obvious that what this little hound needs is some one-on-one time with a real professional. So I wanted to let you know that last night I spoke to Della, and talked her into taking her over to her place for some one-to-one intensives in the evenings."

"No!" Giselle cried out before adding. "Sorry—I didn't mean to shout. It's just that I don't want Scarlett to feel like one more person's given up on her, especially not when…"

"Go on," he encouraged, Scarlett wriggling in his arms. Wriggling to get back to Giselle, just as he'd expected.

"Not when…" Giselle said, the plea in her tear-filled gaze as she held her arms out prompting him to hand over the beagle. "Not when I already love this little mess so much."

He reached out to touch her cheek. "I know you do. Just like I'm totally onto the fact that you've been letting her sleep with you at night instead of in the crate the way we discussed."

Giselle looked down into Scarlett's face. "Did you rat us out, girl?"

"She didn't have to. When that smoke alarm malfunctioned last night, and you came out to see what was up, I spotted all the dog hair on your pajamas while you were pulling on your robe."

"So you were checking out my oh-so-sexy pj's, were you?" she asked, her smile revealing a dimple he'd noticed the night before. A dimple he'd had trouble getting off his mind when he'd later returned to bed alone.

"Hey, how would I have figured out you liked baby

pandas otherwise," he asked, "and that you'd been spoiling our houseguest?"

"I will *never* apologize for my baby pandas, but I *am* sorry if I broke some kind of serious Colton house rule by sleeping with the dog," she said. "You won't report me, will you?"

"To who, exactly—presuming that Mr. Pacer here's never set a paw on any furnishing without an invitation?" He smiled at his own hairy sidekick, who'd been known to hog the sectional while he, his father, and a brother or two were all watching football. "For one thing, my dad's asked everyone to give us a break from any more visits for a little while."

"But I've enjoyed seeing Lizzy, Greg and Briony. And those veggie tartlets Hannah dropped off were delicious," Giselle said.

"It was great they came to check in on us," he allowed, "but even I'll admit my family can be a lot at times. And my dad could see it was getting a little overwhelming for you."

She blushed. "I hope I didn't hurt anyone's feelings."

"Don't worry. You were polite as could be to everybody. But you're also healing—and grieving your friend. So the only other family member we'll be seeing over the next few days will be Sarah, since she'll be briefly stopping by tomorrow to drop off something here at the house."

"Sarah's your mother and uncle Robert's daughter, right?" Giselle said, thinking back to what he'd told her about the two recently discovered Colton siblings.

He nodded. "You've got it. Anyway, back at the time her mother left my father, she took this old Victrola stand record player with her. I suppose it was to spite him since she always told Sarah and Nate it was some sort of valuable family heirloom. In truth, those things aren't actually worth that much, but this one has a lot of sentimental value to my dad since it belonged to his late mother. So Sarah's had it packed up and taken it to her place. She's just been waiting for a chance to bring it by here, to surprise my father."

"That's really thoughtful of her," Giselle said. "It's a shame your father isn't going to be here when she comes by."

"I know, but with Markus coming out of the woodwork the way he did to attack us, he didn't feel right leaving Mama Jen alone at her home unprotected."

"He's so smitten with her." Giselle smiled. "And when she came by the other day, I could see she feels the same way about him."

Malcolm nodded. "I swear to you, it does my heart good, after watching everything they've both been through, to see them find so much happiness together. But I can see your friend there is getting restless." He nodded toward Scarlett, who was pulling at her lead. "So how about we head on back inside now?"

After opening the door and following Giselle and Pacer inside, Malcolm hung their jackets before they headed for the kitchen, where they always stopped to grab drinks following their training sessions.

Once Malcolm gave each of the dogs a chew and had them lie down on their mats in the great room, Giselle brought him a glass of water while holding another in her hand.

"Just look how well she's picked up on that after-training routine you've started with her," she said, clearly not finished advocating for the little beagle. "Look at her, enjoying her own treat so calmly instead of trying to jump on top of Pacer and grab his, too, the way she did at first."

Malcolm wandered toward the leather sectional. "I think we mostly have Pacer to thank for teaching her that bad canine manners aren't going to fly at all. There's nothing like a stable, mature dog for teaching a pup boundaries."

"And she's really picking up fast on going out when she should and releasing off-limits things she's grabbed and trading them for an approved toy," she continued, trailing after him, "so we've *definitely* made progress. And that's in just a few, short days."

Finishing a swallow of water, he lowered his glass but didn't sit. "I was thinking the same thing."

"What on earth?" She made a sound of pure exasperation. "Then *why* would you call Della and ask her to take Scarlett?"

Malcolm took a deep breath. "Actually, I *didn't* call her or have any such conversation."

Giselle scowled at him. "Are you serious?"

Immediately realizing his mistake, Malcolm said, "I'm sorry. I only meant to check the temperature on how close you two were really getting, but I can see now that I should've told you from the start it wasn't Della I really spoke with last night about you and Scarlett. It was Sebastian."

"Sebastian? I don't understand why you would—"

"Please, just hear me out," he said, holding up his uninjured hand. "It was because I saw something in the two of you. The spark of what could be an amazing bond, one of those perfect pairings you can't force and wouldn't trade for anything once you find it."

"Do those usually begin with the puppy leaving the human sprawled out in the grass?" she asked. "Because the way you put it sounds as if it ought to feel a little more like magic."

Malcolm chuckled. "Trust me, things didn't start out with Pacer the way you see them now. He was a cute pup, but a handful, and Kate loved to pamper him, so he started to look at me as the spoiler of all fun. But after the accident, once it was only him and me—"

When his throat clamped tight, Giselle went to him and put a hand on the small of his back. "I know," she said simply, in a voice as gentle and reassuring as her touch.

He slanted a look down into her gorgeous blue eyes. "I thought that maybe—maybe I could convince Sebastian that Scarlett could be for you...what Pacer once was to me, an anchor to help tether you to life."

Chapter 15

As upset as Giselle was about Malcolm manipulating her emotions, the raw fear she saw in his gaze—so close to hers now that she saw his green eyes dilate as she studied them—short-circuited her anger. Not fear for himself, despite the risk he'd taken in exposing his greatest vulnerability in a way so few strong men would dare to, but a bone-deep terror of what he'd recognized in her—and refused to sit still and allow to go on. Because of an attraction so clearly written on his face and every action.

An attraction she felt burning in her own blood, as well, one she'd felt intensifying with every moment she spent in his presence these past few days, for all her efforts to picture Kate's face each time she found her gaze lingering on the solid masculinity of his movements or the working of his throat as he drank water. Moving her hand from his back, she dropped her gaze to avoid his, scrambling to summon a memory of her sister.

But Kate wasn't with them in this room. There was only Malcolm, the warmth of his presence and a lingering scent of sunshine and the outdoors still discernable, as close as they were standing.

Finally finding the courage to speak, she said, "I *am* getting attached to Scarlett—" *And* only *Scarlett…* "and of course, I've fantasized about having the kind of job and living situation where keeping her for myself would be the right and fair thing, if that were even remotely possible…" *Because* he *isn't possible…*

"I have to tell you," Malcolm said, "as sympathetic as Sebastian was to my argument, he did remind me that he has protocols for a reason. He didn't completely rule out the possibility, though, so I believe there's still a chance I might convince him, especially if he sees the two of you together."

She shook her head. "It's fine, really," she said, telling herself it would have to be. "I'll just love on her for the time I have her."

"But you *need*—"

"Stop it, please," she said firmly, prompting him to go still. "You're telling me what *you* needed, in those first truly horrible months after Kate's death. And I truly understand how deepening your bond with Pacer, in addition to your dad's making sure you got the other help you needed, was life-changing—maybe even lifesaving—for you."

He nodded. "Yes, and that's why I want to—"

"Malcolm, I *know* you're worried about me, and all right. I'll admit, I've allowed everything that happened—and how guilty I felt for living through that accident when it should've been Kate who made it—"

"Please, never say that again," he begged her, "because I'm *glad* you're here now, Giselle. Don't you understand that? I look at you and—I feel—I feel alive in a way I never imagined I ever could again."

She wanted to tell him that knowing how much he cared for her was opening the world to her, too, to explain how much it had meant to her, being invited into the warmth of his loving family's circle. But she didn't know how to say it—how to do anything except to reach up toward him and trust that he would meet her halfway between temptation and desire.

He pulled her into his arms, the kisses hungry, hot, and desperate to a degree Giselle could never remember feeling with any man before. For a split second, she told herself to slow down—to slow her questing hands and try to register the wrongness of what it was they were doing. But when Malcolm's mouth nipped her neck and he cupped her breasts, her body rebelled against the impulse, charging ahead in a desperate race to feel, to taste, to savor every bit of him before one or both of them came to their senses.

Yet only moments later, she was pulling him with her down onto the cushions of the sectional and pulling off her top.

Malcolm had almost forgotten what it was like to be overtaken by sensation—the demands of his body running miles ahead of anything that any lingering doubts might have to say about the subject. And his heart was more than willing to go along for the ride. It was pumping now, faster than ever as she reached behind her, clearly meaning to unhook that tantalizing rose-colored bra of hers, a lacy little number that held her breasts so temptingly just beyond reach.

"Hold up a second, will you?" he said.

"Why's that?" she asked, her blue eyes sparking with impatience.

"Just trying to imagine if you're this gorgeous now," he told her, "how much better the view's about to get."

Straddling his hips, she leaned in to kiss him nearly senseless, making him forget everything but the taste and heat and welcome pressure of her body bearing down against his pelvis, and his desire for far more.

When she came up for air and smiled down at him, he repeated, "Absolutely gorgeous…"

"I could say the same of you, but I'm not here for the compliments."

"You have something else in mind?"

She looked around the room, with its large, uncovered windows and the walkway just beyond it. "Something in my room I need to show you…"

Rolling off him, she hopped up and started walking toward the staircase. Before she reached it, he saw that she had the lacy, rose-colored bra trailing like a promise from her fingers.

He wasn't far behind.

Chapter 16

Giselle snuggled deeply into Malcolm's arms, unable to recall the last time she'd awakened feeling so contented. But it wasn't only remembering how completely cherished he'd made her feel, with his unselfish attention to her pleasure, but the knowledge that she'd helped ease Malcolm's loneliness in the same way, that filled her with a happiness so intense and unfamiliar that she wasn't certain she could trust it.

"Hey there, you awake, sleepyhead?" Malcolm asked before gently kissing her temple.

"I am," she said, adjusting her position to lean back into the pillows.

As she pulled the sheet to cover her breasts, Malcolm grinned. "It's too late, you know. I've already committed them to memory for life."

"I'm glad at least one part of my anatomy made some sort of impression," she said.

Shaking his head, he told her, "I don't want you to have a single doubt about it, Giselle. I could rattle off a whole list of your body parts that I'm quite fond of, but it's *you* I've fallen for—no matter how hard I've tried to fight it."

"Malcolm, no. This has been wonderful—so much better than I ever could've imagined. But both of us have been alone for such a long time, so what you're feeling isn't really anything like what you had with—"

"Please, Giselle," he said, passion roughening his voice. "I'm not expecting you to feel the same way I do. That's all right with me. But don't try to tell me what's in my own heart."

"I'm sorry. It's just—this is all so new to me. My brain keeps wanting to default back to—to the way I've always known you." *As Kate's,* she thought. But she couldn't say that part aloud yet. Couldn't allow herself to name the chill that passed over her when she even thought about her sister, lying in another bed beside this man who'd loved her so deeply that he had vowed to make a life and family with her.

Malcolm nodded, his expression softening. "That's completely understandable. So let's talk about our plans for this afternoon, then, shall we? Did you still want to drive over to Conners to go car shopping the way we'd planned? Because there's still plenty of time for us to clean up and head that way."

She made a considering noise before saying. "I really *would* like to keep that test-drive appointment I made for that hybrid model I liked so much at four thirty. Those have been in such demand, it's been hard to even locate one anywhere to look at."

"Sure thing. And after we've finished up, how about if I take you out to Barbieri's? You still like Italian, don't you?"

On hearing the name of one of the area's finer restaurants, Giselle shook her head. "That's awfully nice of you to ask, Malcolm, but I don't have anything appropriate here to wear. And even if I did, I can't imagine being in the mood for anywhere so high-end while Markus is still out there somewhere—"

"You're right, of course. I'm sorry. I'm just—I feel like you deserve a nice distraction."

"You've done a pretty amazing job with that already," she reminded him, "but let's choose someplace a little more casual we can both agree on. And we'll celebrate at Barbieri's once Markus has been arrested, or over at The Tides if you like the food there better. Deal?"

"Sounds like a plan," he agreed. "Now what about a shower?"

"What? *Together*, you mean?" she asked, slightly taken aback despite the things they'd done already.

He shrugged. "Why not? I mean, it does stand to reason that someone as interested in animal welfare and the environment as you are would care, too, about water conservation."

She snorted at his reasoning. "You and I both know that if we tried it, the two of us would never make it past the lathering stage together without getting water *all* over that bathroom."

Grinning, he said, "That sounds like *such* an excellent idea—"

"But think of all the cleanup. *And* I'd definitely miss my appointment."

"I have some pretty good ideas about how I could make it all up to you," he said, leaning in to lay a blazing trail of kisses along her neck—before they were both distracted by the sound of both dogs barking from downstairs.

Sitting up on the bed's edge, he sighed. "As much as I hate having to give up my plans to sidetrack you, I'd better go check to make sure Scarlett isn't demolishing some major furnishing or disgracing herself on a rug."

"Oh, no! *Scarlett*…" Giselle felt her face heat. "I completely forgot she wasn't crated downstairs while we, uh—"

"Were otherwise occupied," Malcolm finished for her as he reached for his jeans. "Don't worry about it. I'll go down and deal with the situation and then take both dogs out to the outdoor covered run so they can enjoy this pretty spring afternoon for a little bit while each of us cleans ups in our own rooms."

Nodding, she said, "I'll meet you downstairs, then. Thanks."

When he bent to kiss her before leaving, though, something made her present him her cheek rather than her lips.

On her way to the shower a few minutes later, she happened to catch sight of Malcolm's phone peeking out from just beneath the edge of a blanket on the floor. Realizing it had probably fallen from the pocket of his jeans, she bent to retrieve it and saw a notification on the screen for a missed called from Ajay Wright.

Thinking that it might be something important, she stepped out into the hallway wearing only a T-shirt, meaning to call down to Malcolm. But at the same moment, she heard the back door close, and she soon realized that he must have gone ahead and taken both the dogs out to their enclosed run.

Remembering what he'd said about heading right back upstairs for a shower, she thought a moment before heading around the corner, where he'd previously invited her to knock anytime if there was anything she needed. Though she was wildly curious about what lay behind that door— and whether Malcolm was really as neat in his personal space as he appeared to be when working in the kitchen and picking up around the house's common areas—she couldn't bring herself to try the handle. So instead, after standing the cell up against the bottom of the door and telling herself he'd have to be blind to miss its safety-orange protective case leaning against the dark wood, she retreated to her own suite.

While she showered, she tried to tell herself the awkwardness she was feeling might be less a result of how very long it had been since she'd allowed any man to get so close than it was the fact that someone as caring, thoughtful, and attractive as Malcolm saw her as someone worthy of his attention. And not only his sexual attention—which, taken on its own, had made her realize how much pleasure she'd been missing out on with her choice of partners—but with his insistence that someone who'd lost everything that had once defined her as a person— her family, her career, and nearly all her friends—might still actually have value.

Of course he thinks that you have value, some small, mean-spirited voice inside her whispered. *You remind him just enough of the only woman he's really interested in having sex with.* But even as the thought occurred, she realized it was really just the self-loathing she had listened to for far too long talking. Or maybe it actually *was* some version of the same depression that Malcolm, too, had struggled with, like so many others.

But what if she'd had it wrong these past few years? If the so-called facts she'd been telling herself about her failures had been skewed so badly that they bore little resemblance to the objective truth of who she was: a woman with as many strengths as flaws. A woman who had made the best choices available to her during a time that she was weathering devastating losses. A woman worthy of the same grace that she herself had always been willing to give others she'd seen stumble.

By the time she left the shower, Giselle was determined to stop looking for reasons to doubt whatever happiness she felt and simply enjoy those moments that came to her. After choosing a pair of navy chinos and a pink top that helped to brighten her fair complexion, she fussed a little with her hair, something she hadn't done in some time, and found herself unexpectedly humming as she did so.

Pleased with the results, she dug out her purse, where she unearthed and actually made use of a few cosmetics she'd neglected to toss. Though she used a light touch, once she finished, she smiled, catching a glimpse of her old reflection, as if she'd just spotted an old friend for the first time after a long illness. Definitely changed, she thought, but surely on the mend.

As she returned her lip stain and mascara to her purse, the cell phone she'd had on the charger nearby dinged a notification for an e-mail. Hoping she wasn't about to find out the vehicle she was scheduled to test drive had been sold already, she picked up the phone, only to find a number of unread e-mails waiting.

Scrolling past the unsolicited automotive ads—which kept springing up like toadstools thanks to her online searches—she zeroed in on a message bearing the name *Colton* in the sender column before remembering how, just the evening before last, Malcolm's sister had pulled her aside during her visit to say, "I have some lovely photos of Kate I've been meaning to share with you—that is, if you'd like to have them."

"Absolutely, Lizzy. Thank you!" Giselle had immediately responded, giving her a hug. She'd meant it, too, since she treasured every opportunity to add to the trove that she'd compiled to preserve the memory of her sister.

But now, as her finger hovered over the message, with its paperclip-shaped icon indicating its attached files, Giselle hesitated, her usual excitement mixed up with dread and guilt. Because the Kate that Lizzy had known so well, the one she would undoubtedly be faced with, would be a woman brimming with love and hope, with trust and anticipation for a future with Malcolm that would never, ever happen.

Not for her, at any rate.

Delete them, all of them. Pretend you never got them, Giselle thought, memories cascading through her mind: Kate posing with her new fiancé, both impossibly photogenic as they flashed a pair of gorgeous smiles, or Kate alone showing off the beautiful diamond-flanked emerald engagement ring she had been so very proud of.

A click, and they go away. Giselle could then text a separate note to Lizzy: Thanks for the pix! Some nice ones in there!

Then, she could move on with her life. And a man who had been meant to be her sister's.

But Giselle didn't have the strength to make such a decision. Or maybe letting herself off the hook had been a right she'd ceded the day she had accepted a breath from Malcolm's lungs as the price of her survival.

So instead, she found herself sitting on the bed, looking through photo after photo, and smashing her own heart to pieces one image at a time.

When Malcolm had first headed downstairs to check on the dogs, he'd found no damage with the exception of a single crime in progress. He winced at the sight of one of the running shoes, which he recalled having kicked off somewhere near the sectional, being masticated beyond recognition by one very small but extremely contented-looking beagle.

Looking over at Pacer, who lay curled up on his bed

pointedly ignoring the destruction, Malcolm said, "Man's best friend indeed. You could've at least *tried* to stop her."

Pacer chose to ignore him, too—probably sulking, Malcolm figured. His K-9 did perk up, however, watching Malcolm chase Scarlett around the room for several minutes before he was finally able to pry the slobbery remnants from the pup's jaws to assure himself that the little miscreant wouldn't end up choking.

"Glad to see you're entertained, at least," he told Pacer before looking down at the sharp-toothed beagle. "You'd better count yourself lucky that Giselle's so crazy about you. And that *I* adore Giselle. Let's go on outside for a bit, so both of you can enjoy a little playtime."

Once he headed back upstairs, he was surprised to find his cellphone lying propped up on the floor in front of his closed bedroom door. In the time it took him to wonder how it could've gotten there, the screen lit up, and he could see—although the sound was off—that it was Ajay calling.

Picking it up, Malcolm asked, "How's the search going?"

"You'd have a whole lot better idea, if you'd ever answer your phone," Ajay complained. "I've been trying to reach you for the past hour."

"Sorry about that. What's up?"

"What's up is I need you and that dog of yours to come over to the staging area as soon as you can get here," Ajay said.

"Meet you? But I thought—Aren't I suspended?"

"I promise you, I'll still be paying careful attention to how you handle yourself as a team member," Ajay assured him, "but right now, we have a critical public safety situation, and I can't afford to leave one of our top trailing teams sitting on the sidelines when we've got Markus Acker on the run on foot and headed straight for town—"

"What are you talking about?"

"We've found your stolen truck wrecked just off the road, in those tall timbers north of Owl Creek. After Archer collected a scent item from the cab, Pumpkin and I started trailing him down into that low creek bottom area—"

"The area where we found that Silver Alert woman last year?" Malcolm asked, speaking of an elderly person with memory issues who'd become disoriented while taking what had been meant to be a short walk.

"Right," said Ajay. "We lost the scent trail, but I'm almost positive he's headed back toward one of the residential neighborhoods near the river. Probably looking for someplace he can jack another vehicle—and we both know he won't leave behind a living witness if he can help it, either."

"You don't have to tell me. I've seen his handiwork in that department," Malcolm said, his thoughts turning toward the bloody handprint on the barn door. "So where exactly should I meet the team?"

"I've already texted the location of the city park where our team's staging. There'll be a law enforcement checkpoint at the entrance, but just tell them you're with the SAR team and they'll let you in."

"Pacer and I will be there as soon as possible," he promised, knowing Giselle would understand.

"Thanks. And, Malcolm?"

"Yes?"

"Before you head out on Acker's trail today, I want you to check in with Fletcher. He'll have a ballistic vest for you, and I want you wearing it."

Malcolm thought about it for a moment before asking, "Are you handing those out to our whole team—or only to the ones named Colton?"

"You're the *only* Colton on the SAR team, Malcolm— as well as the only member of the team Acker's already gone after. But you already know that, don't you? So quit worrying about whether I'm showing you some kind of favoritism or whatever strange idea you've got into your head and just trust that I'm looking out for a valuable asset, the same as I would any other."

"Got it," Malcolm told him, hopeful that he could live up to Ajay's expectations and still be a part of bringing down the man who'd cost his family so much grief.

Before he could start doing that, however, he would need to let Giselle know about the change in plans. When she didn't answer his knock, he decided she must be in the shower, so he headed to his own suite to quickly clean up and change into his SAR gear.

Afterward, another knock at Giselle's door went unanswered, even after he called out her name. Feeling the low hum of anxiety, he trotted downstairs, frowning with confusion when he didn't spot her in either the family room or kitchen. "Did you go check on the dogs?" he asked aloud, jogging over to the back door, his pulse picking up speed.

But he found the deadbolt locked, as were the other two doors—a safety measure his family members had all agreed to follow until Markus was finally behind bars, and he saw that both dogs were still outside lounging. Genuinely worried now, Malcolm headed back upstairs once more—this time at a run.

This time, he pounded on the door hard. "Giselle, can you hear me?" When no answer came, he pictured her lying on the bathroom floor, unconscious after falling after slipping on damp tile. "I'm coming in to check on you unless you tell me otherwise."

He barely waited another second before he was through the door, where, to his relief and bewilderment, he immediately spotted her. Though her back was to him, she was fully dressed and perched on the bed's edge as she stared down at her cell phone.

"Giselle?" he said, upset she would ignore him while surfing social media or something. "You scared me half to death. How did you not *hear* me?"

Her head snapped up, her red-rimmed eyes so miserable, he knew immediately that something was terribly wrong.

"What's happened?" he asked, his anger shifting to alarm. "Are you sick—or has someone sent you some sort of threat or—" He tried to imagine someone from her past, like the obnoxious Nico, attempting to make trouble for her at this juncture, but reasoned that the rock star had been distracted by any number of other, more outrageous scandals since the one in which Giselle had figured.

She shook her head. "I've just—I'm so sorry, Malcolm, but I've—I've made a terrible mistake."

"A *mistake*? I don't under—"

"With you, I mean. I just can't. I—I can't be Kate's sister and your—whatever you've convinced yourself this might be between us."

"What are you talking about?" he asked. Thinking of the phone in her hand, the way she'd seemed so fixated on it, he asked, "Did someone—did someone say or send something to you, something to change the woman I left here in this room such a short time ago into—"

She shook her head.

"Then just what was it you were staring at on your

phone?" he demanded. "Seriously, Giselle. What is it? *Please.*"

"Only a reminder. Pictures of Kate that Lizzy asked me if I'd like to have."

"Oh, no. Not Lizzy and her pictures..." Malcolm ground the heel of his hand into his forehead. "I adore my little sister. Her heart's *definitely* in the right place, but I can remember a similar offering of hers sending me to a very dark place the Christmas before last."

Giselle sucked air between her teeth, looking sympathetic. "She sent you a bunch of photos of Kate at the *holidays*?"

"Right before them, yes," he said. "The thing is, as much as you and I both might want to remember, there are times it's dangerous, poking too much at the tender places underneath the scar tissue. Times when you risk undoing all the healing that's already underway."

"But maybe I'm not *ready* to heal yet, Malcolm. Not if that means betraying the love that I felt for my sister. And everything she felt for me."

After picking up her phone, she touched the screen and showed him the photo she'd been looking at when he'd entered the room. Though he'd been steeling himself—and in some ways dreading—seeing an image of himself with Kate, it wasn't a photo of the two of them together. Instead, it was of Kate, taken on the day of their engagement cookout, reaching to pull in the visiting Giselle into a welcoming embrace. Both of them were so beautiful, so vibrant, and so filled with the joy of their reunion, it nearly took his breath away. The skirt of Giselle's summer dress was flared, captured mid-whirl with her movement, and her nearly waist-long blond locks were fanned out, glowing in the sunlight.

Visually stunning as the shot was, he had to look away, overcome by a gut-wrenching vision of that same long hair, floating detached in the waters of Blackbird Lake after he had cut it. Recoiling from the memory—and from the recollection of the loose strands left clinging to Kate's pale flesh as he'd pulled her from the water to give her mouth-to-mouth resuscitation—he realized, *Heaven help me, I can't do this either. Giselle's been right all along...*

Screwing shut his eyes, he struggled to re-center himself on the present. A present that required his strength, his courage, and all the determination he could muster not to let either Giselle or his SAR team down.

Focusing on those responsibilities, he forced himself to cover Giselle's hand with his. Ever so gently, he prompted her to turn the phone face down. When she looked up at him, a question in her eyes, he said, "I know we need to talk, and I'd like to be able to stay right here and have that discussion with you. But right now I really need to—"

"You're leaving, aren't you?" she asked, her expression changing as she shook her head. "I should've realized—I saw earlier, when I found your phone, that you'd missed a call from Ajay, and I see now that you're dressed for trailing. Is it—is it *him* again?"

Understanding that she meant Acker, Malcolm nodded before sharing the highlights of his phone conversation.

"Then you and Pacer had better get on the road right now," she said. "I'm only sorry I delayed you so long with my..." She gestured vaguely.

"You have absolutely nothing to be sorry for," he assured her. "I hate leaving you here on your own, though. What if I dropped you over to hang out with Greg and Briony at their place down the way on my way out? I'm sure they're home right now and—"

"They're really nice, and I'm sure those little ones of theirs are as adorable as the pictures they showed me the other day when they stopped by. But look at me—" She gestured toward her swollen eyes. "Do I look like I'm in the mood for happy-family company right now? Just let me lock the doors and veg out with some TV with Scarlett and try to forget that this day ever happened..."

He grimaced, hearing her say that. But there was no time to even sort through his own emotions, much less delay any longer, so he said only, "I'll pop Scarlett back inside her downstairs kennel before I leave, then, so you can get her once you're ready. But please, just promise me that you'll keep the doors locked and stay inside. And well away from those photos."

She nodded. "I will. But only if you'll promise me you'll be really careful out there, Malcolm."

"Don't worry. Ajay's insisting that I wear a vest like law enforcement, and all of us trailing will most likely be accompanied by an officer as well."

"That's good," she said, the sadness in her blue eyes holding him a moment longer, "because, no matter where I end up once all this is over, I'll always want to know you're back here, strong and safe and whole."

"We—we'll talk more later, all right?" he managed—barely—now more upset than ever to hear the rejection of everything he'd tried to show her, everything he'd tried to tell her and meant to spend a lifetime proving, of everything they might have been together, that lay in ashes behind the goodbye he'd heard in her words.

It left him frustrated, too, not only with the circumstances forcing him to leave now, but with her, for allowing her own pain to blind her to her capacity to wound him.

So it was that when Giselle nodded and said, "Sure. Please, text me with updates when you're able," he didn't hug or kiss her, instead only answering, "Will do," as he headed out the door.

Chapter 17

Giselle stared at the open doorway, a heaviness growing in the pit of her stomach as she heard his footsteps receding down the staircase. She thought of hurrying after him, throwing her arms around him, and taking back what she'd said. She'd seen it written on his face, how she was hurting him, yet she'd kept on digging the hole deeper. Telling herself he'd be better off set free of the encumbrance of someone who would only serve as an enduring reminder of the most traumatic moments and the greatest grief of his life.

Still, she felt a cold heaviness inside her, a growing doubt about the way they'd left things. Worried about him going off to face a killer who'd already come after him once with his mind on their issue, she finally rose from the bed and rushed for the stairs, intent on apologizing— or at least giving him the goodbye kiss he'd deserved.

But by the time she reached the landing, she could only sigh as she spotted his ranch pickup's lights receding down the long drive.

"That's what you get for dawdling," she scolded herself, wondering if she should call and try to speak with him while he was on the road.

But she had no idea what to say—how to make things

right without giving him false hope for a future she couldn't honestly promise. And it wouldn't be right, or necessarily safe, to further distract him at a time when he needed to focus on both the road and his work with the SAR team. Better that she use this time planning her own next move—and think about what she wanted her future to look like after Markus Acker was captured.

One thing she knew for certain: returning to the isolated life she had been living before Malcolm showed up at her cabin was no longer an appealing option. She'd been floundering for too long—so mired in her grief, she'd been unable to even imagine that any of the skills she'd spent years honing would apply to any other career field, let alone exploring and acting on her options.

Maybe she could start by at least opening some of the unread messages she'd allowed to pile up in her email's inbox. Then she would thank those who'd taken the effort to check in with her and write a brief note asking if anyone had heard of any opportunities that might be a good fit for her, regardless of the location.

She decided the idea felt right, even if a new position required her to sell the family cabin to finally loosen the past's painful grip on her life. Daunted by the thought of leaving Owl Creek and everyone here that she'd come to care for, however, she instead headed downstairs to free Scarlett from her crate, deciding that for the moment, some puppy therapy sounded like her first order of business.

The two played and cuddled until the knot of anxiety inside her loosened. They then practiced Scarlett's commands—so successfully that Giselle wished she'd set up her phone to take a video to show off the pup's skills later.

Just as she realized she'd forgotten about canceling her

test-drive appointment—now ten minutes past, she heard a low rumble. Looking toward the window, she noticed a couple of the hands headed toward the ranch gate in a pickup, towing a livestock trailer. Moments later, the phone inside her pocket started ringing.

Checking it, she saw that it was Detective Ariana Rodolfo from the sheriff's department. Eager to hear what more she might have learned about the two men who'd put the red boat into storage, Giselle was quick to answer.

"Please tell me this is good news," she blurted, the hope she'd worked so hard to manage bubbling up again in spite of years of disappointments.

"I'm doing quite well, thank you," Rodolfo said dryly. "I hope you're having a nice day, too."

"I'm sorry if I sometimes seem impatient with you," Giselle told her.

"Considering what you've been through, that's understandable," Rodolfo said. "And I hope you didn't feel I was making light of something that's so important to you."

"It's fine." Giselle hugged herself. "But please, have you learned any more about the suspects you and Detective Danvers ID'd?"

"I was hoping I might come by to speak to you and Mr. Colton—Malcolm—about that personally if you're available?"

Something important, then, Giselle realized, so anxious she could scarcely breathe. Shaking it off, she turned away from Scarlett's attempt to gain her attention by jumping up against her leg and headed into the kitchen. "I'm sorry, but he's just left to join his search and rescue team. They're assisting the task force right now, trying to keep Acker from reaching—"

"Our department's been updated, and we've sent every

deputy we can spare to help cut off his access to the neighborhood where they believe Acker might be headed."

Giselle got herself a clean glass. "It sounds like they're pretty confident they know where he is, then,"

"There are never any guarantees, but it sounds as if this time, Acker's boxed himself into a half-mile-wide, wooded wedge between a four-lane divided highway where he'll be immediately spotted either by helicopter or one of the drones they've sent up if he tries to cross the river."

"Couldn't he just make a swim for it?" Giselle asked.

"Not there he can't. Even if this past week's snow melt didn't have the river running so fast and cold that it would drown him, the opposite bank is so steep and rocky, you'd practically have to be a mountain goat to climb it."

"He has a gunshot wound as well." Giselle filled her glass using the fridge dispenser. "They're pretty sure that Malcolm at least nicked him in the parking-lot shoot-out."

"I hadn't heard that happy news," Rodolfo said brightly, over the sound of another phone ringing in the background and the muffled rumble of men's voices somewhere nearby. "But it certainly doesn't bode well for Acker's chances of pulling off another miraculous escape."

"I'm praying you're right," Giselle said, "and, selfishly, I'm hoping that someone in law enforcement slaps about six sets of cuffs on him before Malcolm gets within a mile of him." If anything happened to him, she'd never get over it, especially not knowing that she'd hurt him as she had.

"I'm with you on that," the detective told her. "Listen, I understand you're nervous right now, and you have every right to be, but I know Ajay Wright, who's not only working with the task force but the SAR team too, and I can't imagine him taking any chances when it comes to his people's safety."

"I know he cares," Giselle said.

"You'll see," Rodolfo told her. "Malcolm's going to come home safe and sound, and once the two of you have finished celebrating Acker's arrest, then you can call to let me know a convenient time to come out and see you about this other investigation—"

"Oh, no. Please, detective," Giselle said, nearly choking on the water she'd swallowed before setting the glass back down on the counter. "Whatever you've found out, just tell me. Whether it's good news or bad, I can't deal with one more mystery hanging over my head."

"You—you're not alone now, are you?" Rodolfo asked, raising her voice a little to speak over what sounded like male conversation in the background.

Giselle glanced down at Scarlett, who was sitting politely at her feet, as she'd been taught, instead of jumping for attention. Her heart warming at the sight, Giselle squatted down to pet the pup. "I definitely have company," she said, though she realized she'd been played when the pup rolled over on the tiled floor and pawed at her hand, angling for one of the belly scratches that the beagle lived for.

"All right, then," Rodolfo said, "but let me step into this conference room so I won't have to out-shout my colleagues."

A door clicked closed, and she said, "That's *much* better. Now, I have what we believe to be some answers for you. Answers about what really happened regarding the red boat."

Giselle's stomach swooped. "You've tracked down the real owner?"

"Thanks to that faded receipt found by Larry Willets, we were able to determine that his name was Alan Broussard—"

"That's not the same Broussard who owns the big car dealership in Conners, is it?" Giselle asked, chills running down her spine at the realization that she was late for an appointment at the same spot at this very moment.

"It is, though I believe it's his brother who's running the family business these days—unless Broussard's widow's taken up the reins."

"His widow?" Giselle echoed, as Scarlett pawed a reminder at her to keep up with her scratching duties. "Then he's—"

"Money can fix a lot of things, but not the kind of cancer that took him out last July. Although the way that his wife tells it, it was the disappearance of his only son that really did him in."

"Maybe his son wouldn't have gone anywhere if his father hadn't hired him and his friend to do his dirty work and hide that boat that killed my sister." Giselle gave the dog a final pat before once more rising.

"I'm afraid you have it wrong if you think it was the old man who hit you," the detective said. "Broussard's son, Zach, it turns out, was actually the one driving."

"That's the red-haired college kid who had the breakdown? How'd you figure that out?"

"The friend who lawyered up on us before came back. Only this time, Joss Ryan showed up looking like he hadn't slept in days, and he'd ditched his attorney. He took out some pictures of his fiancée holding their newborn baby daughter and told us that now that he's a dad, it's time for him to be a man, too. And a man would own up to the truth about what really happened on the lake that day."

"Wait a minute. So he's admitting he was *there* now? And that he was on board when the boat hit us?"

"Joss was there, all right, standing right next to his good friend Zach Broussard, who'd decided that instead of pulling the new speedboat his dad had just purchased out of the lake and trailering it back home the way he'd been asked to, it would be a lot more fun spending the day tearing around the lake and drinking with a couple of hot babes, as Joss put it, that the two of them had met at the marina."

"So you're telling me the accident—Kate's death—really was all about a couple of idiots joyriding and showing off for girls?"

"I'm sorry, yes. Apparently, the babes in question thought better of the whole thing and no-showed on them. According to Joss, Zach was furious about it, since he'd bought all this alcohol for the four of them to share. He started drinking pretty heavily, going off about 'entitled bitches,' and ripping around so close to water-skiers that Joss finally got scared enough to try to force him to take a break from driving."

"Or so he's claiming now, since Zach's nowhere around to contradict his story," Giselle said bitterly.

"I learned long ago in my line of work that you always have to assume that whoever's telling the story is going to try to make himself look better," Rodolfo told her.

"Same here," said Giselle, thinking about how the versions of the truth her celebrity clients gave her had so often failed to stack up to any fact-checking she might do with others who'd been present at the time of the events described.

"Joss may very well only be trying to get himself off the hook by claiming he tried to do the right thing, saying that Zach yelled how it was his father's boat and shoved him back right before they cleared that point and struck the towrope of the raft that you and Kate were riding."

Giselle felt the world tilt on its access as the truth she had waited so long to hear was finally laid bare. "And then they kept right on going, despite the screams and shouts for help."

"Joss says they both panicked. He was underage and had been drinking, and at the time, he claims Zach was terrified his dad would kill him for taking out his brand-new boat without permission."

Unable to hold her tears back any longer, Giselle asked, "Would *kill* him? But what about *us*? I was left trapped beneath the water. And when Malcolm had no one—no one to help him cut me free, my sister—she slipped out of her vest and drowned—because of the head injury from what they'd done!"

"I know, and I'm sorry," Rodolfo said. "Joss claimed he felt worse and worse, worrying about what might be happening. He tried to tell me he even attempted at one point to get his buddy to turn back."

"I'm sure…" Giselle scoffed.

"Whatever weak protest did or didn't come out of his mouth," Rodolfo said, "you and I both know that those boys pulled that boat out of the water that day. From there, they ended up hauling the thing back to Zach's parents' home."

Wiping her eyes, Giselle said, "I don't understand. I thought they immediately took it and hid it at that storage unit."

"Zach could be a bit of a hell-raiser, but he'd never cross his dad by simply making off with his new boat without explanation. Then the two boys heard about your sister's death, and they realized their troubles could be far more serious than they'd imagined. So they both went to Zach's father and basically threw themselves on the old man's mercy."

Detective Rodolfo then went silent, giving Giselle a few moments to process all she'd said.

Impatient as ever, Giselle couldn't help but focus on what remained unspoken. "So you're telling me it was the late Alan Broussard who put those two young men up to hiding the boat under a fictitious name?"

"So Joss Ryan is claiming. And after my conversation with Mrs. Broussard, I'm inclined to believe that her husband really was involved—and that he very much came to regret it, along with his insistence that neither of the pair even *think* of jeopardizing their futures by allowing their consciences to overwhelm their sense of self-preservation."

"So he blamed himself for Zach's breakdown later and his disappearance?"

"His wife claimed that he was acting out of love and fear for their son's future, but yes, he did blame himself. As she blamed him, when she found out about it later."

"Yet she didn't see fit to end my suffering and Malcolm's by doing the right thing herself and reporting her husband's crimes or her son's to the authorities," Giselle said bitterly.

"If what she claims is true—and I happen to believe the woman—by the time she had all the facts, her son was missing and her husband was terminally ill," Rodolfo said. "I believe she was too caught up in her own pain and her family's to think beyond them."

"I hope she's not expecting sympathy from me, not after what her family's selfishness and silence cost me. And now—" Giselle shook her head as frustration washed over her. "I can't believe how much time I've wasted, imagining that getting these answers was going to somehow make things any better."

"I want you to know, we're not giving up on finding Zach Broussard and bringing him to justice, since he told his father as well that he was the boat's driver. If he's still alive, he can be held accountable. The DA will look at charging Joss, too, for his part, since they both bore a responsibility in the failure to render aid and in keeping the boat hidden for all these years."

"It's not that I don't appreciate all your hard work, you and everyone from your department, because I definitely do," Giselle said, "but how's any of this supposed to even feel like justice any longer?"

"I'm sorry, but the truth is, it probably never will, exactly. But that doesn't mean we should ever give up trying to come as close as we can get."

Already sweating beneath a layered combination of T-shirt, ballistic vest, and SAR jacket, Malcolm was grateful when Pacer's nose quickly took the two of them into a deeply shaded patch of riverside wood. Though the visibility was poor—and would soon grow worse, as the sun was rapidly descending—he decided the relief of the cooler temperature was well worth the trade-off.

As Pacer pawed at a thick patch of ferns before pulling Malcolm deeper into the underbrush, he answered the question the young police officer who'd been paired with him for security had asked about how the SAR dogs worked.

"At this point, Pacer here's just seeking, filtering through an entire world of scents in the environment—the white noise of the scores of animals and humans who've recently hiked through here, along with all kinds of incidental odors, while trying to sniff out the proverbial needle in the haystack that matches the dirty sock collected from my wrecked pickup earlier this afternoon."

"Lucky thing the evidence team found a few of Acker's things abandoned in the wrecked truck today so we could track him, isn't it?"

"Very," Malcolm said. "It's a sign he's breaking down—whether it's from his injury, exhaustion, or the pressure of the three-week manhunt."

"In other words, he's making mistakes that'll make him easier for us to take down," Ramirez said eagerly.

"Easier could still prove lethal," Malcolm reminded him, somewhat concerned about how keyed up the younger man seemed. "Remember, you and I and the other SAR teams are here to narrow down Acker's position then send in the rapid response team for the take-down. They're the only ones properly trained and geared out to deal with the kind of threat he represents."

Ramirez nodded. "Yes, sir. I do understand that."

Dismissing his lingering suspicions about Ramirez's attitude toward being in a supporting role, Malcolm went on to tell him, "If one of the search teams working another area ends up picking up the scent first, we may hear the barking from here. Provided it's not drowned out by the noise from the river."

Ramirez shrugged. "Either way, they told us at the briefing the law enforcement member of the team will send out a GPS-tagged alert to everyone's cell. But that'll only summon the rapid response team and task force leaders—cutting out the working stiffs like us."

Malcolm reminded himself that he, too, had once been in his early twenties—although he didn't recall ever having been so irritating. "But if Pacer hits a scent, things here are going to start moving *very* quickly."

An eager grin erupted on the rookie's tanned and handsome face. "That sounds *just* like what I signed up for."

"I'll be doing my best to keep up with my K-9," said Malcolm, who cared more about getting the two of them and his dog through this safely than he did this rookie's hunger for excitement. "As soon as you've sent out the locater alert to the team, I'll be counting on you to try to catch up and keep up with me as best as you can. You'll definitely need to watch your footing, though. The last time I didn't pay close enough attention, I ended up with this brace as a souvenir."

Lifting his still-healing left hand as a warning, Malcolm surveyed the deeply shaded downslope to their right, which was thick with protruding stumps and understory vegetation.

"My legs might be a little shorter than yours, but I promise you, I'm plenty quick enough to keep up." Hand resting on the butt of his gun, Ramirez nodded toward the shadowed gloom, his dark eyes gleaming with excitement. "You just make sure to get down fast if Acker pops up, so you don't get hit in any crossfire."

"You don't have to tell me twice," Malcolm said. "But Pacer—he means a whole lot to me, too."

"I'll be looking out for your partner, too, I promise," Ramirez said.

You'd better. "And watch out for yourself, too."

As Pacer continued investigating on a loose lead, Malcolm kept an ear open for any signal from other teams. Soon, however, the background thrum of swiftly flowing water drowned out all other sounds as they moved steadily closer to the river, though it remained well hidden by the trees. Most of his attention, however, was centered on shifts in his dog's behavior as he began to pull, more and more insistently, along a rightward-leading track.

As they worked their way deeper into the woods, Ramirez's interest perked up. "Your dog seems to be moving faster. Is he on to something there?"

"Maybe just a skunk in heat," Malcolm said dryly, his standard line for when he wasn't certain. But before Ramirez could respond, the beautiful, rich sound of Pacer's booming howl startled some crows out of the nearby treetops.

Barking away, his dog pulled hard to the right, and for the moment, Malcolm forgot all need for conversation. Forgot everything except the pleasure of running with his best friend, joining Pacer in an activity that sent the pure animal joy of the chase thrumming through his veins as, even in the dark green shadows, he managed to jump logs and dodge saplings to keep up with his K-9 partner.

Remembering his instructions, however, Malcolm forced himself to pull up short, coming to a halt where the sloping depression began to run back uphill toward a ridge that he knew would lead them back toward the river.

"Hold up, Pacer, will you? Settle," Malcolm said, getting out some chicken treats to help distract him from his obsessive need to find his quarry.

"Giving him a rest?" The rookie panted as he caught up.

As Pacer ignored the treat and whined to go on, Malcolm shook his head. "Just waiting for you to catch up. But I think we'd better hold up here instead of heading over that ridge completely blind when we'll have help available in just a couple of more minutes."

Ramirez scowled at him. "But *we're* the ones who

caught Acker's scent—and now you *really* want this rapid-response team to swoop in and hog the glory?"

"What I *really* want is my uncle's and my mother's killer apprehended without adding any more corpses to his body count. Including yours, you little—"

Before Malcolm could further escalate the situation, a breeze rippled through the woodland's understory. Pacer lifted his head and sniffed at the air before pulling in the direction of the ridge and barking wildly, his muzzle moving from left to right as if he were tracking—

Ramirez shouted, "I've got movement on the right! Gray jacket!"

Malcolm saw nothing at first. Then their target crossed a relatively open spot among the trees, sporting the same stained, hooded jacket Malcolm had last seen him wearing in the parking lot. Turning toward the river, Markus ran along the top of the ridge, sprinting faster than Malcolm would have imagined an injured, middle-aged man could possibly move. There was something else that seemed off as well, some troubling aspect that almost immediately evaporated as Malcolm tried to work out whether it was more dangerous losing sight of the man or trying to follow him.

Ramirez made the decision for him, racing toward the threat and bellowing, "Stop, police!"

Malcolm wasn't in the least surprised when Acker only accelerated, disappearing over the far side of the ridge.

"Hold, Ramirez! Don't go!" Malcolm shouted, his instincts—along with everything he'd learned about their adversary—screaming that the moment Ramirez crested that ridge, Acker would be waiting to deal him the swift death of a waiting bullet.

Instead of heeding Malcolm's warning, the rookie only

tucked his head and continued charging forward, as if he were running for a winning touchdown. Clipping Pacer's lead to his belt, Malcolm drew his own gun for the first time and then raced after him with Pacer bounding at his side.

"If that fool rookie gets us killed, I swear I'm going to thrash him," he told his dog.

Though he'd been primed to fling himself to the ground at the first crack of gunfire, Malcolm was pleased to find himself still moving moments later. On the other side of the ridge, the ground was more level and the trees considerably thinner, allowing him space to run unimpeded and better lighting for safer footing. Led by Pacer, Malcolm soon caught up with Ramirez, who had stopped in a grassier area not far ahead.

Ramirez held up a hand before looking back over his shoulder and signaling Malcolm to come no closer. A moment later, the young officer pointed out Acker, about thirty yards ahead and slightly above the two of them, his back turned to them as he struggled to climb onto an overgrown embankment.

Just as Malcolm realized that Markus had decided to take his chances attempting to swim the dangerous river, the right sleeve of Acker's gray coat snagged in the thick brush.

Ramirez, who had his weapon trained on the fugitive, shouted over the sounds of Pacer's barking, "Hands up, now! Police!"

Ripping his sleeve free, Acker turned in their direction. As he raised a pistol of his own toward them, the hood he was wearing swung wide with his movement. Malcolm felt a superheated jolt go through him, causing him to hesitate at the deep-red hair he imagined he had spotted.

But it was hidden again before he could be certain, and Ramirez got off a shot—followed by a second. Malcolm saw the man in the gray jacket twist around, spun to the left by the impact of a bullet ripping through his shoulder.

When the shooting ended, it took Malcolm a moment to register that neither he nor the suspect had gotten off a single shot. But both Ramirez and the man in the gray jacket had climbed up onto the weed-choked embankment.

"Colton! Hurry!" Ramirez called from somewhere among the weeds. "He's going to fall if you don't come help me hold him!"

After pausing to clip Pacer's lead to a thick tree branch to keep his dog out of harm's way, Malcolm climbed up and pushed through the tight space to join Ramirez where he was sprawled near the river side of the embankment, struggling mightily to hold on to the leg of the suspect, who was dangling above the torrent.

Tossing a desperate look back toward Malcolm, the rookie shouted to be heard over the thundering flow. "Get over here and help me! Grab him! Otherwise, he's going to fall for sure."

"Working on getting through these damned weeds," Malcolm said, briars snagging at his clothing as he maneuvered himself into position.

As the injured man's arms waved above the spray, the torrent crashed and tumbled its way among a gauntlet of boulders that Malcolm couldn't imagine anyone with at least one fresh bullet wound possibly surviving.

"Stop your thrashing, you damned fool, before you get yourself killed!" Ramirez shouted at him as Malcolm wormed his way closer.

Malcolm made a grab for the man's leg—only to get the side of his head kicked for his trouble, hard enough that his ears rang and the rushing water below seemed to be inside his head.

But something else filled his head as well—the certainty that the young face and the red hair he'd glimpsed when the gray hood had swung sideways had not been Markus Acker's.

"Hurry, please!" Ramirez shouted. "His boot—he's coming out of it! He'll fall. And we can't let him—*Nooo*!"

With no time to weigh the odds of his own survival, Malcolm dove, both arms reaching desperately toward a risk he prayed would lead to answers.

Chapter 18

Too nervous to do much more than pick at a few left-
overs and try to delete some of the more obvious junk
from among her backlogged emails, Giselle checked her
messages for at least the tenth time to see if she might
have missed a reply from Malcolm.

She'd known, of course, that he wouldn't see her text
since he would have his phone zipped inside his pocket
and his full attention on the dangerous mission he was
part of. But she was hoping that at some point—whether
because the search had veered in some other direction or,
in the best of all scenarios, had come to a successful end,
he would eventually pull it out and check it.

Mostly, though, she needed to know that he was safe,
especially now that a look through the back door's window showed the rose-streaked twilit sky was fading into
a soft violet.

When the phone did ring, however, the Caller ID showed
the name of a Colton she had never met.

"Hi, this is Sarah Colton," a friendly-sounding voice
said following Giselle's greeting. "I hope I'm not disturbing you, but Lizzy suggested I reach out when I couldn't
reach Malcolm this evening. She did tell me he was likely
occupied with the search for Markus."

"He is, but I'm happy to chat. Malcolm's told me a bit about you and Nate," Giselle told her. "Before anything else, though, I want you to know how sorry I was to hear about your mother's passing."

"Thanks," Sarah said. "It's been—our relationship could be...challenging. But in the end, she left me no doubt that in her way, she really cared about me."

"Hold on to that part, then. I understand you're dealing with her—with her things now—I'm so sorry. Please excuse me," Giselle added before covering the phone for a moment and shushing Scarlett, who'd begun barking furiously at something outside.

Picking up a toy, Giselle distracted her from a fat tabby-and-white barn cat out prowling in the grass outside. "Sorry for my puppy problem. Or maybe I should say my problem puppy—not that I'd trade her for the pick of any litter."

Sarah chuckled. "I'm sure you wouldn't. But the reason I'm calling is I was wondering, if it wouldn't be too inconvenient, would you mind if I dropped off that record player from my mother's house this evening? I know Malcolm and I talked about tomorrow, but it turns out, I need to cover a sick friend's shift at the library and then—"

"Of course you can stop by this evening. No one else is around at the moment, but I'll be happy to help with the unloading," Giselle said before, once more, Scarlett began barking at the window.

After returning to the phone, Giselle said, "Once more, sorry about the noise. I look forward to meeting you in person—and having what I hope will be our first uninterrupted conversation."

Laughing, Sarah said, "Can't wait to meet you and your puppy, too. Look for me in about an hour."

After ending the call, Giselle decided she'd better run upstairs and at least wash her face, which probably still bore evidence of smudged mascara. As she started through the kitchen, however, Scarlett yipped to get her attention and went running to the back door.

"I hope this isn't about that silly cat again," Giselle warned.

But when Scarlett sat and yapped again, Giselle realized that the pup was signaling her need to go out to relieve herself. Reassured by what Detective Rodolfo had said about Acker having trapped himself in an area Giselle knew to be some distance from the ranch, she hooked Scarlett to her leash before unlocking the deadbolt.

Outside, a smattering of stars had emerged, and a few automatic solar security lights had switched on to light her path. As she walked Scarlett out onto the grass, she spotted the front end of a truck parked around on the other side of the house. Deciding it must be the ranch pickup she'd seen leaving earlier, she wondered why the hands would have left it there this evening instead of at the working barn, as usual, upon returning from their earlier errand. Taking a few more steps to get a better angle on the silhouetted shape, she realized, *That's not the truck at all. It's an SUV.* At the same moment, Scarlett whirled around and started barking aggressively at something she heard moving behind them.

Instinct had Giselle scooping the dog up and bolting for the door, not knowing the how or why or how close the threat might be, only guessing *who* it must be. And knowing that her sole chance of survival lay in beating Markus Acker to the door.

Within seconds she heard the footsteps, hard on her heels and the panting sounds of his exertion—so close that she imagined she could feel the heat of his breath. As she imagined his fingers closing on her shirt, adrenaline gave her a burst of speed, and she surged ahead to reach the door ahead of him. A hot wave of relief cascaded through her as she fumbled with the knob to push it open.

As she was stepping through, he bulldozed her from behind, his bodyweight slamming her in a flying tackle. As she cried out, the last thing she was aware of was Scarlett spilling free from her arms. Then her head smacked down against the tile floor, and darkness overtook her.

Shoving his damp hair from his eyes, Malcolm looked up from where he sat wrapped in a blanket after being checked out by EMTs and then encouraged to change into a pair of dry sweats supplied by one of his SAR teammates. Exhausted to his bones, he watched the Med-Evac helicopter disappear into the dark sky with both the suspect and Officer Ramirez, who had been sent along in the unlikely event the man came to in transit. As the sound of the chopper's receding rotors merged with the roar of the nearby river, Malcolm shifted his gaze—and spotted Ajay Wright and his Lab Pumpkin striding his way.

Ajay looked down and shook his head. "You know, just because you're the luckiest man in the state of Idaho doesn't mean you're not still out of your mind. When you dove in after your target, there's no way you could've possibly known that you and he would end up washed into the shallows where Fletcher and Officer Phillips would be able to haul you both out. You could've *died* in there—and then what would I have told your sister?"

"That I didn't actually *dive* in so much as I fell," Malcolm explained as he stroked Pacer, who had sidled up in front of him, offering both moral support and the warmth of his dry body. "I was making one last hail Mary of a grab for the suspect when I realized that he wasn't Markus, and his body weight ended up pulling me down after him."

Ajay's golden-brown gaze bored into his. "Because you took things one step too far, as always."

"That could very well be," Malcolm allowed as he climbed stiffly to his feet, his body aching in a dozen places. "But I knew that if he died here, we'd end up losing whatever information he might have on Acker and his plans forever."

As Malcolm was speaking, Fletcher, who'd been on a call nearby, rejoined them. "Sorry to tell you both, but it doesn't sound as if that gamble's going to pay off. That was Ramirez calling from the chopper. He tells me our suspect started crashing almost as soon as they were in the air. They're working hard to try to get his heart restarted, but things aren't looking very promising."

"Tough break," Ajay said.

"On several levels," said Fletcher. "I was pretty sure I recognized the suspect's face and that red hair when I saw him being loaded, so I took a quick pic and conferred with other detectives. They knew who he was right away."

"Let me guess—he's the red-haired college student reported missing three years back in Boise," Malcolm said.

"Zach Broussard, yes. How did you know?" Fletcher asked.

"I was never told the name, but this kid's disappearance from his college came up during the investigation of my fiancée's death at Blackbird Lake. Sheriff's Department Deputy Ariana Rodolfo can give you all the details. But from what I heard, this kid and one of his friends stashed the boat involved in the collision under a false name shortly before heading back to campus. A few months later, the red-haired guy vanished into thin air."

Ajay said, "Interesting how this kid goes missing and then turns up here, more than three years later, acting as some sort of stooge for Markus Acker."

Fletcher said, "I wasn't personally on his case back in Boise, but I do remember hearing that he had some kind of a breakdown before disappearing. I know, too, that a pretty substantial inheritance he'd had access to went missing at the same time."

"Sounds a lot like Acker's M.O.—getting his hooks into a 'lost sheep' and draining them of all their assets," Ajay said. "In return, he would've given the kid a place to run to—"

"But run from what?" Malcolm asked. "Unless Broussard did a lot more than just participate in a cover-up for some rich boat owner to earn a little extra money—which, bad as it is, is hardly enough to trash your whole life over."

Fletcher's gaze connected with his. "I think you probably know, if you think about it, what the kid was *really* running from, Mal."

Malcolm nodded tightly. "So you're telling me I just nearly got myself killed trying to save the man who cost me—*Hell...*"

Ajay clapped him on the shoulder. "He might've taken the future you thought you had ahead of you, but you can at least be sure he didn't take your humanity as well."

"Even if it's kind of reckless at times?"

"I'm still grateful to have you as a friend—and a member of my team," Ajay assured him.

As glad as Malcolm was to hear it, before he could thank Ajay, the task force leader excused himself and stepped away to take a call.

Fletcher said to Malcolm, "I have to head off myself to check back in with Archer about how he's coming on getting that search warrant for the phone that was collected from your pickup—"

"Acker had a cell phone on him? I'm surprised you weren't able to use it to track him before now," Malcolm said.

"His personal cell was found smashed shortly after he went on the lam. This one's probably stolen—but the hope is, it'll yield enough data to give us information on his recent movements," Fletcher said, "or possibly lead us to other past associates he's recently reached out to for help."

"Or other victims—like maybe the owner of that cell phone and whatever vehicle he happens to be driving now," Malcolm added.

"Unfortunately, the thought's occurred," Fletcher said. "I'll check back in with you in a bit."

Instead of leaving, however, he stopped at the sight of Ajay heading back toward them, looking as if someone had slugged him in the stomach.

"What is it? What's happened?" Fletcher asked him.

"It's Acker, isn't it?" asked Malcolm, a chill that had nothing to do with the plunge into snow-melt-charged floodwaters he had just survived washing over him. "Please tell me this whole thing with the Broussard kid wasn't simply a diversion so he could go after another member of our family." He glanced at Fletcher, whose father's stroke a year before, had set off this entire nightmare.

"Just let Ajay speak," Fletcher ordered, his professional training overcoming the emotion Malcolm saw blazing in his green eyes.

"I'm sorry to have to be the one to tell you both this," Ajay said, his gaze moving from Fletcher to Malcolm, "but there's been a 9-1-1 call from the ranch. Your sister Sarah stopped by just a little while ago. She'd spoken with Giselle about three-quarters of an hour ago about a change of plans—an item she needs to drop off."

"Our late grandmother's record player," Malcolm said, his pulse pounding as his dread built.

"The thing is, though, when she arrived," Ajay continued, "Giselle didn't answer. But Sarah spotted a small, frightened-looking beagle running loose with its leash dragging."

"Giselle would *never* leave Scarlett unattended." Malcolm tried to tell himself that, most likely, she'd accidentally lost the pup somehow and gone off looking for her. Maybe this was all some terrible misunderstanding and the same gentle Giselle who wouldn't put bullets in a gun or eat anything with a mother would show up at any minute laughing about how she had simply dropped the leash.

"Sarah thought the same thing," said Ajay, "which is why she went around back to see if she could spot Giselle out looking for her puppy. Instead, Sarah found the back door standing open. There were streaks of what looked like fresh blood, still wet, smeared across the tile inside. That's when Sarah locked herself inside a bathroom and called Greg from down the road, along with 9-1-1."

Malcolm had never been slammed by a tsunami, but for the second time in his life, he felt the earth ripped out from underneath him, replaced by a wave of fear and grief and regret so huge, it squeezed the breath from his lungs.

"I—I never should have let her stay alone," he said. "I should've known, after Markus came for me once, that he might—"

"We had every reason to believe Acker was right *here*,

completely surrounded by dozens of law enforcement and search and rescue personnel," Ajay said. "And we had no reason at all to think the attack on you and Giselle earlier might be personal. But whatever mistakes any of us might've made, we can't afford to waste time on guilt or blame now. Do you hear me, Malcolm?"

Something in his tone cut through the ringing in Malcolm's ears, pulling him back from the spiral of guilt he'd been heading for. It was a damned indulgence, he warned himself, one he dared not give in to—not as long as hope remained.

Over the ringing in his ears, he heard Fletcher, somehow functional enough to ask, "Have they searched the house and barn yet, do you know?"

Some detached fragment of Malcolm's shocked brain understood that those on the scene would be looking not simply for evidence but a body. *Giselle's* dead body, left behind like refuse, exactly as Claudette Hogan's had been following her murder. But he refused to allow himself to believe in the possibility that they would find it. He wouldn't, *couldn't* lose Giselle before he had the chance to make her understand that whatever pain their past held, in her, he saw a future worth staking his heart on a thousand times over. He felt only shame that he'd lost sight of that for even a moment before when he had seen her last.

"Greg and Sarah have done a preliminary search of the house's interior. Other than a single, round hole in one of the top kitchen cabinets, they found nothing—"

"A *bullet* hole?" Malcolm flashed on an image of Giselle's pale face, after she'd been grazed before.

"Unconfirmed at this point. First responders are still en

route," Ajay said. "I'll be heading there with the rapid-response team to join them and take command of the scene."

"Pacer and I will be coming with you," Malcolm insisted. "Wherever that bastard's taken her, we're going to find her—and I swear to you, I'm going to bring her home alive."

Chapter 19

Thirty-five minutes earlier...

"**W**ake up, damn you. Look alive." Markus booted the side of the unconscious woman's thigh, angry with her for running from him and forcing him to tackle her so hard that he was now left with this mess. Not only that, but he'd smacked down painfully against his wounded ear when he had jumped her—a pulsing, overheated pain that had been growing more miserable by the day instead of better, and now he felt something hot and thick and putrid-smelling dripping from his bandage.

"And, *you*, shut up." He kicked at the barking beagle, which deftly dodged his mud-caked shoe to race from the room with its tail tucked tightly between its legs.

Glad he wouldn't need to waste a bullet on it, he knelt down and rolled the limp blonde onto her back, eager to see which of the younger female Coltons he had gotten.

Whoever she was, he saw that she was definitely a looker, despite the large bump already going purple, high on the right side of her forehead. Definitely not Sarah—the troublemaking daughter that Jessie Colton had taken a bullet for rather than allowing him to shoot dead the way he wished he had—and definitely would if he ever saw her treacherous face again.

Whether this was Jessie's other daughter or some cousin didn't much matter, he supposed. Since the lot of them were all so pathetically attached to one another, he was certain she would serve as the hostage that he needed to finally reclaim the life that he deserved…

But if she were too badly damaged to speak into a phone—to cry and plead for her life before sharing his demands with her distraught family members—it was time to cut his losses and find himself a sturdier hostage. Eager to find out, he bent to scoop up the cell phone he saw she had dropped. After tucking it into his own shirt pocket, he reached over and roughly shook her shoulder.

"If you're only playing possum on me," he told the helpless woman, "I'm going to give you this one warning. An unconscious victim's as much use to me as a dead one right now, which is exactly what you're going to be if you don't open your eyes and start cooperating, right—*awfgh!*"

His shout transformed into an expletive as two sharp jaws—the small piranha of a dog's—clamped down painfully onto his bare ankle.

Kicking the beast free, he drew his gun and took aim at the barking, snapping menace.

"Don't you *dare* hurt her!" the woman cried out, shoving his legs out from under him so unexpectedly that he crashed down onto one knee, sending a wild shot into an upper kitchen cabinet.

With a shout of rage, he spun around to point the muzzle only inches from her pale face, a wave of dizziness making him realize the infection working on him must be worse than he'd imagined. "You ever lay another hand on me, and I swear to you, I'll leave what's left of you strewn across this kitchen for your precious family to find! Now get that barking stopped, or I swear to you that I will."

"Scarlett, hush, girl. It's all right," the woman pleaded, her voice reed-thin.

When the animal went quiet, he noticed the red smears on its muzzle. Realizing it was *his* blood on the dog's fur, he gave it a glare that sent it darting behind the kitchen island, at least for the time being.

As he returned his attention to the woman, Markus wiped away the sweat dripping down into his face. "Have you—have you seen an antique record player lately, from Jessie's home? Do you know what's happened to it?"

"An old record player? Why would..." She sounded so bewildered that he wondered for a moment if either shock or the blow to her head had rendered her incapable of comprehension.

Then she shook her head. "I'm sorry, but I've never been inside her place. But if there's something you were particularly attached to that was accidentally packed up, I'm sure I can help you get it back, if you'll only tell me where to have it sent—"

"Are you joking?" His laughter sounded like a dry wheeze. "And I don't give a damn about your stupid Colton family heirlooms, only the—"

"*My* heirlooms?" she echoed.

He eyed her with suspicion. "You *are* a Colton, aren't you?"

She seemed to weigh her answer momentarily before her blue eyes turned disdainful as she looked him over, from the hat that partly obscured his dripping ear to the clothes that he suspected were by now only being held together by the layers of grime and sweat embedded in their fabric. "Oh, I'm Colton enough," she said, "to know *exactly* how big of a mistake you're making in daring to come here, Acker. And if you imagine that one little dog and I are trouble, just you *wait* until you see what's coming for you next."

Furious to be treated with such contempt by a woman whose life he could snuff out in an instant, he rounded on her once more, pressing the gun's muzzle to her temple as he hauled her up off the floor. "You're damned lucky I need you for a hostage for the moment, to trade you for what I'm really after, do you know that?"

"A hostage?" she echoed weakly.

"But you're right about one thing, though," he said. "It's time that you and I get moving. First, though, I'm going to bind these hands of yours and cover your eyes. If you fight me, I may need to tape your mouth, too—"

"Please, no…" she said, her eyes gone huge and glassy.

Empowered by her helplessness, he felt a hot surge of satisfaction. "Only, the thing is, I can't guarantee you I won't get sloppy with it. Sloppy enough that I won't accidentally cover up your nose, too, with that tape and leave you to smother underneath the blanket in the back of the SUV where you'll be riding. Then maybe I'll dump your body in the lake before I turn around to find myself a more compliant Colton. Or will you save me the trouble?"

She only stared in answer, completely unresisting as he bound her, her lips slightly parted and her face as pale as death.

I'll dump your body in the lake…the lake…thelakethe-lakethelake…

The words looped endlessly, the soundtrack of Giselle's dread and horror as she lay curled on her side beneath a musty-smelling—and profoundly itchy—blanket in the SUV's cargo area with her arms bound tightly behind her. The rough ride of the speeding vehicle—an older model whose engine was a throaty rumble—was brutal, battering her head, already throbbing from its impact with the kitchen floor, against what felt like bare metal as they jolted over every bump.

Willing away her nausea, she told herself that whatever happened to her now, she could at least take some comfort in knowing that Acker had taken her away before Sarah had shown up with the very record player he seemed so eager to get his hands on. Guessing that there had to be something critically important to him hidden inside—and that the moment that he had it, he would have no more incentive to keep her and Sarah breathing—she'd told whatever lies she'd thought might buy her a little more time. Time to come up with some hope for extricating herself from this nightmare.

She held out hope that Sarah would quickly raise an alarm over her failure to be at the house as they'd arranged this evening. But Giselle had no idea whether there were any cameras around the ranch property that might have shown the vehicle that she'd been loaded into. She thought about her cell phone, with its GPS, but she couldn't feel it pressing into her body when she rolled from side to side, so she supposed that Acker must have taken it from her pocket while she was unconscious and tossed it somewhere to make it impossible to track them.

Desperately, she fought against whatever he'd used to tie her up. Her bonds barely gave at all. He'd tied her wrists so tightly, the rope or cord felt as if it was cutting into her flesh, and her hands ached with the restricted circulation. Frustrated by her inability to loosen the binding, she instead wriggled around and used her shoulders until the blanket finally slipped off her. Pushing her face against it even harder, she gradually forced the torn tea towel he'd used to blindfold her down from her eyes until the still-tied cloth dropped down around her neck.

Blinking in the darkness, she peered all around her but saw little, other than a few hazed reflections through the SUV's filmed rear windows. Her exertions must have stirred the dust, however, for she sneezed reflexively. Afterward, she froze, terrified that he might have heard and that he'd pull over and beat her bloody for making a sound, the way he'd threatened when he had dumped her back here. Fortunately, however, he'd turned on the radio— she'd caught the muted tones of some advertising jingle and now, a couple of male voices chatting about the forecast for the upcoming weekend.

Would she be alive to see if they were right about their prediction of "great weather for tennis, hiking, or boating," she wondered, or would that only matter to the searchers out looking for her remains?

A wave of grief washed over her as she pictured Malcolm out with Pacer, knowing he'd insist on being part of the operation, even though she was certain he would be beside himself with worry. And knowing that, if he did find whatever Acker left of her, it would certainly destroy the man she'd come to love.

Her heart breaking at the thought, she told herself, *No. I'm not doing this to him—and Markus isn't destroying our chance to make things right between us. Whatever I have to do, I can't let this happen...*

She wasn't certain whether minutes or hours passed her by in the rear of that SUV, only that time seemed glacially slow as she came up with and discarded dozens of plans—each one wilder than the last—to plead, bargain, or fight for even the slightest chance of saving her life. Eventually, however, they turned, and the jouncing battered her sore head worse than ever as the ride grew rougher and the truck took a tight corner.

This is it, she sensed, a moment before she heard the loud squeak of the brakes, and she heard as well as felt the SUV's shift into park. Her every nerve ending standing on alert, she strained her ears, listening as he shut off the engine and opened his door.

As an eddy of fresh air reached her from the front, Giselle dragged in a deep breath, desperate for any clue of what might be coming. But all she smelled was the acrid scent of her own terror mingled with the damp breath of a lake that chilled her to the bone.

Chapter 20

Markus had driven around and around the back roads, the plan that had seemed so clear in his mind a few hours earlier fraying at the edges as waves of heat and chills vied with the pain for his attention. If it were only the discomfort, he told himself, he would fight straight through it to head to the Wilderness Chapel, where he knew that a secure supply of clean and edible, if not gourmet, food and a medical kit he'd personally ordered kept well-stocked to protect his church from lawsuits lest some member of his sect perish while left to contemplate the error of his or her ways on the isolated island.

But Markus hadn't beaten the odds his whole life—and outmaneuvered the authorities for most of the last few decades—by being stupid, and he was smart enough to know that, with pain, fever and fatigue nipping at his heels, he wasn't thinking straight now. That he was forgetting something. That this plan for exchanging the sealed pack containing his passport and a million-dollar ransom for the location of the Colton woman, which he would offer to provide via text message once he was safely beyond the country's borders, was as full of holes as a wasp's nest with an even greater potential to end up with him getting fatally stung.

So he continued driving, mentally running through each step, trying to come up with where he'd gone wrong. Soon, however, he became sidetracked, imagining the Coltons opening the photos he meant to send the worried family from the phone of their loved one. Bruised, bound, and terrified, the young woman would make quite the horrifying picture. Or better yet, he thought, he could tear her clothes off before he started—add that layer of humiliation to punish her for the way she'd dared to shove and threaten him back at the ranch house instead of simply cowering and complying the way a woman ought to from the start.

On some level, he knew there was something dangerous about using her cell phone to send such messages. But now that he'd come up with the idea of playing god once more, shocking and hurting the Colton family with the kind of photos they could never erase from their minds, the less he could focus on the risk and the more excited he became about the idea of getting started with his plan.

By the time he finally parked the old Suburban beneath the low-hanging limbs of the huge black walnut tree near the dock where the Ever After Church kept several rowboats tied, a fresh wave of anticipation had him floating high above the pain. Hurrying around to the vehicle's rear hatch, he popped it open and gestured with his gun at the still-bound woman—who was staring at him with the blindfold dangling down around her neck—and sitting propped up on one elbow.

Ripping the blindfold off her, he slapped her hard enough to knock her over—less because he was angry than because he imagined that another mark on her face would look good for his explicit photos.

"Did I *tell* you you could take that off?" he demanded. "Did I?"

"I—I'm sorry," she said quickly. "I swear I didn't mean to. It just—it fell off. From all the bumping around these roads."

Another lie, he knew, but at least he'd shocked her enough that she gave him no trouble when he pulled her from the rear of the vehicle. Grabbing one of her bound arms, he began forcing her quickly downhill, frog-marching her ahead of him through the overgrown grass.

As they approached the lakeshore, she dug in her heels and shook her head, staring at the half moon's reflection off the inlet's shimmering waters. "If you're—if you're planning to drown me, j-just go ahead and shoot me here. Because I'm not going one step closer."

"You think I've driven you around for hours just to toss you in the damned lake? If that was all I wanted, I would've killed you back at the house," he said. "Now get moving. Boat's right over here to take us where we're going—then you and I have some proof-of-life pictures that need taking."

"Proof-of—for your ransom?" she asked.

He sent a cruel smile her way, warming even more to the thought of repaying a fraction of the suffering this family had forced him to endure. "For the ransom, a few porn sites—there's honestly no telling where the sort of shots I have in mind might end up…not that you'll be alive to worry about your precious reputation."

Predictably, she tried to bolt then, but he slapped her again before dragging her down onto the pier. When he tried to fling her in the boat, though, he fumbled the gun he had been holding on her.

In an instant, everything sped up: Markus ducking and

reaching for the dropped gun—the woman kicking it out of reach and into the dark water before diving after it to avoid his fist arcing through the air above her. And then there was the sound of shouting from the shoreline—deep-voiced men barking out harsh orders.

But Markus Acker wasn't about to end his life withering away in some prison, so with a roar of pure rage, he made one more wild leap in the direction the woman had taken…

Only to have a hail of bullets catch him before his body hit the water.

"I've got her!" Malcolm shouted to the others, his heart pounding like a piston as Pacer bounded into the shallow water just ahead of him. The K-9 grabbed Giselle by the shirt where she struggled, facedown, a moment before Malcolm lifted her, coughing, choking, and sputtering in his arms.

"You're all right now. You're safe. You're safe," he kept telling her as Fletcher came to help him carry her to the grassy bank, now illuminated by the headlights of several emergency vehicles.

At the edge of his awareness, he caught sight of Ajay on the dock, directing two of the strike force team members, who were hauling an inert form from the wine-red water. But Malcolm returned his attention to lowering Giselle—who continued coughing—gently before noticing, with a flare of fresh rage, the way her arms were bound behind her.

"Her wrists," he said, his voice rough with emotion and the understanding that she would have certainly drowned had it taken them even a few minutes longer to track down her location after requesting an emergency ping from her cell phone provider. "You have a knife to cut her loose?" And for just an instant, he was back again on that deadly August day, sawing through her hair.

"You keep her supported so I can reach her hands. I'll get this," Fletcher said, pulling a blade from his pocket.

Nodding, Malcolm let him free her, instead focusing his energy on reassuring Giselle as he held her. "Fletcher, Ajay, and I are all here with you. You're safe now, safe forever. I promise you, he can't hurt you or any of us any longer."

Glancing back over at the dock, he saw no activity to indicate that Ajay had ordered any resuscitative efforts, and realized with a start that Markus Acker would never again threaten any of his loved ones. Still, when Malcolm got his first look at the bruising on Giselle's face, he felt a surge of such overwhelming rage that it still took all his restraint not to rush straight over and beat the living hell out of the lifeless corpse.

He shook off the foolish impulse, reminding himself that right now, the living woman in his arms deserved every scrap of his attention. She gave a moan of relief as her wrists were finally freed.

"There you go," Fletcher told her gently. "I see a pretty good-sized knot on your forehead. Any other injuries we need to know about right now?"

"Don't think—so—no—" Her words splintered into another round of coughing.

Patting her shoulder, Fletcher said, "Let me go check on the ETA for the ambulance and see if I can round up a blanket for you. Anything else you need or want, just name it, and I'll do whatever I can to make it happen."

"Th-thank you," she choked out.

Concerned about how much lake water she may have

inhaled, Malcolm gently gave her back a few thumps. Pacer chose that moment to move in and sneak a couple of face licks before Malcolm was able to push him back.

"All right, you. Give her some space," he complained, pulling the dog back from her cheek. "I haven't even scored my own kiss."

"So now..." Giselle wheezed out a laugh as she reached to pet the shepherd. "So now you two are in some kind of competition?"

"I've already accepted that I'll always be runner-up behind that handsome mug of his," Malcolm said. "You know, he led me straight to you—even after—after Acker threw you in the water."

"He—he didn't throw me in. I—I dove in myself. Because he was going to kill me. I saw it in his eyes when I—when I punted the gun he'd dropped off the dock."

Pulling her into his arms, he let her cry, gently stroking her hair and telling her, "I'm so sorry that he hurt you, that he ever laid a finger on you."

"It was—it was all my fault. I thought it would be safe to take out Scarlett. Oh, no—Scarlett! I know the door was left wide open, and she—" Giselle coughed briefly before quickly regaining control. "She was so frightened when he tried to shoot her. I think—I think she might've bitten him—when he was hurting me."

He drew back to look into her face, still so beautiful to him despite the marks of violence. "First of all, Scarlett's safe—Sarah and Greg found her. And if she *did* bite Markus, she deserves a big, fat T-bone."

Giselle's face contorted. "She might need an extra rabies shot, though. He was *so* horrible! I never should've let him take me—"

"Please don't say that. No part of this is in any way your fault. Why would you imagine for a moment that—?"

"Scarlett was crying to go out, and I thought, since Detective Rodolfo had told me on the phone that Malcolm appeared to be surrounded at the search location miles away, it would be more than safe to take her for a quick walk."

Malcolm grimaced, shaking his head. "Believe me, we were *all* fooled. But it turned out we were chasing an impostor. Acker had sent the missing red-haired guy Rodolfo was looking for, Zach Broussard—who's apparently been in hiding all this time as one of his cult members—to lead us on a wild goose chase in my truck."

"Broussard's a member of the Ever After cult?"

"He *was*," Malcolm said. "He ended up shot by an officer himself. Our last update was a text on the way here saying that he'd just been pronounced dead at the trauma center."

"Detective Rodolfo said—she told me that Broussard—that he was the one who was piloting the—"

"I've already put together that he had to have been out joyriding with his buddy in the red boat that day," Malcolm said, drawing her in closer once more as he felt her shiver. "But now that we know the truth about the past, the real question is, are we going to keep allowing it to keep us from claiming the kind of future we deserve? Because we *do* deserve to know real happiness, Giselle. I think we both know that Kate would want that for us."

"Of course she would, because she loved us." Giselle sighed. "So maybe what's been getting in the way is that we haven't been willing to show ourselves a measure of that same love…"

"I think so, yes," Malcolm said just as Fletcher returned, tearing open one of the emergency space blankets that so many first responders carried in their vehicles.

He passed it to Giselle. "About five minutes on that ambulance."

She thanked him before he excused himself when Ajay called him over.

Returning her attention to Malcolm, she said, "When I was tied up in the back of that SUV, all I could really do—other than dream up a lot of really unworkable ideas for how I might overpower and escape an armed psychopath—was regret how afraid I've been of my own feelings for you—"

"Afraid?" he echoed.

She nodded. "Afraid of trusting in the positive things you saw in me, since I couldn't even see them in myself. And believing that after years of settling for immature, self-centered men when I was younger, I might really deserve to love someone so driven, so focused, and so absolutely loyal to the bone—because I *do* love you, Malcolm. I can't help but love who you are. I even love seeing my mess of a self through your eyes."

In the distance, he spotted flashing emergency lights approaching. But his attention remained riveted on Giselle.

"You're absolutely perfect as you are to me," he told her, "but if there are some issues for both of us to work through, what do you say the two of us throw in our stakes and tackle them together?"

"Together?" she asked.

"Absolutely," he said, as someone directed the ambulance to pull up nearby, "because whatever challenges life hands out, it seems to me, they'll be a whole lot easier to face, knowing I have someone as brave and bright and beautiful as you are standing by my side."

She stared at him a moment before gesturing toward

her face and muddy clothing. "You *really* need to have that ambulance crew give you an eye examination if you imagine I look beautiful covered in lake muck, bumps, and bruises—"

"And one more thing," he said, reaching over, as if to pull something off her shoulder.

"What's that?" she asked, looking down to see what he'd found.

"Just this, my love," he said, lifting her chin to claim a kiss that began sweetly, only to tip quickly toward a heat that he took as a promise of far better days—to say nothing of the nights—to come.

Chapter 21

Two Weeks Later...

A satisfied grin stretching across his freshly shaven face, Malcolm looked down from the window of the bedroom suite he and Giselle were now sharing and pointed out the long line of vehicles coming up the ranch's drive and heading for the house. "Judging from the response to his Saturday-afternoon summons, the old man's definitely still got it. Looks like every single member of the family's arriving for the Buck Colton Show right on time."

Giselle finished affixing an earring and smiled back at him, her healing bruises now scarcely distinguishable beneath the light dusting of powder she'd applied—mostly, he knew, because she was more than ready to move on from discussing her abduction with anyone besides him and the counselor she'd begun seeing last week, a woman who specialized in the processing of trauma.

"You sound almost surprised to see them," she said as she straightened the lower hem of the pretty spring top she was wearing with a pair of ankle jeans. "Was there ever really any doubt this family would be ready to celebrate, after nearly a year of the kind of stress you've all been put through?"

Malcolm patted Pacer, who had walked over to check on the action outside the window as well. "Oh, I'm sure everyone's more than ready to let their hair down for once. It's just the *on-time* part that's left me so impressed. Let's just say we have a few chronic stragglers among our ranks—and between those juggling little ones and my cousin Frannie being so close to her due date, I'm sure that's added an extra layer to the challenge of keeping to a schedule."

"Speaking of Frannie, I ran into her at the bookstore a few days back. She looks amazing."

"I'm surprised she was even there. Dante's told me that she's been a bit uncomfortable on her feet just lately, and the doctor's advised her to take it easy for the duration."

"Dante has nothing to worry over. She was sitting in a comfy chair, enjoying her time visiting with everyone and looking positively radiant while the staff and the store manager handled all the real work. I kept trying to ask her about the baby, but everyone there was too excited about that big Cami Carlson TV interview to talk about anything but my 'big moment.'"

Malcolm couldn't help but smile at the way Giselle rolled her eyes. "I don't know why you find it so embarrassing. People are proud of you. *I'm* proud of you—and have been, since long before 'My Lioness' became such a megahit."

"It's a wonderful tribute to her mother, who's devoted her life to teaching her daughter how to become her own independent woman, and Cami really deserves the success she's found with the song becoming such a huge crossover hit. But it was *totally* unnecessary for her to publicly name me as 'the other lioness' in her life, especially in front of one of the biggest interviewers out there. I became a ghostwriter for a reason. I've never personally wanted this kind of attention. It's been crazy."

"I'll admit, it's not at all what I expected either," Malcolm said, thinking of the avalanche of requests for interviews from other media outlets. In addition, so many cards, bouquets, and gifts had been sent by Cami's grateful fans that Giselle had been having a ranch hand check her cabin for them daily and donate everything that was appropriate to a local nursing home.

He said, "Once the media sees you're not willing to trade in juicy stories to get your face and name splashed worldwide—"

"Heaven forbid." She made a face.

"They'll move on to their next target."

"Now that it's been announced that a certain previously unnamed 'wolf' is facing multiple charges related to his history of 'mentoring' other musically gifted girls, they can focus on the whole sordid history of his scandals instead. Then I'll be able to quietly get on with working on Cami's book helping other young people figure out how to become the lions and lionesses in their own lives—and to recognize and avoid those looking to exploit them."

"So you've decided to go ahead and ghostwrite for Cami?" he said, not at all surprised by her choice, though he knew that Giselle's new agent had received at least two other celebrity tell-all offers, either of which would have paid more up front.

Giselle smiled. "How could I say no to something with the potential to make a real difference in so many young lives?"

"I think it's the perfect choice—especially since you'll be able to do most of your work from here," he said. "Speaking of which, we'd better hurry up and get downstairs before everyone else beats us inside and we end up getting counted as the late ones."

"Or worse yet, missing whatever this huge announcement is your dad keeps teasing everyone about."

"I've been wondering exactly what he has up his sleeve myself," Malcolm said.

Giselle squatted to give Scarlett a final pat before opening her crate door. "In you go, my sweet girl. I'll be back to check on you soon."

When the pup trotted in obediently, Giselle gave her a fresh chew and sighed happily. "I still can't believe she's really mine. That was so nice of Sebastian, bending the rules to let me keep her."

"He couldn't technically allow anyone else to adopt her, since she'd bitten Markus," Malcolm told her. "But I think we would've come up with some way to make sure you got her regardless, considering the ordeal you'd been through together."

"This is why I adore you both," she said, giving him a quick kiss before they hurried downstairs to join the joyful chaos of Malcolm's siblings and his cousins, their loved ones and their littles. For the next half hour or more, there were numerous hugs and greetings, reunions and introductions, laughter and the rising din of happy chatter as drinks were passed around and the pre-meal snacks set out.

Malcolm couldn't believe how much he'd missed the wonderful normalcy of it all, after all these months of stress and danger. Or maybe it just seemed better, having Giselle at his side.

Then his father, looking more at ease and—somehow—younger than he had in ages, in a new pearl-button denim shirt, and a pair of neatly creased jeans went to the antique brass dinner bell that hung on the wall. When the crowd failed to quiet in response to his throat-clearing, he rang the bell so loudly that all those nearest him clapped their hands over their ears and Pacer gave a single hound-like howl of protest.

As everyone fell silent, Buck put his arm around Mama Jen, who was all smiles in an embroidered turquoise dress that complemented her silver-streaked dark-blond hair.

"All right, everybody," Malcolm's father said. "Simmer down, or *next* time, I'll make a bad noise even worse by singing along with it."

There were answering calls of "Please, have mercy!" and "We'd rather hear more howling!" followed by laughter as Buck pretended to peer around angrily in an attempt to find the culprits.

Malcolm—who'd been one of them—bit down on the inside of his cheek as Giselle elbowed him in the ribs and then returned a wink sent to him by his cousin, Ruby, from across the room, next to Sebastian, who held their infant son.

"All kidding aside," his father said, "Jenny and I wanted to thank all of you for taking time from your busy lives to be here today. We thought it was important to mark the memory of the struggles we've shared and observe a moment of silence for those we've said goodbye to this year."

They did so, a solemn stillness descending until, a short time later, baby Sawyer cooed and babbled, prompting an outbreak of smiles and then giggles from Greg and Briony's children and Hannah and Archer's daughter, Lucy, as the contagion spread.

Always a pushover with the youngest Coltons, Buck Colton didn't scold, but instead asked in a teasing voice, "What's all this, during our serious moment?"

Answering for him, Mama Jen said to everyone, "It's a wonderful reminder that along with its challenges and sorrows, this past year has also brought us so many blessings. Some fine new grandchildren to love with all our hearts; delightful new daughters- and sons-in-law or in-love, and I can't tell you how very happy and proud we both are of every single one of your amazing choices." Her gaze and Malcolm's father's traveled from one couple to the next, brimming with a full measure of love, pride, and approval that excluded no one.

"And now it's time to tell them, my love," Buck said, "that we've made some choices of our own. This coming June, Jenny and I would like to invite you all right back here for…" He drew out a long silence, milking every moment of the building anticipation before booming out the very words that everyone present had most hoped to hear: "our wedding!"

Wild cheers, whistles, and shouts of congratulations erupted, with so many rushing toward them that Malcolm found himself protectively pulling back Giselle, explaining at her protest, "Sorry, but I was afraid I'd lose you in the crush!"

Squeezing his hand, she smiled and assured him, "In case you haven't figured it out yet, Malcolm Colton, you couldn't lose me if you tried."

He was kissing her when the dinner bell rang out once more and his father shouted, "Everybody, back off for a minute, please. Because we aren't quite done with the announcements."

From near the back of the scrum, Malcolm's brother Max called, "Let the luckiest man in Owl Creek speak!"

As the room once more fell silent, Buck beamed, saying, "I really *am* the luckiest man, aren't I?" and locked lips with his bride-to-be, provoking another round of applause.

Coming up for air, he said, "While I still have your attention, I wanted to let you know, too, that Jenny will be moving out here to the ranch with me—just a hop, skip, and a jump from the new place that Malcolm and Giselle will soon be breaking ground on. And as much as I know it means to everyone, I'm afraid that for practical reasons we've decided to put Jenny's home on the market—unless any one of you here would like to buy it for your own family."

A hush fell, and when people began whispering, Malcolm told Giselle, "I have so many fond memories of all us cousins running around that place as kids together. It's going to be really tough to see it leave the family, but it's awfully big for most—"

"We want it!" came a familiar voice. Malcolm turned his head just in time to see that it belonged to his *very* pregnant cousin, Frannie, who was being helped from her seat by her husband Dante, whose dark beard bore the slightest trace of silver.

At the moment, however, they both looked excited and perhaps a little nervous as his blond cousin went on to explain, "We could definitely use the space, you see," she said, "because we've been holding back some big news of our own. News we had to—shall we say—*process* for ourselves for a little while before we were ready to finally share it with everybody."

When she inhaled deeply, as if for courage, the whole packed room seemed to hold its breath in anticipation.

Dante grinned and blurted, "Send diapers, everybody, lots and lots of diapers!"

Frannie cut in, finding her voice to add, "Because… we're having triplets!"

Once more, the household erupted into a riot of cheers, hugs, laughter, and congratulations. Only this time, no one even tried to shut down the ensuing celebration, which kept right on rolling through the afternoon and well into the happiest of nights.

* * * * *